TWO TEXAS HEARTS

"Jodi Thomas is at her remarkable best in *Two Texas Hearts*."
—Debbie Macomber

TEXAS LOVE SONG

"A warm and touching read full of intrigue and suspense that will keep the reader on the edge of her seat."
—*Rendezvous*

FOREVER IN TEXAS

"A great western romance filled with suspense and plenty of action."
—*Affaire de Coeur*

TO TAME A TEXAN'S HEART

Winner of the Romance Writers of America
Best Historical Series Romance Award

"Earthy, vibrant, funny, and poignant . . . a wonderful, colorful love story."
—*Romantic Times*

THE TEXAN AND THE LADY

"Jodi Thomas shows us hard-living men with grit and guts, and the determined young women who soften their hearts."
—Pamela Morsi, *USA Today* bestselling author of *Doing Good* and *Letting Go*

PRAIRIE SONG

"Thoroughly entertaining romance."
—*Gothic Journal*

THE TENDER TEXAN

Winner of the Romance Writers of America
Best Historical Series Romance Award

"[A] marvelous, sensitive, emotional romance . . . spellbinding."
—*Romantic Times*

P9-CES-995

continued . . .

WHEN A
TEXAN GAMBLES

JODI THOMAS

JOVE BOOKS, NEW YORK

This is a work of fiction. Names, characters, places, and incidents either are the product of the author's imagination or are used fictitiously, and any resemblance to actual persons, living or dead, business establishments, events, or locales is entirely coincidental.

WHEN A TEXAN GAMBLES

A Jove Book / published by arrangement with the author

PRINTING HISTORY
Jove edition / November 2003

Copyright © 2003 by Jodi Koumalats
Excerpt copyright 2003 by Jodi Koumalats
Cover art by Wendi Schneider
Cover design by George Long

For information address: The Berkley Publishing Group, a division of Penguin Group (USA) Inc., 375 Hudson Street, New York, New York 10014.

ISBN: 0-515-13629-8

A JOVE BOOK®
Jove Books are published by The Berkley Publishing Group, a division of Penguin Group (USA) Inc., 375 Hudson Street, New York, New York 10014. JOVE and the "J" design are trademarks belonging to Penguin Group (USA) Inc.

PRINTED IN THE UNITED STATES OF AMERICA

10 9 8 7 6 5

ONE

❦

Sᴀᴍ ɢᴀᴛʟɪɴ ʀᴇᴍᴏᴠᴇᴅ ʜɪs ʀᴀɪɴ-sᴏᴀᴋᴇᴅ ᴄᴏᴀᴛ ᴀɴᴅ shirt, knowing they would never get dry before morning. He neatly folded his trousers over the chair before he turned and noticed his new wife had slipped from the bed. She had disappeared, along with one of the Colts from the holster he'd hung on the rusty bedpost moments before.

The pale lightning of a dying storm blinked in the small room, offering him enough light to see. Far away thunder echoed, barely a rumble through the night as it blended with the tinny piano music of the bar across the street.

He was bone tired, so cold he would never get warm, and now he had lost the woman he just married. She couldn't have gone far, not in these cramped quarters. He stood between where he had set her atop the covers and the door leading into the hotel hallway.

She was either under the bed or folded into one of the dresser drawers.

He found little comfort in discovering his new bride might be insane as well as armed. But bad luck had been running a wide streak through his life lately, so he did not bother to be surprised by the possibility.

He knelt on one knee and stared into the shadows beneath the iron railing of the bed frame.

"Now look, Miss . . ." he began, knowing she was no longer a 'miss' but forgetting the name the sheriff used several hours ago when Sam paid her fine, got her out of jail, and married her. "There's no need for you to hide."

He expected she would have the good sense to be grateful that he coughed up the money to save her from a life behind bars. But she hadn't said a word since they left Cedar Point. He might as well have bought a china doll for all the company she offered on the trip.

The barrel of his Colt poked out from under the bed.

"It's been a long night," he mumbled without moving. They'd driven through the worst storm he had seen in years in a flimsy rented buggy. "I'd like to get some sleep in the few hours we have left before dawn. Then I'll buy a good wagon that can take us the rest of the way to my place."

No answer.

"Lady." *Lady* didn't sound right. A man couldn't go around calling his bride *lady*. Sam straightened his large frame, hating the way his body always ached when he had to cram into a buggy. Man was meant to ride on a horse, not behind one. If he had been alone today, he would have braved the weather on horseback. But his new bride looked so weak, a dozen raindrops would have probably drowned her.

Sam decided to take the direct approach. "Get out from

under that bed, lady. The sheriff said you've been married before. You should know by now what's expected on a wedding night. Stop this foolishness and climb under those covers."

The barrel pointed at his heart. It occurred to Sam how her first husband might have met his end.

She had looked like an angel when she stepped up and pulled his name from a hat back in Cedar Point. He'd won. A bride for the price of her fine. He thought it fair when he read about the wife lottery. Three young women had confessed to a murder, but the sheriff hadn't found the body they'd admitted to killing. So, in the name of justice and because the county couldn't afford to hold them indefinitely, Sheriff Riley had held a lottery.

Sam had gone more to watch than participate, but one look at Sarah changed his mind. He had to at least put his name in the hat. The likelihood of winning had seemed more of a wish than possibility.

"I'm not goin' to hurt you." Sam tried to sound kind, but kindness was not something he wore easily. "I've never hurt a woman in my life," he added, then decided that didn't make him sound much better.

He thought he heard her sniffle. If she didn't show some sense, they would both catch pneumonia. The room offered little warmth, only a block from the icy wind. The owner downstairs had laughed when Sam asked if the room had a fireplace or a tub.

He wished suddenly that he'd been able to take her to a good hotel, but this had been the shortest way to his land, and he wanted to get home before trouble caught up with him.

"Come out and tell me what's the matter," Sam said as if he wasn't too tired to care. He already knew the problem. The lady figured out she married him and would have to look at him every day for the rest of her life. All six-feet-three, two hundred pounds of him. If his size didn't frighten her, wait until she found out what he did for a living. He figured *bounty hunter* ranked right below *undertaker* in most women's minds.

He pulled his wet shirt back on, hoping to cover a few of the scars across his chest before she noticed them.

"You are not going to touch me" came a whisper from beneath the bed.

"Well, of course I'm going to touch you. That's what husbands and wives do. They touch each other. Everyone knows that, lady." Maybe she was simpleminded. Sam remembered old man Harris's daughters, who'd grown up down the road from him. They were all fine-looking girls who developed early and fully, but there wasn't a complete brain among them. Their pa's only hope of getting them married off was to encourage it while the girls were too young and shy to say more than a few words.

Sam hadn't thought about his bride being turned that way when he decided to marry. He just thought about how much like an angel she looked, with her pale blond hair and light blue eyes, and how loneliness weighed down on him like a rain-soaked greatcoat. It had been so long since he'd said more than a few words to anyone, or ate a meal across from another person. He wasn't sure he knew how to act. Half the people in Texas thought him the devil, so why not marry an angel?

He tried again. "Look, miss, if you don't want me to touch you, I won't for tonight. I give you my word. Come on out from under the bed." He thought of adding that he wasn't all that interested in anything but sleep, but he didn't want to hurt her feelings.

She didn't move.

"You could keep the Colt if you like. Just for tonight, of course."

The shadow shifted. "What's my name?"

He'd been afraid she might ask that question at some point. "Mrs. Sam Gatlin." He smiled, proud of himself.

"My first name?"

He didn't answer. There was nothing he could say that would hide the fact he'd been only half-listening to the sheriff who married them. He'd been staring at her, and that had taken most of his attention.

Sam walked over to the chair and started putting on his trousers, since it didn't look as if they would be crawling beneath the covers anytime soon. He might be just guessing, but he figured wives didn't warm up to husbands who couldn't remember their names. They might be married, but it didn't look as if there was going to be any wedding bed tonight.

The wet wool of his trousers had grown cold and stiff. He tossed them back over the chair and grabbed one of the blankets from the bed.

Sam wrapped it around his waist. The barrel of the Colt shook. He knew she was as cold as he. "Come on out, Mrs. Gatlin, and get under the covers. I won't come near you, if that's what you want." His new bride made no sense. Why would she marry and leave town with him if she didn't plan to be his wife? She acted as if he had abducted her and forced her here.

As he pulled the blanket up over his shoulders, she slipped out from beneath the far side of the bed.

"Sarah," she said. "My name's Sarah and I won't hesitate to kill you if you come closer, Mr. Gatlin."

Sam sat down on the chair and folded his arms, locking the ends of the blanket around him. "You've killed before, have you?"

"That's right." She lifted her chin. "A man my friends and I met on the way to Cedar Point." She took a deep breath, as though she'd said what she was about to say one too many times in this lifetime. "Because we were three women, Zeb Whitaker tried to steal our wagon and take my friend Lacy away with him. We all three clubbed him with a board Bailee brought to Texas for protection. So we all killed him." She stared at him. "I'm a cold-blooded murderer, that's a fact."

Sam fought down a grin. The angel lady fascinated him with her sunshine hair and her soft southern voice. She was so beautiful, even now, damp and tired and barely able to stand while she confessed. He found it hard to believe such a creature could swing a board hard enough to hurt anyone.

"Why didn't you shoot him?" he asked more to keep her talking than out of interest.

She slipped into the bed, covered herself, then wiggled out of her wet dress. "I would have if I'd had a gun, but the wagon master took all our weapons when he threw us off the wagon train. I guess he figured we'd be dead soon and didn't want to waste a rifle."

Her dress hit the floor with a wet plop.

She was good, he thought. Her story became more unbelievable by the second, but she wasn't backing down. He'd hunted outlaws who were like that, so good at telling lies they made people want to believe them even when proven false.

"What wagon train?" It wouldn't take him long to trip her up and find the truth.

"The last one to leave Independence for California last summer. They called it the Roland Train with a wagon master by the name of Broken-Hand Harrison. I don't remember much more; first my husband got the fever a few weeks out, then my baby. They both died while we were moving across Kansas." A tear rolled down her pale china face. "If Bailee and Lacy hadn't saved me, I would have died, too. I had a fever so bad, I didn't care one way or the other if I woke up every morning."

"Bailee and Lacy?"

"The two women kicked off the wagon train with me. Broken-Hand thought I had a fever that would spread, so he didn't want anyone around me, but Bailee let me ride in her wagon after people from the train burned mine." Her words slowed as she warmed beneath the blankets. "Everyone figured Lacy for a witch just because all the folks she nursed died, except me. Some said she danced with the moon, but I never saw her do that. She is little more than a child, but when they left Bailee and me, they left her, also."

Sam watched his wife lean her head against the pillow and close her eyes. The sheriff mentioned something about her feeling better since she'd had regular meals, but she looked as fragile as cottonwood seed blowing in the wind.

"What about the one named Bailee?" he said louder than he'd intended. "Why did Broken-Hand Harrison kick her off with you?

Sarah jerked, as if in the moment while she paused, she'd fallen asleep. "The wagon master thought Bailee killed someone back East. But she's a real nice person, even if she does have this habit of clubbing men when she's angry. Maybe whoever she killed needed killing as bad as Zeb Whitaker did."

The angel closed her eyes again. Sam watched her grip on the gun relax. He waited a few minutes, then stood and carefully lifted the weapon from her hand and pulled the covers over her shoulder.

For a moment, he thought of returning to the chair. But the empty space beside her invited him.

He spread his blanket atop her and moved to the other side of the bed. When he slipped beneath the covers, he smiled for the first time in a long while.

Come morning, he would probably face the wrath of Sarah for taking up half of her bed. He almost looked forward to the clash. But right now, in the cold dampness of the tiny room with music filtering from the saloon across the street, he felt almost at peace lying by her side.

Sam turned his head and studied her in the shadows. She was too beautiful to be real. The lady had no idea yet that she didn't have a chance of bending him around her finger. No woman ever had, no woman ever would. Within a few days he would let her know how their marriage was going to be. He would set the rules and she'd follow. She'd give him a home to come to, a place to rest between battles, and he'd keep her safe. She'd do his cooking and cleaning, and he'd see that she had enough to eat. What more could either of them want from the other?

Sarah shifted, moving toward his warmth. In sleep she laid her hand atop his heart.

All thought drained from his mind as frail, slender fingers slid through the hair on his chest and then relaxed as though her touch had found a home.

Breathe, he reminded himself. Breathe.

TWO

SARAH ANDREWS STRETCHED BENEATH THE LAYERS OF blankets and opened her eyes to sunshine filtered through ragged curtains. For a moment she had no idea where she was. Shadows dominated the room. The air smelled musty and damp, as though the place had been shut away for a time.

She listened as she had all her life. Listened for the day's approach. "Be still," she told herself. "Don't move. Don't make a sound and you might hear dawn tiptoe in."

Granny Vee, an old woman who finished raising her, used to whisper that if Sarah sat still long enough, she could hear the changes in the world, the changes in her life. And Sarah tried. She always tried, yet she could never hear them. She sensed change coming, sometimes she swore she almost tasted it, but she never heard anything. Not dawn tiptoeing, or spring yawning, or age lurking.

Granny Vee was a crazy old fool for believing such

things. She'd made her living helping with the birthing of babies and watching the dying pass on to the hereafter. She always told Sarah she knew things other folks would never know, just because she paid attention. Sarah wasn't sure she always believed Granny, but listening became a habit just the same.

She stretched, enjoying the silence. Yesterday had been endless. First, she endured being raffled off in the sheriff's lottery. Then a strange man with dark hair and black eyes swept her away. The sheriff, her friends, even the town melted in the rain.

Sarah glanced around the room, just in case the dark-haired man hid somewhere in the shadowy corners. "No," she said to herself. "I'm alone. Probably abandoned again."

It had become a way of life for her. When she was only a few days old, someone left her on Harriet Rainy's steps. Sarah imagined her mother had been the one and how she must have held her close one last time before she disappeared. Her mother might have prayed that whoever lived inside the farmhouse would open their hearts to a child, not knowing that Harriet Rainy didn't have a heart.

By Sarah's sixth year Harriet had defined her as "too frail to bother to feed" and passed her along to a neighbor everyone called Granny Vee. The old woman was kind, but so poor Sarah often said she wasn't hungry because she knew there was not enough food for two. Granny Vee never made Sarah feel like family, but more like a stray cat she let live with her.

Years later Sarah thought she finally found a place to belong when she married Mitchell Andrews. She dreamed of a family and the possibility of a home of her own. Within a year he sold his farm for the adventure of heading west.

Sarah fought back a tear. Mitchell hadn't even asked her. After all, he'd said, it wasn't her place.

Once on the trail Mitchell succumbed to a fever before they reached the Rockies.

Even the baby she delivered shortly before his death hadn't stayed with her on this earth. Her tiny daughter died before Sarah had the strength to give her child a name.

A few weeks later Broken-Hand Harrison deposited her, and two other women, in the middle of the wagon trail to find their way back to civilization. However, after being in Texas several weeks, Sarah felt sure she was nowhere near finding a civilized world.

Now her new husband, a man named Sam Gatlin, had abandoned her in a shabby hotel room.

It had been raining when they stopped last night, but she'd seen what little there was to see of the town. A few stores, a two-story hotel, a saloon, and a livery. When she asked the clerk the name of the place, he'd said no one had bothered with a name. The local resident added that the mercantile had once been a trading post for buffalo hunters and the first cattle drives. Back then everyone called it the Scot's Stash, but no one thought that was a proper name.

Slipping from the bed, Sarah searched the room. Her husband had taken everything, even the wet dress she'd dropped on the floor beside the bed. Only her tattered, muddy shoes remained and her small bundle of "necessities" she kept tightly wrapped in an old handkerchief of Mitchell's. A sliver of honeysuckle soap. A comb. A pack of herbs Granny always claimed would lessen pain.

It wasn't much, she realized, but all the things in the bundle were hers. She tied her belongings to a string sewn to the waist of her undergarments.

Sarah didn't have to be still and listen to life's changes. They shouted at her this morning. Her situation would have to get better before she could die. She wasn't about to be buried in her worn petticoat with so many patched holes the hem looked like cheap lace.

"I should just kill myself," she mumbled old Harriet Rainy's favorite refrain. But without a gun or a knife, Sarah would have to jump out the second-floor window and drag herself back upstairs, over and over, before the ten-foot fall finally broke her neck.

Harriet Rainy would sometimes add, "But if I killed myself, who would take care of you?" as if giving Sarah an old quilt in the corner of the room were a great burden.

Sarah paced the room. Last night she should have shot the cowboy who married her while she held his Colt in her hand. What kind of man chooses a wife from a jail cell? He either had something seriously wrong with him, or he was as dumb as kindling. If she had shot him during the storm, folks might have thought it was thunder. Maybe she could have escaped with his guns and sold them. Or robbed a bank, assuming she could find one in this town named Used-to-be-called-the-Scot's-Stash. Now that she found herself on the path to a life of crime, Sarah saw no need to stop.

She tried to remember what Sam Gatlin looked like. Tall, very tall. And strong. He'd carried her as though she were made of straw. And mean, she decided. He definitely had a mean look about him. Eyes so dark they looked black when he watched her. Though he couldn't be thirty yet, his jaw was square and set. She'd bet a smile never crawled across his face.

Sarah fell back on the bed. She'd married the devil. It was her punishment for marrying Mitchell Andrews when she didn't love him. Granny always told her never to marry a man unless you love him something fierce and can't help yourself, 'cause men are like apples, they don't do nothing but rot once you take them home.

Since Granny had never married, Sarah wondered about her advice. When Mitchell took her back to his farm after Granny died, Sarah thought she'd grow to love him. But it hadn't happened. She didn't even cry when he died. What kind of heartless woman doesn't cry when her husband dies?

Sarah shook her head. "Me!" She answered her own question as she continued analyzing her crimes.

"Then I clubbed Zeb Whitaker," she mumbled. Killing a man, even a worthless one like Whitaker, couldn't be a good thing to do. Now her sentence would be spending the rest of her life married to a cold, heartless man who stole her one dress. With her luck she'd live a long life.

There was no choice for Sarah other than to believe that Harriet Rainy had been right. Maybe she was a worthless nothing who washed up on the porch one night during a storm.

Someone shouted from down the hall.

Sarah listened. A woman swore and ordered a man out of her room. Footsteps suddenly thundered toward Sarah's door.

She panicked and pulled the covers over her head. Maybe he wouldn't get into her room. Maybe, if he did, he wouldn't notice her beneath the covers.

The door creaked open. Someone stomped in.

Sarah tried to be perfectly still. Maybe if she didn't breathe, the intruder would simply go away.

"Mrs. Gatlin?" came a man's voice that sounded vaguely familiar. "I hope this is the right place and that lump in the bed is my wife. I forgot to look at the room number when I left, and guessing which door is not the healthiest game to play around this place."

Sarah peeked out from under the covers. Sure enough, there he was, the demon she'd married. He didn't look any less frightening in daylight than he had last night. So big, she could cut him in half and still have two fair-sized husbands.

When she didn't say a word, he tossed her the bundle he carried.

"Your dress was ruined, so I got you another one." He watched her closely with his black eyes.

"Thank you," she whispered as she glared down at the plain brown dress with not even a touch of lace at the collar. It reminded her of old Harriet Rainy's clothes, simply cut, made of coarse linsey-woolsey. Harriet always combined cotton for the warp yarns in the loom and wool for the weft. Serviceable fabric. Warm. Scratchy. Ugly.

Sarah didn't want to put it on. Afraid that if she did, she might somehow come an inch closer to sharing old Harriet's hatred of life.

"They didn't have much of a selection." Her new husband waited for her to respond. "It'll be warm. We need to get going. I've ordered a wagon and supplies. With the rain last night, the road may make the journey longer than I'd planned."

She couldn't bring herself to touch the material. Somehow, an inch at a time, she'd finally sunk to the bottom. She had nothing, not even her own clothes to wear.

A tear slid down her cheek. She still had her pride. What little belongings she'd gathered for her first marriage had been burned when the people on the wagon train thought Mitchell sick with the fever. The dress she'd worn last night was all she owned, and it was little more than a rag. But it was better than this.

"Thank you for the offer, but please bring me back my dress. I'll wash it. My dress will do fine."

Sam Gatlin raised an eyebrow and looked like he might argue. "I can afford to buy my wife a new dress. I wanted a wife and I plan to provide for you."

"Not this one," Sarah whispered. "I won't wear this one." How could she ever tell him about the woman who raised her until she'd found someone else to pass her along to? She barely knew his name. She'd never be able to describe memories of running to Harriet Rainy and folding into the skirt of her scratchy dress, only to have the woman jerk her up by the arm and slap her. "I'll give you something to cry about!" Harriet would shout. "I'll show you fear."

Sarah steadied herself, bracing for a blow. He looked like the kind of man who would beat his wife. If so, she might as well find out right now.

To her surprise, he turned and walked out of the room without another word. Sarah pulled a blanket over her shoulders and ran to the window in time to watch him go into the saloon across the street.

He's a drunk, my mean husband, she thought. That was plain. What kind of man goes into a place like that when the sun isn't even high in the sky? Mitchell Andrews might have bored her to death some days with his silence, but he never drank before noon.

She stared at the dress still spread across the bed. If she put it on now, she could run. Who knew how many miles she could be away before he sobered up enough to notice? The wagon he had rented in Cedar Point was probably at the livery, and she could drive a team as good as anyone. She could ask which way she could go to get back to Cedar Point. Maybe Bailee or Lacy married a kind man who'd let her stay for a while. Or maybe the sheriff would help her. He said it was her choice to marry. She would just tell him she changed her mind. She didn't want to marry Sam Gatlin.

Moving closer to the bed, she stared at the dress. It had been handmade by someone without skill. She was foolish not to put the garment on with the room freezing. But she couldn't. If she did, she'd disappear.

Curling into a blanket, Sarah sat on the uneven window ledge watching clouds crowd out the sun. Noises from the other rooms drifted around her, but she paid them no mind. She didn't care what happened in this no-name town.

Sarah drifted to sleep, leaning her head against the rain-cooled windowpane.

She longed for the dreams that took her away as they always had. Dreams of color and light. Dreams Harriet Rainy's cruelty or Granny Vee's poverty could not touch.

A rap on the door startled her. When she jerked, she almost toppled off the window ledge.

Stumbling, Sarah hurried to the door. "Who is it?" She knew it wasn't her husband; he would have just turned the knob and entered. That is, if he remembered the room number. Maybe alcohol had already rusted his brain.

"Let me in, hon," a female voice whispered from the other side of the door. "It's Denver Delany. I'm the owner of the saloon across the street."

Sarah knew no Denver Delany, but she opened the door a few inches. "Yes . . ." Sarah managed to say before a huge woman shoved the door wide and hurried in.

"There ain't no time for introductions." Denver was large enough to be named after several cities, with hair the color of a harvest moon and eyes rimmed in black paint. "You'll just have to trust that I'm a friend of your husband's and you got to get him out of town fast." She pushed her sleeves up to her elbows, as if thinking she was about to have her work cut out for her.

Sarah stared as Denver grabbed the ugly brown dress and headed toward her. "Your man's been stabbed by a no-good, low-life, cattle-stealing, worthless . . ."

The dress went over Sarah's head, blocking out the rest of Denver's description.

When Sarah fought her way through to the neck opening, she asked, "Is he dead?"

Denver snorted a laugh. "If he were dead, hon, we wouldn't need to be getting him out of town, now would we?"

Sarah nodded, as if seeing the logic. "Shouldn't we be taking him to a doctor?"

"Ain't no doctor for fifty miles. You'll have to take care of him. Phil, the bartender, is rearranging the supplies in the wagon Sam ordered from over at Mr. Moon's place." The huge woman stared directly into Sarah's eyes. "Can you drive a wagon, girl? You don't look strong enough to carry a half-full bucket."

"I can manage."

Denver pulled her along as Sarah frantically tried to slip into her shoes. "Good. Don't worry about the doctoring. Just plug up the hole as best you can and give him whiskey until he stops complaining. That's always been my method of treating gunshots or stabbings. It seems to work about half the time."

The woman glanced back at the room. "You got any luggage, hon?"

Sarah held her head high. "No," she answered, daring Denver to say anything. Her bundle of belongings was now hidden beneath the folds of the brown dress.

Sarah changed the subject. "Shouldn't we doctor him before we try to move him?"

"Hon, if he's not out of town fast, he'll be dead for sure in an hour. There's probably men strapping on their six-shooters right now itching for a chance to gun down Sam Gatlin, and they don't give a twit that he's bleeding a river." Denver paused at the bottom of the stairs and patted her ample bosom in an effort to breathe easier. "Don't you know? Your man is famous in these parts."

Sarah wasn't sure she wanted to know. Her gut feeling told her that whatever his claim to fame, it wouldn't be good.

Denver towed Sarah out the hotel door as panic flooded Sarah's brain. "But where will I take him?" She didn't even know the man, or like him, for that matter. How could his life suddenly rest on her shoulders? She wasn't sure which way was north from here much less how to take him to safety.

Denver stopped so quickly Sarah bumped into her back. The strange woman turned around and whispered, "You'll take him to Satan's Canyon. No one will find you there." Denver stared at Sarah as though gauging her bravery. "If you can't get him there, we might as well bury him now, for he's a dead man if he stays here."

THREE

Sarah fought down panic as she followed Denver into the saloon across the street from the hotel. The place looked far worse than Sarah imagined such places would look. The odor of rotten whiskey and stale cigar smoke hung in the air like thin, colorless moss. Her eyes watered while she battled to keep from breathing deeply.

The floor was filthy with the worst spot being a three-foot area around the bar's only spittoon.

When she first peered around Denver, the stained floor was all Sarah saw. Slowly she became aware of people moving through the thick air like shadows on a wall. There were men dressed in the color of dirt and women whose faces seemed painted on. But, mostly, they were shapes without solid form. She heard the clank of glasses, the shuffle of feet, the murmur of questions no one bothered to answer. They skirted her, staying well away, as though they thought she might turn and strike like a rattler.

The door creaked just behind her. The volume of the crowd lowered slightly as the mob turned to register the new arrival.

"Move out of the way, lady." A boy bumped against her as he elbowed his way inside. "I don't want to miss seeing someone gun down Sam Gatlin."

Denver backhanded the boy with one mighty blow, sending him flying. "Have a little respect for Gatlin's widow." She smiled down at Sarah and nodded, indicating she'd straightened the youngster out, right and proper.

Without reacting to being called widow, Sarah glanced at the kid to make sure he was all right.

The boy didn't look hurt, but he appeared terrified as he backed away from a lone man sitting at a nearby table.

"Gatlin!" the boy whispered and joined the other silhouettes lining the room.

Sarah followed his stare. The man who'd married her last night sat so still she wasn't sure he was real. His dark eyes, full of anger and pain, met hers.

She'd never wanted to run so badly in her life. She didn't care where. Any place was bound to be better than here.

But she didn't run. She couldn't. She was the devil's wife. No matter what he'd done, or was, she owed him. He saved her from a life in prison and she hadn't even bothered to thank him. It wasn't his fault the dress reminded her of Harriet Rainy. He had tried and all she'd repaid him in was trouble.

No one else in the room moved as Sarah walked toward Sam Gatlin. "Good morning," she said calmly as though she'd said the words to him a hundred times over breakfast.

He didn't move. He didn't even blink, though sweat dripped from his forehead.

She knew he'd been stabbed. Denver told her. But he didn't look a fraction less powerful or deadly than when she first saw him.

"Sarah." He said her name low, as though he didn't want the others in the room to hear. "Would you pull the knife out of my back?"

She slowly circled behind him. The wide handle of a hunting knife stuck out from just below his left shoulder blade. It had sliced through the leather of his vest. Thick drops of blood dripped from the bottom of the steel to his waist.

"I hate blood," she mumbled, thinking of all the times she'd cleaned after Granny Vee had patched up someone, or delivered a baby. Even though Sarah scrubbed, the one-room cabin smelled of blood for days.

Glancing up at the twenty people watching from the other side of the room, she asked Sam, "Why hasn't someone pulled it out before now?" How could people simply move away from a man with a knife in him?

Sam didn't turn to look at her, but remained perfectly still. "They think . . ." He took a moment before he continued with slow, measured words. "They think I'd kill the man who pulled it out, if he makes it hurt more than it already does."

Leaning around him, she tried to read his face. "And would you?"

"I might," he answered between clenched teeth.

"What about me? Will you kill me if I make it hurt more?"

"That's not possible," he answered.

"But will you kill me?"

A hint of a smile pulled up the corner of his mouth. "I might."

She straightened and moved directly behind him, not

knowing him well enough to guess whether or not he was kidding. She wasn't sure she wanted to know him any better. From the looks on the faces of the twenty or so bystanders, everyone in the room believed him capable of such an act.

"Well." Sarah gripped the handle of the huge blade with both hands. "I never wanted to live long enough to worry about growing old."

The knife didn't budge.

Sarah took a deep breath and widened her stance. "If I get this out, you owe me one, Sam Gatlin."

With a mighty tug, she yanked the knife from him, tumbling backward with the effort. Thick, dark blood bubbled from the opening on Sam's back.

Sarah stared at the knife and fought to keep from fainting. How could a man not be dead with such a wound?

"Is it out?" Sam's voice sounded tired.

"It's out," she answered, surprised he couldn't tell. She hoped he didn't ask how the wound looked as she wiped the blade on a dirty rag.

"Sarah"—his voice came low, mixed with his shallow breath—"come closer."

Moving cautiously, she marveled he still had the strength to kill her. The blade sliding out of his flesh must have been painful. He was a big man. Killing her would probably take little more effort than snapping a match between his fingers.

She thought of using the knife to protect herself. But threatening a man with the weapon that had just been embedded in his back seemed overly cruel, even for a murderer like herself.

"Yes?" she whispered close to his ear.

He still didn't move, and she wondered if she guessed that any action on his part might be his last.

"I'd owe you another favor if you can get me out of here before I hit the floor."

His words were so low, she wasn't sure if she heard them, or just thought them.

Determination flickered in his eyes and Sarah understood. The pain didn't matter, or the fact that he was losing blood with each beat of his heart. His life, and probably hers, depended on him being strong enough to walk out of this place.

Carefully she lifted his right arm and placed it over her shoulders. He braced himself against the table and stood, leaning heavily against her.

She didn't bother to ask if he could make it. She knew he would. He had to. "Well, Sam," she said for all to hear. "We'd better be going. You said you'd like to get an early start."

Slipping her hand around the back of his waist, she felt the warm blood against the leather of his vest. It trickled through her fingers and puddled on the floor behind them.

The men staring at them didn't offer to help. They watched like vultures waiting for an animal to fall. She didn't know Sam Gatlin. Didn't understand what he was about or why he was so feared. But as they moved across the room, she made up her mind that if Sam fell, she'd somehow pull his Colts from his gun belt and kill any man who stepped toward them.

Denver held the door. "The wagon's loaded and ready. I even tossed your old dress in there in case you need something to change into on laundry day."

The huge woman made her voice sound higher, brighter than her face told Sarah she felt. She was a lady used to putting on a show.

"Sam ordered the wagon supplied before he got stabbed. Phil's pulling it up now." Her hand patted

Sarah's arm as her voice lowered. "Everything's packed, including a loaded rifle under the seat, hon. The hard part's over now. He made it out of the saloon. Won't many men be brave enough to follow."

"How much do we owe you?" Sarah wondered how she could repay the woman.

"Nothing," Denver answered, backing into the street ahead of them. "Sam's account is still black with me and with the store owner. He's traded with us many a time over the years."

As the two women lifted him into the back of a wagon, the bartender hurried out with several bottles of whiskey. He helped lay Sam facedown on a bed of blankets and straw, then placed the Colts he wore on either side of the blanket close to Sam's hands.

"Just in case you need them," the bartender whispered as he moved away.

There looked to be enough supplies for a month, maybe longer. The bartender turned to Sarah and added, "I'll see the rented buggy gets back to Cedar Point with the first folks I know heading that direction."

Sarah had no time to worry about the buggy but nodded her thank-you anyway.

Denver Delany opened one bottle of the whiskey and dribbled it across Sam's wound. He didn't make a sound. Sarah guessed him beyond feeling the pain, for his eyes were closed. It had taken the last of his reserves to walk out of the bar.

She watched as Denver covered the wound with several towels and wrapped him with a dusty buffalo robe. The scraggly hide looked so nasty Sarah doubted the original owner would wear it.

The bartender handed Sarah two more bottles of whiskey. "He'll be needing this when he wakes up, ma'am. If he wakes up."

Sarah nodded. She placed the knife on the bench before she climbed into the wagon. If trouble followed she knew little about using a rifle, but the knife might prove useful. She didn't bother to question whether or not she would be able to defend herself. She had once before. She would again if need be.

Denver's bloody hand patted Sarah's fingers. "Go north to the breaks, hon." She pointed with her finger. "Then turn west on the first trail you come to. When any sign of a road runs out, you know you're close to Satan's Canyon." She leaned against the seat of the wagon and lowered her voice. "You'll come to a shallow river. Turn your horses upstream, staying well in the water so as not to leave any tracks. When there is a fork in the river, always stay to the left. Before dark the canyon walls will rise up around you. You'll think it's a dead end, but keep going until you spot a clearing. That's where I've left supplies a few times, so Sam's cabin must be close. He never told me where it was; he wouldn't."

Denver winked. "When you get there I reckon you're in the mouth of Satan's Canyon, so don't let your guard down."

"Thank you." Sarah wasn't sure she should have thanked the woman at all. "I'll be careful," she answered as she told herself the place could not be as bad as Denver pictured it.

"Don't mention it." Denver stepped away and added, "To anyone. If he's alive when you get there, he's got a chance. If he's dead, bury him and don't tell a soul, not even me."

"But why?"

Denver smiled. " 'Cause legends aren't suppose to die."

The saloon owner pulled her huge shawl from her shoulders and circled it around Sarah. "Don't trust anyone, hon. Far as I know, Sam Gatlin doesn't have a friend in this world."

"He has one," Sarah said. "You."

The large woman shook her head. "Today maybe, while he's flush on my accounts, but don't put no stock in me. I've made a habit of letting folks down all my life."

"But not today." Sarah took the reins and gripped them tight so her hands wouldn't shake.

She smiled at the owner of the bar. "No matter what happens in the future, I'll remember what you did today, Denver Delany."

Denver returned the smile, then headed back inside mumbling, "You've been warned, hon. You've been warned."

FOUR

SARAH FOLLOWED DENVER'S INSTRUCTIONS. WHEN she reached the river, she turned upstream, fighting the horses along with the current. The water wasn't deep, but the rocky bottom made it unpredictable. The reins tugged and jerked so many times Sarah feared they would pull her arms from their sockets. Within an hour her back felt as if it might snap with the next sudden twist.

Finally, with a bend in the river, bluffs replaced shoreline. The river branched out, and she veered to the left. She knew that if anyone followed, she would have appeared to vanish amid canyon walls lined with different colors of the earth as they rose.

Heavy clouds roofed the cliffs on either side, creating a misty foglike visibility. Sarah didn't bother to look ahead as she pulled the shawl over her hair. She watched the water's edge, trying to stay deep enough in the river so the current erased the wagon's tracks along with the echoes of the horses' splashing.

Every few minutes she glanced back at Sam. He swayed with the movements of the wagon. Dampness claimed the corners of his blankets. Sarah feared he would be soaked by the time they reached his cabin. She wrapped the edges of her shawl around her palms to keep the reins from cutting into her hands and pushed on, fighting time as well as water.

As Denver foretold, the walls of the canyon rose around them, offering protection from the wind, but blocking the pale sunlight that filtered through the clouds. With the shadows came a damp cold that penetrated to her bones.

Sarah's fingers froze to the curve of the rawhide strips.

Sam groaned once in pain, but there was no way she could stop to check on him. The shoreline grew rocky and so jagged not even a horse, much less a wagon, could climb from the water. With no room to turn the wagon around, she had to move on.

Sarah knew if she didn't reach the clearing before dark, she would have no chance of finding Sam's cabin until morning. He needed to be inside, out of the weather; near a warm fire.

Shadows layered on one another as she finally twisted with the river one last time and spotted a small clearing between cliffs. Sensing safety, the horses bolted toward the dry land. Sarah almost tumbled from her perch on the wagon's bench.

The wheels slid across the sandy bank, then stopped on solid ground. For a moment, Sarah did nothing but breathe. She'd made it to Satan's Canyon. She looked back toward the stream, watching, listening. If she'd been followed by someone who also knew the secret to turn left, they'd be rounding the bend soon. Denver had warned her not to let her guard down.

Nothing. No one followed.

Sarah climbed down from the wagon and faced the clearing. Knotted, ancient cottonwoods thirty feet from the water's edge greeted her like twisted sentinels. She saw no opening between them large enough to drive the wagon through. Branches crisscrossing above would knock riders from their mounts, and the huge roots would break any wheel that tried to trespass.

She paced in front of the trees with wide steps that crushed the layers of dried leaves. Waist-high brush blocked her path in the few places she might have walked between the cottonwoods.

"This must be the clearing." She glanced back, hoping for a comment from Sam. When none come, she added, "But where's the cabin? You said you had a place. Denver thought it was near here." Sarah circled, her arms wide. "But where?"

Sarah waited, half expecting him to answer, but he didn't move. She unhitched the horses and let them graze on the grass that grew almost to the water's edge. Grabbing a dead branch, she dragged it toward the wagon. "I don't care if this is the wrong clearing. Do you hear me, Sam Gatlin!" she yelled, suddenly enraged. "I don't care. I'm not getting back in that water today. So I guess we are camping right here. Any objection?"

Dumping the branch beside the wagon, she stormed back for another, angry at the entire world. Nothing ever went right. She'd started out without a father or mother to love her. The one man who'd ever asked to marry her up and died before she had time to get used to him sleeping beside her. She had nothing to her name but an ugly dress and a drunk husband so mean someone stabbed him in the back. She didn't have to think about this not being her day; this wasn't even her lifetime.

"And I'm sick!" she yelled at the body wrapped up in

a buffalo robe. "Bailee says I'm fragile. I should take care of myself."

He didn't move.

"Fragile people can die anytime, you know." She pulled another log forward. "They're breathing one minute and the next thing they're gone. Snuffed out like a candle with too much wax and too short a wick. That's me, husband. Near death and I still have to haul the wood for a fire so you won't die on me, too."

Back on the wagon train she'd tried wishing herself dead, but it appeared neither heaven nor hell wanted her, for she still breathed.

Glancing at Sam, she remembered something Lacy said about how every person has to live until they've fulfilled their destiny.

Sarah picked up an armful of sticks. "I find it hard to believe my purpose for being on this earth is to marry a drunken, mean outlaw of a man who can't leave my sight for five minutes without getting a knife stabbed into his back. I haven't seen much of this world, but if you are the best man to come out of that hat back in Cedar Point, the whole population is in big trouble. I could have done better marrying the old sheriff. At least he was breathing, which is more then you are probably doing at the moment."

As usual, Sam made no comment.

In less time than she thought possible, Sarah gathered enough wood for a fire and unloaded several of the boxes. Denver hadn't lied about the supplies; with care they might last a month. Everything needed had been packed.

Everything except matches.

Sarah mumbled to herself as she went back through the stash, hoping she'd overlooked them. She came across the knife she'd pulled from Sam's back. After washing it in the river, she tucked it away with care.

It was dark when she finally gave up looking for matches.

"We can survive without a fire, I guess," she told him, as if he listened. "It probably won't freeze tonight, and you're covered with blankets."

When he didn't answer, she added, "I've been cold before, you know. But this kind of damp cold just might be the death of me."

Curling into a ball at the back of the wagon, Sarah remembered the nights Harriet Rainy used to lock her out of the house. She'd pretend like she wasn't cold . . . like she wasn't hungry . . . like she wasn't all alone. . . .

She would build a home in her mind where the cupboards were stocked and a fire blazed in the hearth. Sarah imagined lace curtains on the windows and a wool blanket beside her very own chair. She'd think of details down to the way the air smelled of fresh bread, and how it warmed her lungs when she took a deep breath.

Sarah looked over at the mound of blankets taking up most of the wagon bed. Was she alone, or could some small part of Sam Gatlin still be alive and with her? The sheriff had told him to take good care of her or Sam would have him to answer to. She hated criticizing the man after one day of marriage, but so far he was falling down on the job.

"Hello." She leaned closer. "You still there, Sam Gatlin?"

She wasn't sure he even breathed.

"Are you alive?" She poked his arm.

No answer.

Sarah brushed her finger along the line of his shoulders to his throat. There the skin was warm to her touch.

"You're alive," she whispered more to herself than him. She wasn't alone. "Wouldn't happen to have a match?" As she said the words, hope crept into her voice.

She moved closer. "You might have a few. My guess is they'd be in your pocket. Most men carry them, I think." Her knowledge of men consisted of one husband who never said more than a few words to her and the few men she'd met on the wagon train.

Hesitantly she slid her hand along Sam Gatlin's side until she reached his waist. "You wouldn't mind if I take a look would you?" If she hadn't been so cold, she never would have been so brave.

As the blanket slipped away, she saw a dark spot below his shoulder blades. Blood soaked through the towel bandage Denver had tied around him. He might not be doing anything else, but the man was still bleeding.

"The wound needs to be cleaned," she whispered as she felt for his pocket. "But first we have to have a fire."

She couldn't reach inside the pocket and she doubted she had the strength to roll him over, but giving up didn't seem to be an option.

Bracing her back against the side wall of the wagon bed, she offered, "How about I give you a hand to move over?" Not waiting for an answer, Sarah pushed with both her hands and feet until he shifted with a groan.

It was too dark to see his face, but she felt his breathing as she brushed her hand down his chest to the leather of his gun belt. Slowly she pushed her fingers into his pocket. Nothing but a short comb and some coins, which she kept. Sarah leaned over him so she could reach the other pocket.

His hand moved so suddenly she didn't have time to retreat. His powerful fingers gripped her wrist with bruising force.

"I'm not dead yet, lady. It's a little early to pick the bones."

Sarah tried to pull away. His hold tightened.

"I . . . I was only looking for matches."

He didn't move or show any sign of understanding her words.

"I need to light a fire. I can take care of your wound, but first I have to see it."

Slowly his grip lessened. "In my vest."

The iron in his voice slipped, and she wondered if he'd used the last of his reserves defending himself.

She rubbed her wrist. "You didn't have to grab me so hard. I told you I was fragile. It's a wonder you didn't snap my bones right in two. Then who do you think will clean the wound and bandage you?"

She pulled the small tin of matches from his vest pocket and climbed from the wagon. Anger made her march around the wagon. "Serve you right to freeze to death, Sam Gatlin. I've seen wounded snakes that were friendlier. You haven't even bothered to thank me for pulling that blade out of your back." Frustration flavored her words as she worked. "You'd probably still be sitting in that bar bleeding on that dirty floor if I hadn't helped you."

Even after she got the fire going, she still couldn't stop shivering. What kind of monster had she married? What kind of man, even near death, thought only of protecting himself?

As she added wood, Sarah tried to piece together all she knew about her new husband. The sheriff called him by name when he'd married them. Had he known Sam as a friend? No, she decided. The greeting was too formal to be friendly and held enough respect to discount the two as enemies. Apparently, according to Denver, several people in the town wanted to kill him, or at least watch him die. Gatlin had money, he'd bought supplies, rented a buggy, paid her way out of jail.

She glanced toward the wagon. She owed him for that. No matter how mean a man he was or how many people hated him, Sam Gatlin saved her from a life in prison. Clubbing Zeb Whitaker seemed like the right thing to do at the time, but she'd met nothing but trouble for her effort when she had been honest enough to confess to the crime.

"By the way"—she poked at the fire—"thanks for getting me out of jail. I'll be your wife, just like I said I would, but don't forget you owe me one. You said so in the bar." She wanted to add that being a complete wife wasn't the "way" she had in mind, but there was no use wasting time explaining anything to a man who was busy pounding on death's door.

As the fire warmed the little clearing, Sarah collected all she needed to help Sam. Whiskey, if he woke up. Boiled water for cleaning the wound. Enough wood to keep the fire blazing so she could see. And the pouch of herbs Granny Vee had given her over a year ago. She'd said to use it only if the wound was a matter of life or death, and Sarah decided Sam's wound would qualify.

Bandages would also be needed. The only clothing packed in the boxes was two cotton shirts. They'd been wrapped separately and mailed in brown paper with a note scribbled on the package, "For Sam. Hope they last you through the winter."

Sarah ran her hand over one of the shirts. Unlike her dress, the shirt was well made with extra care taken to add strength. It wasn't a farmer's shirt, or any other kind of working man's garment. Sarah decided it was the kind a gentleman would wear.

It would be a crime to destroy something someone had

spent so much care to make. Sarah lifted the knife. There was no time to hesitate, she needed bandages. With a determined slice, she cut into the scratchy material just below her waist and sliced her skirt all the way to the hem.

She hadn't felt so good about doing something since she clubbed Zeb Whitaker. Cutting the skirt of her dress into bandages was as much fun as opening presents. She didn't even mind that her mended petticoat showed. As soon as she had time, she'd wash her old ragged dress and wear it. Sam could keep his fine shirts, but she had no plan to keep the dress he'd bought her.

Supplies in hand, Sarah climbed back into the wagon and rolled Sam Gatlin onto his stomach.

A complaint slipped from between his clenched teeth. He didn't answer when she asked what he'd said, but she guessed the comment was one she would be better off not understanding.

Working in the firelight, she removed the blood-soaked towel, then his vest. As she cut away his old shirt, Sarah couldn't help but notice the solid wall of muscles running across his shoulders. He was well built, this no-good husband of hers.

He reminded her of a rock-hard statue. Broad shoulders, trim waist, powerful arms. Only this statue, so perfect in form, had weathered many storms. Scars marred the excellence.

She cleaned the wound with a mixture of whiskey and warm water, letting her fingers brush across his back. The warm skin seemed to welcome her caress. She touched his hair and was surprised at its softness. He'd taken her as wife without question; maybe she should try to do the same.

She forced herself to concentrate on the wound. Before Sarah made up her mind if she liked the man or not, she had to keep him alive. Burying two husbands in less than a year seemed a grim prospect.

Blood still oozed in tiny trails from the opening in his back. "A fresh bandage wrapped tightly over the wound might help," she mumbled as she braced herself once more against the side of the wagon. Rocking him in one direction, then the other, she wrapped a strip of her dress around his chest and tied it over the bandage.

"There, Mr. Gatlin, that's the best I can do for now." She leaned forward and listened for his breathing.

It came in a slow steady rhythm.

"You are more than welcome," she said in answer to his silence as she covered him with a blanket. "Would you like a bit of supper now that you're all cleaned up?"

She knew he wouldn't answer, but she needed to hear a voice, even if only her own. The stillness of the clearing wore on her nerves.

Sarah reached for the rifle beneath the wagon's seat as she looked around. The water shimmered silver in the river, mirroring the firelight in places. The trees beyond the clearing were black with night. Fear made her want to look away, but curiosity forced her to study the shadows searching for someone, or something looking back.

If his cabin lay beyond the trees, it was well hidden. If she could get him there tomorrow, they might be safe until he recovered enough to take care of himself. Until that time she'd offer him care, doing all she could. Granny Vee would have told her it was a rule to take care of one's own husband. And Sarah believed in following the rules. Only this time Sam Gatlin had told her he owed her one, and as soon as he came to, she planned to ask for her favor. One slight change in the rules between man and wife.

Sarah grinned to herself. If he didn't honor his agreement, she'd offer to put the knife back.

A few leaves stirred to her right. Sarah pulled the rifle closer. It was only the wind, she told herself. Or a rabbit or a squirrel.

Somehow Sam's warm body comforted her even though she knew he would be no help if trouble rushed in.

"I might just heat up a can of those beans," she said, hoping to convince whatever waited in the shadows that Sam was with her and could help if needed. "There's plenty if you decide you want some."

Something moved in the blackness again, stirring leaves, snapping a branch.

They were not alone.

"What did you say, Sam?" She leaned closer to him without taking her eyes off the darkness just beyond the fire. "You think you'll just rest here in the wagon for a while? All right, but keep those guns handy. I put your Colts within easy reach just like that bartender did back in town."

She slipped from the wagon and tied her shawl around her waist. "If there's anyone out there, he'd be more than welcome to share the fire and supper!" she yelled "Provided you come in unarmed."

Turning slowly, she set the rifle down on a box and pulled a can from their stash of food. With an easy skill, she hit the handle of the knife and slid the blade around the top of the can.

She paused a moment, listening. Maybe she was being foolish. No one would be near. Even if someone had been beyond the wall of cottonwoods, they would have had to stumble and fight their way into the clearing. It couldn't have been accomplished with only the slight rustling of leaves.

Pouring the beans into a tin plate, Sarah turned back to the campfire. As she set the food to warm, she looked up, across the flames into the shadows that had taken on shapes.

Three pair of frightened eyes stared back.

FIVE

On instinct, Sarah reached for the rifle. As her fingers wrapped around the cold metal, her brain registered what sat across from her. Not wild animals, but children. Wild children.

Slowly she turned back toward them without letting go of the barrel of the gun. Of course she would never shoot a child, Sarah reasoned, but she wasn't quite sure she wanted to be unarmed in front of them.

They sat perfectly still on the ground, their clothes and bodies the same shade of brown as the dirt. The firelight danced across their dirty faces and reflected in three pairs of deep blue eyes.

"Hello." Sarah tried to keep her voice calm. If she frightened them, they might disappear as silently as they'd arrived. "Have you come to dinner?"

The oldest, a girl of no more than six or seven, nodded without blinking.

A hundred questions came to Sarah's mind. Where had

they come from? Where were their parents? How had they moved so quietly across the rooted, leaf-packed spaces between the trees? The amount of dirt on them ended any possibility that they might have come from the water. Their presence gave her hope that something did lie beyond the trees.

Sarah returned the rifle to the wagon and opened another can of beans. While it heated in the plate close to the fire, she rummaged through the supplies until she found another plate and two tin cups. Carefully she divided the beans and handed each of the two smaller children a cup filled with beans and a spoon. Sarah gave a plate and fork to the oldest child. Then, watching out of the corner of her eye, she carefully took the hot plate filled with her share of the beans and began eating.

The children watched her for several bites. Finally the oldest one lifted her fork. The two younger children tossed their spoons aside and scooped the beans out with their fingers. They all ate as though they hadn't tasted food in days, maybe even weeks.

Sarah studied the two little ones. She couldn't tell if they were boys or girls or one of each. One was slightly larger, maybe four. The other smaller, younger. Both were so thin, they reminded her of string puppets. At one time their clothes had been well-made. She noticed the outline of where a pocket had once been, and only every other button remained on one child's garment.

"My name is Sarah." She focused on the older child. "What's your name?"

Not one of them answered. They watched her as if they didn't trust her.

When Sarah reached behind her for a can of fruit they could have as dessert, the children vanished as quickly as they'd appeared. Standing at the edge of the campfire's light, Sarah listened for them. She didn't hear a sound. Somehow they'd crossed through the trees once more without crushing leaves or breaking branches.

The thought occurred to her that she might have dreamed them, for she had long ago grown too tired to think straight. While ill on the wagon train, she used to think her husband and child were still alive. She'd talked to Mitchell, asking him simple questions like what he wanted for dinner and would he be in before dark. For days she rocked a baby that turned out to be nothing more than a pillow. Sometimes, when the world of reality and dreams mixed, her arms still ached to hold her newborn.

The reality of losing her family, of watching her wagon burn, or being told she'd have to leave the train; all seemed the nightmare. If Bailee and Lacy hadn't been there to help her, Sarah wasn't sure what would have happened. She drifted so much between dreams and wakefulness, she had trouble telling the difference.

They had cared about her just because she needed someone to care. Sarah would never forget their kindness. They would forever be her friends.

A moan from Sam drew her back to the moment. She climbed in beside him and tried to see his face in the shadows. But he turned from the light, mumbling words about walking over too many graves.

She felt a kinship with him, for she'd spent many hours in the place he now resided.

She touched his forehead, planning to let him know she was near. His skin felt afire.

"Fever," she whispered, remembering Denver telling her Sam would be all right if fever didn't set in.

Forgetting the wild children and her fears, Sarah hurried off the wagon. She grabbed a pot and ran to the water's edge. She had to do something and fast or the fever would take Sam.

Before climbing back into the wagon, she tore another strip from her skirt to use as a rag.

Over and over she returned to the river for cold water, then bathed Sam's hot skin with the damp rag. By the time he'd cooled a little, she had touched him enough to know every curve of his torso.

He was so much bigger than Mitchell, she found it a little frightening, for Mitchell could be cruel and rough. How much rougher could this huge man be when he regained his strength?

But when Sam moved, even in his pain, he never swung at her, or grabbed her. It was almost as if he knew she was trying to help him.

When his fever eased more, he mumbled, "Don't leave, Angel. Don't leave."

Sarah smiled and touched her hand to his cheek. "I'm not going anywhere, Sam. I'm your wife."

He drifted into sleep.

When she checked on him, the fever had cooled.

"Would you like some supper?" Pulling the buffalo hide up to cover him, Sarah noticed his wound had not yet bled through the bandages. Thank goodness he was starting to heal.

Dark eyes, as black as the night, stared up at her.

"You're awake." Sarah smiled because he looked at her as if he'd never seen her before.

"Whiskey," Sam said. "Is there more whiskey."

While Sarah found the bottle, he mumbled on about how someone had to tell Ruthie if he died. "I promised I'd have someone get word to her," he said, as though talking to some invisible person in the shadows of the night.

"Ruthie?" Sarah asked as she handed him the bottle. Could Sam have a love somewhere? "Who is Ruthie?" she whispered.

His eyes met hers and she almost thought he understood that he had been talking out of his head. But then he took the bottle from her as if he hadn't heard her question.

"Ruthie?" she asked again.

"There is no Ruthie anymore," he said as he managed to prop himself up enough to down almost half a bottle. "Ruthie cut her hair."

He didn't bother to thank her for the whiskey, only collapsed mumbling about rattlers gnawing on his back and how he wished the summer would end.

Sarah scooted farther into the wagon, resting her back against the bench. She was so close to Sam she could feel his nonsense words brush along her hand. She pushed her cold feet just beneath the edge of the blankets he used and pulled her knees against her chest. With the rifle within easy reach, she tried to sleep. But thoughts of the children, cold and somewhere in the darkness, kept her awake. Why hadn't she offered them a blanket? Why had they disappeared?

She leaned her head against the wood of the wagon's bench and tried to stop shivering.

Without warning, Sam's big hand circled her waist and pulled her down beneath the buffalo robe.

Fighting down a scream, Sarah searched for enough energy to struggle free, but Sam's arm moved across her middle and rested there, pinning her beside him.

She tried to breathe. Fear claimed her thoughts as her body warmed beneath the blankets. Sam's slow steady breathing brushed against the side of her face. The smell of whiskey whispered through the air. Sarah wiggled her nose, then decided it was better than the smell of blood.

After several minutes she relaxed, deciding he had no plans to ravish her. She allowed sleep to settle over exhaustion.

When she woke, just after dawn, she hadn't moved. Neither had Sam. His hand still rested atop her. It took all her energy to force herself to slip into the cold morning and climb from the wagon.

She almost laughed at herself for even thinking a man so wounded could have been thinking of mating. He probably was only tired of having her shake the wagon with her shivering.

But he dreamed of Ruthie, she remembered. It surprised her that a man so hard, so cold, would mumble about a woman. Maybe he had loved once. Sarah felt suddenly jealous, for she'd never loved. However, he wasn't with Ruthie, and she wondered if that didn't somehow add to the pain he felt. Maybe she was better off having no one to worry about.

The air thickened into gray light, as though a cloud had nestled into the clearing overnight. For an hour she pulled dead branches from between the cottonwoods, letting the fire rage against the cold, but she couldn't seem to warm the clearing. Once, she tried to climb between the roots and see what lay beyond the trees. Only more trees, choking out daylight. She called several times for the children, but wasn't surprised when they didn't answer.

Sam woke once, asking for more whiskey and managing to swallow a little jerky broth she'd kept warm. Sarah ripped another section from her skirt. He sat up without saying a word as she changed his bandage. The wound was red and ugly across his flesh, but at least it no longer bled.

Just before dark, as she set out the cans for supper, the three children appeared as they had the night before.

Sarah tried to act as if she wasn't in the least surprised. "I was hoping you'd join me for dinner." She set the can of peaches where they all could see it. "Maybe you'll stay for dessert?"

Tonight she cut up a large potato and let it cook with three cans of beans. She wanted to make sure there was enough food, for she knew what it was like to leave a meal still hungry. While she cooked, she talked to them, answering questions they never asked. She told them that she and Sam were married, but left out the fact that they met when he bailed her out of jail.

Finally the oldest child set down her empty plate and studied Sarah before she spoke. "I'm K.C. These are my brothers, Dodge and Abilene."

Sarah tried not to smile. "K.C. is short for?"

"Kansas City. My ma named us for the town she was in when we was born."

Sarah finished her plate, then opened the can of peaches and offered each child a peach half. Again the smaller two used their hands while K.C. watched Sarah and tried to use her fork to cut the peach. When Sarah finished, she walked to the water's edge and washed her hands along with the plate she had used.

None of the children seemed to feel the need to follow her example.

K.C. glanced toward the wagon when Sarah returned. "You gonna feed Sam Gatlin?"

"When he wakes," Sarah answered, surprised the child remembered his name. "Is he a friend of yours?" The possibility that Sam might have been the one who left the children at this place crossed her mind. Or maybe K.C. had just listened when Sarah talked to Sam. She must have said his name twenty times in the two days they had been in the clearing.

"No." K.C. giggled. "But I seen him before. I think he might have been Ma's 'happen-along.' "

"A happen-along?" Sarah asked as she collected the children's plates.

"Yeah, you know. Ever once in a while this man happens along and comes to see my ma late at night. The next thing I start worrying about is if I'll get another little brother."

Sarah looked at Dodge and Abilene, trying to see any sign that either could be a child of Gatlin's. They were too dirty to tell much, but neither had his dark eyes.

"Is Sam your father?"

All three children nodded in unison as if they'd practiced their response to such a question.

Sarah added another black mark to her husband's growing list. Drunkard, gunman, probable wife beater, and now no-good father. How had she managed to marry the lowest of the low in several different categories?

"I should have left the knife in his back," she mumbled as she scrubbed the dishes. "Maybe before I stepped up and helped him, I should have asked why someone stabbed him. Who knows? Maybe they had good reason. He didn't bother to tell me, and Denver didn't seem the least surprised that someone would want to kill him. In fact, she hinted men might be forming a line to do just that."

Sarah glanced over her shoulder. The children watched her as if she were some kind of curious animal. She wasn't too sure if K.C. was telling her the truth, or simply saying what she thought Sarah might want to hear.

"Do you know where your mother is?" Sarah asked.

"Nope," K.C. answered without emotion. "Last time we seen her was in Fort Worth. She was dead in a box."

"But how did you get here?" Sarah found it hard to

believe anyone, even a man like Sam Gatlin, would leave three children out here alone.

K.C. wrinkled her face in thought.

Sarah guessed the child debated telling the truth. "It's all right, you can trust me. Even if I wanted to, I have no one to tell any secrets to."

"Tennessee Malone told us not to tell nobody. He said if we want to get to our father, we better not talk to anyone."

Sarah tried again. "Who is Tennessee Malone?"

"He said he was a friend of our pa's and he'd take us to a place where we'd meet up with our pa, but all he did was leave us here."

Sarah tried for another hour, but the child had no more answers, only that the day her mother died, a man they'd never seen before named Malone loaded them in a wagon. Then he dropped them off with a thick wrap of jerky and told them Sam Gatlin would be there in three days.

Only Sam never came and K.C. said she'd watched the moon turn full three times. When the jerky ran out, they'd survived on berries and roots.

"We've been hungry for a long time," K.C. said. "Could we have another peach?"

Sarah knew she should ration the quickly dwindling supplies, but she couldn't say no.

After feeding them another two cans of peaches and all the bread that was left, she wrapped the children in the huge shawl and put them close to the fire so they would stay warm. She spent the second night in the clearing listening to Sam mumble in his sleep and trying to figure out why he hadn't come for the children. Had he thought that if he waited long enough they'd be dead and he wouldn't have to worry about them?

Sarah had no idea if he was their father or why he

hadn't helped them. Maybe he married her so he'd have someone to take care of them. Maybe Malone's message never reached Sam. Maybe it did, but Sam didn't care.

She scooted into the corner of the wagon, next to the rifle, and curled into a ball. She didn't want to touch him tonight, not even to get warm. So far every day she had learned more about her husband. And it was all bad.

As the night aged, she shivered and finally slipped beneath the covers and into the warm place at his side. But tonight there was far too much to think about to sleep.

The next day mirrored the last. Sam seemed to be sleeping sounder and his wound no longer bled, but he never opened his eyes or responded when she talked to him.

Dawn crept through the cottonwoods on the morning of the fourth day with Sarah wide awake. She'd made up her mind that there was only one thing to do. She had to take the children back to town and talk Denver into watching over them until Sam was at least coherent. Maybe he'd have some answers. If he had money for supplies, he might have money to hire someone to watch over the children for a while.

She woke him by pulling the buffalo robe off him. His eyes were rimmed in red and bloodshot, and his face looked pale beneath his weathered tan. He stared at her as though he were trying to remember where he'd seen her before.

He growled like a bear, but Sarah didn't back down. "I can't lift you out of the wagon, Sam Gatlin. You'll have to climb out if you want breakfast."

"Go away. I'm not moving."

"You are if you plan to eat."

"Forget breakfast," he mumbled. "Where's the whiskey in this bar?"

Sarah sighed, realizing he still talked out of his head.

She wasn't sure if he was drunk or in so much pain he didn't care where he was. "The whiskey is a few feet from the wagon, along with your breakfast." She'd made a table of water, whiskey, and jerky. It wasn't much in the way of rations, but she thought it would keep him alive until she returned, or he got strong enough to look for the canned goods.

He didn't seem to see anything but the bottle. When she didn't offer to get it for him, he slowly moved to the back of the wagon under protest.

Sarah helped him down. When he slid off the gate, she almost buckled beneath his weight. Slowly they crossed the distance to a makeshift bed of leaves Sarah had arranged for him.

While he downed a long swig of whiskey, she told him her plan. "I have to take the children to town. With the nights getting colder, they can't stay any longer." She didn't mention that they'd eaten half the month's food supplies. "I left you food within easy reach. If I don't get lost, I should be back by tomorrow night. It's not the best of plans, but it's all I could come up with. You can't go to town in the shape you're in, and the children can't stay out here in the cold."

"There are no children here," he answered as he pulled the buffalo robe over him. "I'll try not to be dead when you get back." From the way he said the words, Sarah guessed he felt so bad he didn't much care one way or the other.

"Good," she answered without feeling. "Be alive. I don't want to have the trouble of trying to bury you out here."

"Bring a shovel back, just in case," he said, already half asleep.

Sarah swore she heard a laugh beneath the blankets. An

hour later, when the children were fed, cleaned, and waiting in the wagon, Sarah checked his wound. If possible, it seemed to have healed a week's worth since yesterday. He didn't open his eyes while she wrapped a clean bandage across him. His skin still felt hot, clammy, and she knew when she returned, she might just need that shovel.

She tried to cover him and make him comfortable before climbing into the wagon. He mumbled, "What children?" once but showed no sign of listening when she explained.

Ten minutes later, when she climbed onto the wagon's bench and picked up the reins, Sarah turned around to make sure the children were still ready to leave.

All three were gone.

Frustrated, Sarah climbed down and called for them, but they had vanished. She tried everything, setting out food, yelling for them, crawling into the brush. Nothing.

After rebuilding the fire, she forced Sam to eat a few bites and began a quest to find where they had crossed through the brush. She worked her way into the foliage as far as she could and still there was no sign of them. Nothing.

They had simply slipped from the wagon while she was tending Sam and disappeared. She waited long after dark, but they never returned. Finally she unhitched the horses once more and sat down beside Sam.

To her surprise he looked up at her with unclouded eyes. "Back so soon?" he asked.

"I didn't go. The children vanished, so I couldn't take them to town. I can't even find them."

Sam looked as if his head had cleared of pain enough to follow the conversation. "You're missing the kids that just appeared?"

"Yes!" Sarah answered, frustrated.

"Maybe you just imagined they were here." He scrubbed his face as if fighting his way out of a hangover. "I've sure been having some crazy dreams."

"Maybe I did." Sarah set her chin on her bent knees. "And maybe I just dreamed we had supplies." Her gaze fell on the empty boxes beside the wagon, then back at the bare table where she'd stacked Sam's supplies. Only the half-full whiskey bottle remained.

SIX

∞

SAM FORCED HIMSELF TO MOVE. THE PAIN IN HIS BACK competed with the throbbing in his head. Slowly, like a man laden with lead, he stood, letting the night's cold add another measure of discomfort to a body he thought had already reached full capacity. His mind floated with the pain.

Move! He took a step. *Keep moving or they'll bury you!* With each stride he stopped and rested, bracing raw will against the desire to retreat. He'd faced this hell before and he knew the way out . . . refuse to give in to the torture. It didn't matter that he couldn't remember where he was, or how he got to this place. If he lived, his head would clear in a few days. All that mattered was controlling the terrible throbbing that broke in waves across his senses.

Whiskey still clouded his mind, blurring dreams with scraps of reality.

Early morning drifted across the clearing without

warmth. Hesitantly Sam staggered toward the water. He thought of bending down for a drink but knew the agony would be too great. He pressed his lips together, holding in a cry, as he unstrapped first his holster, then his trousers. Thankfully, someone had already removed his boots and Colts. He would never have been able to pull off his boots, and he'd not allow his Colts to fall into the sand.

With grim determination he stepped into the river.

For a moment the blast of icy water outran all other pain. His knees buckled from the force, and he crumbled into the current like a warrior made of sand.

The cold water, rushing past his chest and face, made his legs, now somewhat accustomed to the temperature, seem warm. For several heartbeats Sam remained underwater, welcoming the feel of nothing but waves circling him. Finally a need for air forced him up. He planted his feet wide apart on the rocky bottom and stood, allowing a hundred streams to rush down his chest to where the river rounded his waist.

Plowing his fingers through his hair, he lowered once more. This time the current welcomed him as wet-warmth replaced the chilly air's touch. He floated for a while, inches beneath the surface, enjoying feeling weightless. No time. No place. No problems. The thought crossed his mind that he could continue doing nothing. He'd drift downstream like a log, bumping against the shoreline, rolling in the current, until he reached the ocean.

A strange sound, like a bird's cry or a woman's scream, bubbled around his ears. He stood once more, pulling reluctantly from the peace of drifting.

"Are you crazy?" A shout echoed off the walls and bounced back and forth along the canyon.

Sam looked about, trying to tell where the noise originated. At first all he saw was the clearing, the trees, the water.

Then she came into view. A tiny, half-pint of a woman standing at the water's edge with her fists on her hips. She looked every bit as if she planned to wring his neck when she got hold of him. He found it impossible to believe such a dainty creature could have created such volume.

"Get out of that water, Sam Gatlin, before you catch your death!" She paced inches from the shoreline. "I didn't keep you alive for four days to have you drown yourself."

Sam tried to bring her into focus, but water dripped off his hair into his eyes. The woman multiplied like ripples on the waves. Surely she was only in his imagination. She couldn't be real. He'd never even seen a woman like her, curls the color of sunbeams tumbling across her shoulders and skin as pale as moonlight.

She was the most beautiful creature he'd ever encountered and obviously madder than hell at him. All he'd done was stand waist deep in a stream. The past few days were fuzzy in his head. She seemed like part of a dream he'd had, more wishing than real. He knew he could never do anything to hurt such an angel even in his dreams. So why was she so angry?

Maybe she thought this stream was hers and him a trespasser?

"Name's Sam Gatlin!" he yelled by way of introduction.

She stomped her foot and, if possible, rage rose in her tone. "I know who you are, you idiot. Get out of the water!" She leaned closer to the edge, as if irate enough to come in and get him if he didn't follow orders. "I swear, you'd think that knife I pulled out of you sliced right through your brain and not your back."

Sam frowned. He vaguely remembered someone pulling a knife from his back. Someone said there would be a condition, but for the life of him, he couldn't remember what it was. Someone had helped him into a wagon, someone fed him soup. "Do I know you, lady?" He might as well ask before he got close enough for her to take a swing at him. If he'd seen her kind of rage in a man, Sam would have made sure his Colt was ready to pull.

"Of course you know me, Sam Gatlin. I'm your wife."

She showed no sign of kidding.

"But if you don't get back in that bed right now, I'll probably be your widow by noon."

Sam saw no choice but to head toward the shore. She looked as if she meant every word she said. Besides, he didn't know how much longer he could stand. The river must have seeped into his brain along with some of the bottom mud, for his thoughts were muddled.

As he stepped up to the shore, he heard her sharp intake of breath and looked up.

She might be the one who pulled the knife from his back, she might even be his wife, but one thing Sam knew . . . she had never seen him without clothes. She stared at him with a mixture of horror and curiosity.

Sam groaned. He'd seen the same kind of stare from folks looking at freaks at tent shows.

He wasn't a man who thought of himself as modest, but if he could have vanished in thin air, he would have. She looked at him with huge round eyes, and it crossed his mind that this lady might never have seen a man before.

"What is the matter?" He tried to stand still and not act like he noticed her gaze moving over him. He never thought of his body being anything out of the ordinary, more scarred maybe than most. If she was his wife, as she claimed, surely she'd seen him naked.

"Are you all right, lady?" The edges of his brain were starting to clear. She did look vaguely familiar. The past and dreams began to separate in his mind. "Is something the matter with you . . . or me?"

"Nothing," she whispered. Her glance darted the length of him once more, and she added, "You shouldn't bathe with your socks on."

He looked down at the wool socks. "All right," he answered, as if she made any sense. "I'll try to remember that in the future." If she was his wife, he must have forgotten how picky she was. A woman with white-blond hair sitting on a bed crossed his mind. He remembered she refused to put on a dress.

She marched back to the campsite. He followed, wondering if clothes often made her angry.

Without looking at him, she tossed a blanket in his direction. "If you'll sit on the box, I'll rebandage the wound. There is no telling how many bugs or how much mud got beneath the bandage. I've heard of folks getting infections from river water."

"All right," he answered, hoping not to make her angry or shock her again until he figured out who she was. He didn't believe it possible such a woman could be his wife. First, he had no time or place in his life for a wife, and second, a lady like her would never give him more than a glance. But facts were muddled in his brain. He had no idea what day, or even what month it must be, but visions of her lined the corners of his thoughts.

He tried to think back before the pain. He'd been riding south, following a trail of cattle thieves out of Dodge. He remembered being bone-tired when he stopped at Cedar Point and deciding he might learn something about the men he was trailing if he had a few drinks. The sheriff there would loan him a cell for the night if he had too much. Sam could remember Sheriff Riley always kidded him about not being able to hold his alcohol. So why couldn't he remember how he met this woman before him?

The rest of that night in Cedar Point seemed more dream than memory.

While his wife stirred up the fire, he covered himself, then sat on a box and studied her. She was a lady, that he would bet on. He'd never seen the likes of her in a saloon. But her dress was no more than a rag. Sections of the skirt were missing as if it had been quilted and someone had left out a few of the panels. She was thin, but not girl thin. A full-grown woman moved beneath those rags. A woman who hadn't been eating regularly, he'd guess.

"Turn around," she ordered as she knelt behind him. "And keep still while I work."

Wrapping the blanket around his waist, he did as she instructed. He felt her fingers at his back, working with the knot of a bandage tied just below his rib cage. Her hands were warm and seemed used to the feel of him.

"The wound is still closed." Her words brushed against the back of his shoulder. "No more bleeding, but I'll bandage it just in case."

He glanced over his shoulder in time to see her rip a strip of material from the skirt of her dress.

He realized she'd been cutting her own clothes to doctor him. "I'll buy you another dress," he offered.

"No," she shot in anger. "I'll buy my own dress."

Sam frowned. She might be beautiful, but she had a temper. He'd never known of a woman who got mad just because a man offered to buy her something. Yet, her touch was gentle as she spread the cotton around his waist and tied it. Her body leaned close against his, and he felt an ache like he'd never felt before. A hunger for something he'd never tasted. A longing. A hope.

She might call herself his wife, but he'd never made love to her. There wasn't enough pain or liquor in the world to make him forget what this woman would have felt like beneath him.

"Who are you?" he asked as she pulled the blanket over his shoulder.

"Forget my name again, did you, Sam?"

He wanted to tell her that she wasn't someone he would forget, but at the moment he couldn't remember much more than his own name. He'd been hurt enough times to know that in a day or two the world would settle back into place, but he didn't want to wait that long to hear her name.

"Mrs. Sam Gatlin." She laughed. "That's my name."

He frowned.

She took pity on him. "Sarah. I'm Sarah. Maybe next time the sheriff marries us, you'll remember."

Her hand moved along his forehead as though she'd touched him there a thousand times. "How's the hangover?"

"Pounding," he answered, wanting to ask about the sheriff, but guessing it could wait. "How long have I been drunk?" He caught her hand in his and held it a moment before he let go.

"Four days." She didn't seem offended by his action. "Passed out most of the time, which was probably for the best." She unwrapped a white shirt from wrinkled brown paper. "You want me to help you?" She held out the shirt.

He thought of saying no, but he kind of liked the idea of her drawing near again. As she slipped the shirt over his shoulders, she moved close once more, bumping against him slightly, as if it were nothing unusual. He wondered if she knew no one ever came near him. No one dared.

"Want some coffee?" She buttoned the first button, then lay her palm flat against his chest and brushed the material smooth.

The simple action dynamited his senses, shattering a hundred barriers he'd built over the years.

And she wasn't even aware of what she'd done, for she turned and added, "Coffee's all we have, I'm afraid. The kids must not have thought it worth stealing."

He nodded, deciding just to watch her without talking. She wasn't making sense, and he wouldn't, either, if he tried to talk.

What he really wanted was a drink, but if what she said was accurate, he'd had plenty the past few days. She'd be surprised to learn that normally he avoided alcohol. He'd learned long ago that it dulled the senses, and in his line of work that could be deadly.

In less time than he thought possible, she handed him a steaming cup of coffee. He downed half of it in one swallow. As the warmth spread through his insides, Sam leaned back against the buffalo robe and closed his eyes. He could hear her moving around him, but sleep claimed him before he had time to form words to thank her.

She didn't have to touch him; she didn't even have to talk to him. If felt good just knowing she was close.

Hours later, when he drifted back, he was surprised to find her still with him. A part of him hadn't wanted to wake because he thought she might be only in a dream. But there she sat on an empty crate, his freshly washed trousers spread across her lap.

Sam shoved his hair from his face and tried to rise. The

clearing came into focus and he realized where he was as he stood. When he groaned, she looked up.

"Oh, hello." Her voice was soft when she wasn't yelling. "Feeling better?"

He thought about asking "compared to what?" but instead just nodded.

"Good, want to show me the way to your cabin now? We really should find it and get settled in before dark."

He closed his eyes. It would sure help if she were sane or he more sober.

"What cabin? I don't have a cabin."

"Of course you do. You told me you had a place, and Denver directed me this far. If she was right about the clearing, she must know about the cabin. We just didn't have time for more directions."

The fog in his brain cleared slightly. If she'd been talking to Denver, no wonder the woman who claimed to be his wife was confused. "I only told Denver I had a cabin because I needed her to drop off supplies. This was a great place to leave a stash, but the clearing isn't big enough to build a cabin on."

Sarah looked disappointed. "I thought you had a place."

He didn't have to read her mind to know what she could have added. She'd been hoping that if he had a cabin, maybe then she'd have somewhere to stay. Could it be possible that such a lovely creature not only didn't have any clothes but had nowhere to go? If she'd picked him to follow, her other choices must be dire indeed.

"I only told Denver about a cabin because I needed supplies delivered here. I feared she would tell everyone in the state. This place is too hard to find for most to bother with. Denver's lips are so loose, every secret that ever went into her head drips out. You're probably not the only one she told about this spot, so we better get moving."

"I'm not." Sarah frowned. "She also must have told Tennessee Malone."

"Tennessee Malone?" The name sounded familiar, but Sam couldn't draw a face to match.

"He's the man who brought the children out here. You know, your children."

Sam started to wish he was still dreaming or drunk. "What children? I don't have any children."

Suddenly she jumped like a fireball on the sun and headed right toward him. A few inches from his nose, she shouted, "How dare you deny those sweet kids!"

"What kids?" he yelled, figuring if she could act like he was hard of hearing, he could do the same for her. "I never even heard of Malone or any kids he might have brought."

She poked him in the very place she'd patted him before. "They sat right here and knew your name and said you were their father."

Sam glanced past her to the clearing. He wouldn't have been surprised to see children pop up from behind the rocks. He had somehow woken up from this drunk on the other side of the moon and everything was backward.

He took a deep breath and tried to think. "What kids, Sarah? I don't see anyone out here but you and me on this wide spot between the river and the cliffs."

"Of course not," she answered, as if disgusted. "They disappeared."

Sam grabbed his trousers from her and pulled them on, ignoring the pain in his back. He needed to think and he always did his best when he was pacing.

Walking back and forth between the trees and the water, he tried to remember anything that had happened the past few days. Only flashes of her blinked through his mind. He remembered her all wet and cold, the feel of her cuddled against his side, the way she faced him without fear. He knew how she looked in just her undergarments, but he couldn't picture her on their wedding day. If there had been such a day.

She had handed him one of the white shirts Ruthie always made for him. She knew his name. She'd found this place.

Finally he figured it all out. He might be the one who just returned from a four-day drunk and who had been in so much agony he could think of nothing else, but she was definitely the one claiming crazy.

Surely if they were married and had kids he would have at least one memory of it.

Sam watched her closely, thinking he knew the feel of her touch on his flesh, but all the pieces wouldn't fit together.

He feared, in time, he'd get over being drunk, but she would still be crazy.

SEVEN

∞

"GET IN THE WAGON, SARAH," SAM ORDERED, FIGHT-
ing the need to swear. Slowly, over the past two days, he
had remembered the details of their wedding, but most of
the time after he'd been stabbed still floated in fog. In the
bar that morning, she had said he would owe her if she
helped him, but so far Sarah had not named her price.
Maybe once they got to town she would find something
in the mercantile that she considered payment for saving
his life.

"We have to go." He tried to keep the impatience from
his tone.

She stood a few feet away, arms folded, acting as if
she hadn't heard a word he'd said in the last hour.

"I'm not going," she finally answered. "I can't leave
your children."

They'd been over this a dozen times. Every time Sam
woke up, she mentioned the kids. Then he tried to convince her there were none. Surely, if they'd been around,

he would have at least heard them. "What children?" he asked as if he hadn't listened to her reply before.

"The ones who disappeared." She moved her head back and forth as if she were reciting a nursery rhyme.

He stared at her, remembering how he thought she looked like an angel when he'd married her. The angel was sure doing a good job of making his life hell. He wasn't sure he was strong enough yet to drive a team through the water and back to town. But if he stayed here without food, he'd never get any stronger. They'd even finished the last of the coffee at dawn. He either had to take his chances driving down the river or die here in the clearing.

"We have to go." Sam glanced up, guessing they had another three hours of daylight. Even if they left now, it would be late when they got to town. But there was no sense in waiting; conditions would not improve for them here in the clearing.

"No." She brushed the sleeve of an old dress she put on to travel. The faded blue garment looked even more like a rag than the one she'd been cutting on for bandages. The sleeves were an inch too long and had frayed until they were like thin lace covering her wrist.

In his wildest dreams, he never imagined he'd find a woman as stubborn as himself. She might not come to his shoulder in height, but she obviously thought of herself as an even match for him.

"Then I'm leaving you," he threatened.

"Then leave. When you pass out and fall off the wagon, don't float by here and expect me to fish you out."

He'd had all he could take. Slowly he lowered himself from the wagon and walked toward her.

If she had any sense, she'd run. But he knew she'd stand her ground. Something more than memory told him she hadn't backed down from him one step since they'd met. For most people, the length of a room wasn't far enough away from him. She must not have an ounce of self-preservation in her entire body.

When he stood in front of her, he noticed how tiny she was compared to his bulk. Didn't she know he could break her in two as if she were no more than a dried twig?

"Well?" he asked.

"Well." She took a breath and held it as if she were making herself bigger, more frightening.

Sam wrapped his arm around her waist and lifted her up against his chest. "You are going with me, not staying here to care for invisible children."

"I'm staying." She pointed her finger at him as though it were a weapon. "So put me down."

Sam had been fighting the torture of her nearness for two days. The hunger for food was nothing compared to the hunger he felt to touch her. But he wasn't an animal like some men he'd known, who would take a woman just because she was there for the taking.

If he were honest, though, he'd have to admit that he thought about holding her more than once. And a few times he'd wanted to return the touch she had so frequently given him.

She was already his. She'd told him so herself. He even remembered bits and pieces of the wedding. Sarah was his and he'd spent every waking hour not touching her while she'd patted and poked on him like a kid at an ant bed.

"Well?" She glared at him with those sky blue eyes. "Put me down!"

Sam lowered her to the ground without removing his arm from around her. The hint of honeysuckle drifted in the air, and he guessed she'd used the sliver of soap she had left to wash up. Before he thought of why, he leaned forward and kissed her hard on the mouth.

She didn't fight, or try to push away, but she didn't kiss him back, either. She felt stiff and cold, as if his advance had stopped her blood from flowing. He couldn't even feel her heart beating. It was as if he'd caught a butterfly and held it a little too tightly.

When he straightened, he let go of her and said two words he'd never said in his life. "I'm sorry."

If she had yelled at him, or slapped him, or swore to kill him, Sam would have felt better. At least she would have reacted. But she did nothing. The nothing hurt worse than anything she could have thought to do.

She didn't back away from him now, he admired her for that. She stood right where he'd planted her and said, "You got a right, I guess. But don't expect me to take any part of your handling me. I've been told men have needs that sometimes they can't help but force on a woman." Her chin rose slightly. "All I ask is that you don't hurt me overly if you plan on not honoring our bargain."

"What bargain?"

She stared at him with a hint of fear sparkling in her eyes. "You said if I helped you out back there in the bar that you would owe me one."

"I did." Sam had no intention on going back on his word but he couldn't remember. "Name your price."

"I ask one thing only. I probably should have said something earlier, but with you so hurt, I didn't see that there was a need."

"Ask." Sam wasn't sure he wanted to hear her words, but he knew he could wait no longer.

"I ask that we not become fully man and wife. . . . I ask that you not bed me until I'm ready. Just for once in my life I want my body to belong to me for the giving. I'll be a wife to you in all other ways, I promise."

The request seemed simple, but Sam saw the importance of her favor reflected in her eyes. He knew little of her past, but he saw her fighting for control in some part of her world. And here, with them, seemed to be where she drew the line.

He turned away. A week ago he would have sworn he didn't have a heart, but Sarah just cut a chunk out of it. With coldness she spoke of something that was supposed to be special between a man and a woman. With the honesty of her stare she made his kiss less than nothing. And light blue eyes told him she meant every word. She would accept his advance, even his abuse if he chose not to keep his word. All she asked was that he allow her to live through it, like what he offered was a torture.

Half the people in Texas hated him and he didn't care. They could be afraid of him or believe all the legends they wanted and it didn't matter. As far as he could tell, Sarah didn't even know enough about him to fear him. He'd never done anything to harm her.

She just thought less of him because he was a man . . . because he had needs . . . because he wanted her. As if wanting her were a crime. As if she had already decided he gave no honor to his words.

"I'll never touch you again, if that is the way you want it, Sarah." The words tasted bitter in his throat. Despite her stubbornness, she was the first woman in years that his arms ached to hold. A woman he thought it might be nice to come home to. The only one who'd stirred his blood when he looked at her. "I swear."

She stared into the water, and he guessed she didn't believe him.

"It doesn't matter," she answered, pushing her hair off

her shoulder with her fingers as if she dusted away a bad memory. "I only hoped."

"Sarah?" He waited for her to look at him. He couldn't help but wonder if anyone had ever kept a promise to her.

When her eyes met his, they sparkled with unshed tears. "I'll keep my word," he swore. "Or I'll give you back my Colt and you shoot me."

She smiled. "I don't know much about guns."

"I'll teach you just in case." He turned to check the lines on the horses, thinking if he kept looking at her, he might as well hand her the Colt right now.

Sam ran his tongue across his bottom lip, remembering the taste of her. He hadn't given her much of a first kiss, he decided. More like an attack. No wonder he saw fear in her eyes. She probably thought he planned to knock her down and mate with her right here in the clearing. He had his work cut out for him, trying to keep from touching her while figuring out how to hold her when she decided the time was right.

He waited a few more minutes before he said as softly as he'd ever issued an order. "Get in the wagon, Sarah. We'll make it to town tonight, load up with supplies, and come back tomorrow, if that is the way you want it. If we stay here, we'll all starve. You, me, the invisible children. I can drive the wagon on land, but I need help in the current. I can't make it to town and back without you. Leaving is our only option."

She turned away from him and walked to the tree line. After a long pause she yelled, "We'll be back in two days! I'm leaving the blanket and the buffalo robe so you can stay warm!"

When she noticed him watching her, she raised her chin. "All right, Sam Gatlin, I'm ready." She lifted her bundle she'd tied together with her shawl.

"You taking that?" he asked.

"Of course. A lady has to have belongings."

He didn't comment, but wondered what she carried. As far as he knew she was down to near nothing. One dress she'd been using for bandages. The knife she'd pulled out of his back. A half-empty bag she'd claimed an old woman had given her as medicine. Not much in the way of belongings, he decided.

They climbed into the wagon and started off without another word. The first few hours were hard, fighting the currents in the water. Sam held the reins as long as he could. When she took over, he circled his arm around her, bracing her in the seat, making it easier on her to drive without having to worry about tumbling from the bench.

He tried not to think of the way she felt against him. She might have married him to get out of jail, but she wanted no part of him as a husband. And he didn't want her if she thought she was just doing her duty. Sometime soon he'd have to tell her about how he made his living, and then she wouldn't stay with him.

But for now he'd hold her against him, acting like the feel of her didn't affect him. For once he wanted to believe he could be a normal man. He didn't want to think of the handful of outlaws who wanted him dead, or the places where folks swore when anyone said his name.

At first he'd done what he had to for money. He'd told himself he was in the right, he wasn't breaking any laws. He accepted jobs no one else wanted. Fighting on the frontier, bounty hunting. The pay was good, and drifting seemed destined to be his way.

He thought he would walk away when he'd done his part, or made enough, but that day never came. Lately, he had even stopped thinking about the possibility of another life until one night at Cedar Point when he saw an angel.

Only problem was, that angel wanted more than he could give. She planned to be a wife to him, and Sam had no plans of remaining a husband.

Shadows covered the town when they finally saw it along the horizon. The horses didn't speed up as they usually did with the promise of hay ahead of them. Like Sam, they were too tired.

He had to stay alert. Both their lives might depend on it. She didn't know it yet, she hadn't been married to him long enough to understand that a town or anywhere with people was not a haven, but a danger.

Ignoring the pain in his back, he pressed forward. The sooner they got to town, the sooner they could leave. He didn't care where they traveled next as long as it was away from people and for a long enough time for him to heal.

Sam unhitched the team while she got a room with a twenty-dollar gold piece he pulled from an opening in the leather of his gun belt.

Sleep seemed to have settled on the little no-name town. Tonight not even piano music drifted from the saloon.

Sarah thought of getting separate quarters, but wasn't sure how much more money Sam had. It seemed as if he'd drawn his final stash for the night's stay. When she wrote Mr. and Mrs. Sam Gatlin on the register, the night clerk raised an eyebrow, but didn't say a word. She carried her bundle upstairs to the same room where they'd spent their first night. A lifetime had passed since then.

Spreading out her belongings on the bed, she removed the knife she'd pulled from his back, the remains of the dress he'd bought her, and his extra shirt. She also had his comb and the thin box of matches.

Sitting in the only chair, she waited for him with the

door open. If he wandered into the wrong room this late,
she might find herself a widow again. She lit the lantern,
hoping he would see the light when he headed down the
hallway.

Unwittingly, she compared Sam to her first husband.
Mitchell had not been so tall, or as thick as Sam. Mitchell
had never yelled at her, or argued with her over anything.
From the beginning, he'd shown little interest in her or in
what she did all day as long as she did what was expected
of her. They'd married one morning, then she'd moved
her few things into a kitchen that had been set up by his
first wife. By supper she had a meal prepared.

On their wedding day Mitchell had complained about
a late start as they drove home from the preacher's. He
worked until dark that first day. When he finally came in
from the fields, it was as if they'd been married forever.
Like Granny Vee, he believed in rules. Sarah had broken
the first one that night by moving things around in the
kitchen. Mitchell reminded her that everything was to remain as his wife had left it.

Sarah touched her sleeve. Her dress, the only dress she
owned, had once been Mitchell's first wife's. Sarah had
always felt like a poor replacement for someone he had
loved and lost.

He never looked at her with hungry eyes as Sam had
today in the clearing He'd never grabbed her and kissed
her so hard her teeth hurt.

Sarah closed her eyes and fought back tears. But late
at night . . . late at night Mitchell's hands would slide
along her leg and pull up her nightgown. Without a word
he'd climb on her. Cold, almost impersonal, he'd take her.
Then, without a comment or a caring touch, he'd leave.
Rolling over to sleep. Not bothering to lower her gown.
And every time . . . she fought down tears as she remem-

bered . . . every time he hurt her deep inside where bruises never show.

She told herself she hadn't minded the bedding so much. But she dreamed of more. This time she wanted to be a wife, a true partner. She would do all that was expected of her, but she would not be bedded by Sam until he made up his mind to be her husband. This time she would wait until she was ready to be truly married.

Sarah heard Sam lumbering slowly up the stairs like a great tired bear looking for his den. When he reached the door, she saw exhaustion in his eyes.

"Are you all right?" she asked as he moved into the room and closed the door. He hadn't said more than a few words for hours. She didn't know if he was mad about the kiss or simply saving all his energy for traveling.

"Just tired," he answered as he turned and set the rifle by the bed. A dark red stain spread across the back of his white shirt.

"You've reopened the wound." Sarah hurried to his side, hating to see blood once more. The smell of it seemed to fill the room.

"It's nothing." He made a movement with his hand as if to shoo her away.

"I'll be the judge of that. Lie down on the bed and let me have a look."

Sam unbuckled his gunbelt and draped it over the side of the bed just as he had the last time they'd stayed here. "I'm too tired to argue, Sarah. Just shoot me. I'm not sure I can endure much more of your nursing."

Sarah grinned, remembering how she'd thought of shooting him in this very room not so many days ago. "Don't tempt me. Now lie down." She wanted the blood on his back gone as fast as possible.

He almost fell atop the bed as she pulled his shirt from his trousers.

The wound wasn't as bad as she feared. Carefully she cleaned the blood, letting the cold water aid in stopping the bleeding. As she pressed a rag against the opening, Sarah spread her other hand across his unharmed flesh. Lightly she stroked his skin as if her touch could brush away the pain she caused.

He didn't make a sound, but his flesh was warm and seemed to welcome her caress. Strange, how she liked touching him. In a small way, he belonged to her, this powerful man. He didn't have to tell her no one ever touched him. She knew. Just as she knew his soul must be as scarred as his body. But fate had put her in the lion's cage, and she'd lived too long in fear to be afraid anymore.

When she finished bandaging his wound, she heard his slow steady breathing and knew he was sound asleep. Too tired to give it much thought, Sarah curled up next to him and fell asleep.

EIGHT

GUNFIRE RICOCHETED DOWN THE HALLWAY, JARRING
Sarah awake. She heard people running. A woman
screamed. Thuds rattled against the walls as if bodies were
being tossed. Chaos rode full speed toward her door.

"Hurry!" Sam ordered as he pulled on a new white
shirt. "Get dressed."

Since she'd fallen asleep in her clothes, Sarah had nothing to do but stand. "What is it?"

Angry voices drew nearer. Sam didn't bother with the
shirt's buttons as he strapped on his gunbelt.

"My guess is Levi Reed is looking for me so he can
finish the job he started with his knife."

"What makes him want to kill you?" She tried to pull
on her shoes.

"I sent his brother to prison."

"But—"

Sam grabbed her arm and pulled her toward the window. "I don't have time for a discussion, Sarah." He

opened the window. "I'll lower you down as far as I can. You'll have to drop from there."

She stretched for her bundle. "What about you? It's not me he's looking for but you. If you hide, I'll tell him I don't know where you are."

He took her parcel and tossed it out without bothering to look at where her collected belongings landed.

"My things!" she cried as he reached for her next.

"They're waiting for you," he grunted as he lifted her over the windowsill. "And don't worry about me," he said, as if he thought she was still thinking about him. "It will take more than the likes of Reed and his men to kill me."

Sarah glanced at the drop below. "I can't . . ."

He didn't wait for her to finish. He locked his hand around her arm and shoved her off the ledge.

Clinging to him, she whispered as she dangled, "Don't drop me . . . I'm fragile. I'll die!"

"No, you won't. I promise. You're about as fragile as I am lucky."

Her hands slipped along the sleeve of his shirt.

"Go to the mercantile and buy what you need. I have credit there. I'll get the horses and pick you up as soon as I can."

Sarah's shoe slipped off and sailed downward, landing with a plop. "I can't do this!" She clung to his arm. He didn't understand. She wasn't brave.

"You can," he ordered more than encouraged as he swung her away from the building and released his grip.

Sarah held her breath, too frightened to scream as she dropped. The hard hit she expected ended as more of a thump in the weeds growing between the hotel and the wooden walkway.

Jumping up, she straightened her skirt and lifted her

knotted bundle, trying to act as if she hadn't just tumbled from a hotel window. Luckily, the street was deserted. No one saw her graceless fall.

Slowly she moved onto the uneven walk, gingerly testing each bone for breaks. Glancing back, she frowned at the window where Sam had been only a moment before. What kind of husband drops his wife over the ledge? What kind of man figures any trouble coming is bound to be looking for him?

The racket from the hotel window grew. Pandemonium rumbled down to the street below.

Sarah ran toward the mercantile. She heard shouts. An angry voice answered back. Then gunfire.

"He's dead," she whispered to herself as she stomped away in shoes she'd never had time to tie. "My no-good, drunkard, backstabbed husband is dead. Left me with three kids and no roof over my head." She laughed without humor. "Just when I think things are as bad as they can get, they take a turn for the worse."

Ten minutes later she wasn't surprised to learn that she couldn't touch any of the money Sam had at the store. The shopkeeper, a short, barrel-chested man who introduced himself as Mr. Moon, claimed he might need the balance to pay for Sam's burial expenses.

He greeted other women who came in the store to browse, and did his best to ignore Sarah. She guessed Mr. Moon thought, as she did, that Sam must have died amid the gunshots the whole town had heard.

Sarah circled inside the store trying not to listen to the whispers of other customers. "He's finally been killed," one said. "I'm not surprised. Men as mean as him don't live long round here," another muttered. "Did you hear what they say he did in Fort Worth one time . . . ?"

Sarah concentrated on the clocks for sale behind the

counter. Granny Vee had an old clock on her wall. It hadn't worked in years, but Granny still dusted it twice a week, telling Sarah that folks have something fine when they have a clock.

The gossips' voices invaded her thoughts. Sarah focused on the ticking. She didn't want to listen. They said that Sam was no better than a hired gun. "Some men hunt bear or deer," one said. "What kind of man hunts men even if they are outlaws?"

"That's his wife, I've heard," another whispered back. "She'll be leaving him when she finds out about him."

"Not a woman in the state that would stay," the other replied, "not married to Sam Gatlin."

Munching on a cracker from the barrel beside her, she tried to pick out her favorite clock as though she had the funds to consider such a purchase, but each tick eroded her thoughts to worries.

With the coins left from the twenty-dollar gold piece Sam gave her for the room, Sarah would have to make each selection count. Taking her time, she examined every item she put on the counter. Beans, flour, coffee, salt, matches. All musts. Crackers, soap, a little sugar, a dozen eggs, and bread. All needs. With each item Mr. Moon kept a running total, making sure she wasn't spending a penny more than she'd pulled from her pocket.

Sarah looked at a sewing box made of tin and a bolt of sturdy gray wool for winter as she tried to figure out if she had enough money left to buy both. The sewing box was stuffed with supplies, but cost almost two dollars. The wool was three more.

A blue dress hanging beside the blankets caught her eye. Though several sizes too big, it was the kind of dress she wished she had. Not fancy by any means, but stylish with lace on the collar and buttons down the front for no reason other than that they looked good. She brushed her hand over the soft cotton.

"That just came in, yesterday," the shop owner said with a raised eyebrow. "I'd rather it not be handled unless you're buying."

Sarah lowered her arm.

"She's buying" came a voice from the back of the store.

She couldn't hide her smile as Sam's big frame stepped from the shadows. One hand rested easily on his holstered gun handle. He'd slung his jacket over one shoulder like a cape.

"Yes, sir, Mr. Gatlin." The shopkeeper hurried to pull down the dress. "It may be a little big for your woman, but she can take it up, I reckon." Suddenly Mr. Moon was all sunshine.

Sam stood on the other side of a huge table of supplies. "Wrap anything else she needs; I think my account can stand the hit."

He remained perfectly still as Sarah added bacon, canned goods, and the wool to her selections. She touched the bolt. "For the kids?"

Sam grinned. "Invisible children shouldn't need many clothes." But he nodded at the shopkeeper as Sarah set the sewing kit atop the material.

"My wagon's out back," Sam said without offering to help load. "Add a couple bottles of whiskey to the order and a basket of those apples you've been unloading." He glanced along the top row of shelves behind Mr. Moon. "Add a few bars of honeysuckle-scented soap if you have it and the largest carpetbag you got."

When the man disappeared with his first box of food, Sarah moved around the table, noticing that all the women spreading rumors had hurried out the front door far more silently than they had arrived. "I thought you were giving up the bottle." She stood by Sam's side, expecting him to argue with her. "You told me you never drink except when you're hurt, yet the first time we're in a place that sells—."

Without turning to face her, Sam took her hand. "You'll be needing that bag to carry your belongings in." He didn't even act as if he heard her as he squeezed her fingers.

Trying to pull away, Sarah looked down at the huge hand holding hers. Warm blood dripped across her fingers, and she realized his draped coat hid a wound beneath his shoulder.

"You're hurt!"

"Shot," Sam corrected. "And I'd appreciate it if you didn't make an announcement. I took one in the arm, two in the leg. But I think those bullets just passed through muscle."

His dark eyes stared down at her, and she saw the all-too-familiar pain. "Sarah . . ." Sweat formed across his forehead as he fought to remain standing.

"I know," she answered, aggravation blending with panic in her voice. "Better get you out of town before you fall."

He nodded slightly and slipped his arm around her waist.

They moved slowly through the back room of the store. Sarah acted as if she were showing him something when the storekeeper hurriedly passed with another load.

"Oh!" Sarah yelled to the round little man's back as she tried to keep him too busy to notice them. "Could you add six more cans of peaches and three blankets?" They crossed the cluttered storage room, Sam leaning more heavily against her shoulder with each step. "And"—she fought to keep her voice even—"I forgot potatoes." They made it to the opening when she added, "And, Mr. Moon, Sam just reminded me, he'd like a couple of pairs of your best longhandles. Winter's coming on."

They could hear the shopkeeper groan. He'd obviously rather be out bragging about waiting on Sam Gatlin than actually doing so.

Moving as fast as Sam could, they crossed to the wagon. Sarah noticed it was the same old rented buckboard and the same two horses, but Sam had tied a saddled mount to the back. This black stallion was not like any she'd seen for rent at a livery, but there was no time for questions.

Five minutes later, when Mr. Moon finally collected all the extra things Sarah asked for, she and Sam were already in the wagon, their laps covered with one of the new blankets.

When the store owner shoved the last box in the back with an oath, Sam seemed to be forcing his voice to sound calm. "I shot one of Reed's gang when they stormed the room at the hotel. He had a price on his head." Sam took a breath and continued, "Tell the sheriff to take the man's burial expenses out of the reward and deposit the rest of the money with you. I'll pick it up in a month or so."

Mr. Moon brightened. "Yes, sir. You know I'll keep it in the safe for you. Same agreement as always, a five percent charge for handling."

"One more thing." Sam gripped the side of the wagon and straightened so the shopkeeper wouldn't know he was hurt. "The next time my wife comes in here, you'd better be damn sure I'm dead before you turn her down. Understand?"

Mr. Moon looked too frightened to answer.

"And don't go calling her my woman. She's my wife. Anything that belongs to me belongs to her. She can take my entire stash out of your safe if she feels the need."

Sarah glanced at the shopkeeper. He nodded and she knew the next time she came into his store she'd be treated differently.

Lifting the reins, Sarah maneuvered the horses along the back of the stores toward open country. After a few minutes Sam pointed at a path veering off the main road and not north in the direction they'd entered town.

"Take that trail as far as you can," he whispered under his breath. "I want to make sure we're not followed."

She didn't question, guessing he had his reasons and she'd find out soon enough. He might be bleeding, but there was still a power about him. A wounded lion was still a lion.

They traveled half a mile down the path before she turned to him and asked, "So, what did you do before I came along, just die every time you went to town?"

Sam didn't laugh.

Sarah knew the pain must be bad. "We need to stop and let me take a look at those wounds."

"Not yet," Sam said with clenched teeth. "Not until we're out of sight of the town. I'll show you a place. Try to miss as least one of the mud holes between now and then."

"I was driving a team before I could walk," Sarah lied. In truth she had only learned to drive a team when they started out on the wagon train. There, every wife drove, everyone walked from time to time.

Sam grunted at her claim as she managed to roll over another mud hole.

Ten minutes later Sarah turned a bend in the road and pulled the wagon off to the side onto a grassy area near a stream. She spread one of the new blankets over grass already brown and helped Sam down. Blood coated one side of his leg like thick paint.

"I hate blood," she whispered more to herself than him.

"I'm not too fond of it myself." He smiled. "I don't mind other people's, but the sight of my own doesn't sit well with me."

"Take off your clothes and let me count the wounds this time."

Sam hesitated.

Sarah collected supplies. "Take them off, Sam Gatlin. I'll not be seeing anything I haven't seen before."

He pulled off his once white shirt slowly, trying not to raise his left arm more than a few inches. He stumbled when he stepped out of his pants while trying to hold a blanket up to allow a bit of privacy. Sarah hurried to steady him, but ended up tumbling with him. He twisted as they fell, taking the blow of the ground while she landed atop him.

For a moment Sarah didn't move. She lay atop the wall of his chest, listening to his heart pound beneath her ear.

"Are you all right?" she whispered as she struggled to sit up.

He didn't move. His eyes were closed. The corner of his forehead looked purple.

She stood and circled him. The blanket he still held by one corner lay across his waist, barely covering his private parts. "Sam?" Even without his gun belt or clothes he still looked like a mighty warrior. "Sam!"

He didn't answer. He was one bloody, magnificent creature, she thought, even out cold. Not one ounce of pretty or even handsome on him, but two hundred pounds of solid muscle and power.

Tripping over the new tin sewing box, she found what his head must have hit when it fell. "You dented my sewing box," she complained as if he could hear her . . . as if it mattered.

Sarah pulled their canteen from beneath the seat, thankful she'd refilled it when they'd left the river yesterday. Looking back at him, she shook her head, not knowing where to start.

"You are doing your best to turn me into a widow again, Sam Gatlin, but I've got news for you, I'm not going to make it easy on you. If I learned anything from living with Granny Vee, it was how to patch up folks. She always told me doctoring was easier than picking cotton, so that's why she learned it. But then, she never ran across the likes of you."

She jerked the linsey-woolsey dress from her bundle. He'd bought her the dress the morning after they'd married, and she was running out of places to cut strips along the skirt. "I've made up my mind that I don't have any place to go, so I might as well stay here with you and be your wife." Sarah washed away blood so she could see how much damage he'd done to himself getting into a gunfight. "Devote my life to patching your already beat up body."

She smiled, remembering what the women in the store had said. "I guess I'm the one woman in the state who'll stay married to you. But I'm giving you fair warning, you need to think about changing your habits."

Sarah let her fingers slide along the unharmed muscle of his thigh. Touching him was like brushing over fine mahogany; she could feel the solidness with her fingertips. The scars only added character to him.

"All my life, all I've ever wanted was someone to love, and it looks like you're the only one who applied." She continued to touch him, hoping he'd know that someone cared. "So I'm going to love all six foot of no-good, drunken, worthless inch of you. I've heard folks say not to try to make a man over when you marry him, but they never met you."

She dusted a little of her herbs and wrapped his leg where one bullet must have slid along his thigh. He'd been right, the bullets had passed clean through.

"You see"—she pointed her knife at him as she moved to the next wound—"I figure anything I do is an improvement 'cause you're about the most low-down, mean, worthless man I could ever hope to run into. You're less than not-much-of-a-father to those kids, you got people trying to kill you at every turn. Even respectable ladies gossip about the mean things you've done. Far as I know, not a soul cares if you live or die."

Sarah smiled. "Except me, Sam Gatlin. There's something good left in you or you wouldn't have bought me a dress or told that shopkeeper I was your wife. So I've made up my mind, and there isn't anything you can do to change it. I love you." She knew she made no sense, but Sarah had to start somewhere. If she was afraid of him, or hated him, she'd just be standing in the crowd. For some reason he'd married her, and he hadn't forced himself on her. It wasn't exactly a long list of good traits, but it was a start.

She cleaned the next wound while noticing his back had healed nicely. None of the bullet holes were as bad as she'd feared. The lead only grazed his arm deep enough to cause bleeding. His legs would heal as soon as scabs formed.

Finally all the blood was removed and the damaged skin doused with whiskey, sprinkled with Granny Vee's herbs, and wrapped. She flattened her hand against his heart and felt the warmth of his skin along with the steady pounding. She'd done the best she could do. Maybe, if they ever made it into town again, she'd buy a medicine box.

Looking up, she found dark eyes staring at her. Pain still clung to the edges, but his gaze was clear.

His eyes were brown, she thought, deep chocolate brown.

Neither of them moved. They just looked at each other as if they had never seen the other before. She left her hand resting against his chest as she lifted her chin, slightly challenging her right to touch him.

"I'm not dying, Sarah." He rubbed the bump on his forehead. "These were no more than scratches." Bracing himself, he sat up slowly, nursing his bandaged arm.

"You can't promise that." She let her hand fall away, brushing against scars as she moved. "We've been married less than a week, and you've been attacked twice. I'd say you were accident prone, but none of these wounds are accidents."

Sam stared at the bend where they'd turned off the road, then checked to make sure his Colt was within reach. "I'm not dealing with anything new here, Sarah." He closed his eyes, as if dreading what he had to say. "I was ten when my father was killed in the War Between the States. I was big for my age, so I went along with my uncle and grandfather to bring his body home. My mother had died a few years before in childbirth. I guess the Yankee scouts thought we hauled supplies when they ambushed us. Within minutes the fighting was over. All my family, except my baby sister, died that day."

His voice remained flat as if the memory had grown too old to stir emotion. "A Confederate scout found me a few days later on the road, a bullet wound in my chest. I told him I was walking home."

Sarah's fingers brushed over the scar on his chest. The twisted flesh lay only an inch from where she'd felt his heart pounding.

"The Reb took me to a doctor working behind the lines. The doc just glanced my direction and asked me to rest outside the hospital tent. I heard him say that with the amount of blood covering me, it wouldn't be long. There was no use wasting time patching me up."

Sarah felt a chill. "What are you saying?"

He continued as if he hadn't heard her. "I fought along the frontier line near Fort Griffin soon as I got old enough to sign up. Twice I was left for dead by war parties, the only survivor in a scouting company. The first time the men welcomed me back to the fort, thinking I escaped death, but the second time they avoided me as if I'd somehow cheated it. The blessing became a curse."

"Maybe you were just lucky."

"No, if I'd been lucky, I wouldn't have been shot in the first place. A few years after the army, an old doctor in San Antonio patched me up after a gunfight. He told me that I heal faster than most. He said some men get a scratch and die of poisoning in the blood, but with me it's going to have to be a straight shot to the heart before I drop."

"So, what are you trying to tell me?"

Sam frowned. He looked down at her hand resting on the blanket only a few inches away. "It seems I've been trying to die for years, Sarah. For a long time after I saw my family die, I wanted to go with them. Then when I grew up and watched my friends shot while I stood right beside them, I thought nothing made sense."

"So you became a bounty hunter?"

He laid his fingers over hers. "Life lost all reason. I didn't really care if I lived or died."

"And now?"

His dark eyes met hers. "You gave me a reason to care."

NINE

Sam sat on the back of the wagon and watched his new wife as she walked down the creek's bank. Eventually she'd turn around and come back. Then she would have to talk to him no matter how much she hated the idea.

He seemed to have found the one thing that would make her think less of him. In truth, if he had any good traits, he might have told her about them. But he was a loner who had few friends. And the good he'd done, he couldn't tell anyone, not even Sarah. Lives depended on his silence. He'd buried more than one coffin filled with rocks to give an outlaw a second chance. Now he only wished he had another chance with her.

She knew all of it now. He was a bounty hunter.

Hell, he thought, he would settle for a first chance. She hadn't liked him from the start. The silence right after they married had been their best time together. Now that she knew half the outlaws in the state would gladly kill him, conditions between Sarah and him were not likely to improve.

But in his line of work, every year he made a few more enemies who thought they would be doing the world a favor if they killed him. Every year more tried. Sometimes he thought he was the one with his picture on a Wanted poster. Folks thought the bad guys should be brought to justice, only no one wanted to get too friendly with the man who did the job.

He'd lived the life of a bounty hunter for so long he hardly knew how to talk to normal folks. Maybe he should have tried to visit with her the night they married. If she'd learned about him then, she might not look so angry now.

But she seemed so frail and frightened, he decided to wait. Then there had been no time to explain why a man like him would even want a wife.

"One question?"

Sam hadn't noticed Sarah turning around and walking back to the wagon. Now she stood eye level to him almost bumping his knees as she leaned toward him.

"Just one?" he asked, trying to act as if the sight of her standing so close didn't bother him. People usually made a point not to get within reach of him.

"Why'd you marry me?" She narrowed her eyes as if she planned to evaluate his answer carefully.

Sam wasn't sure he knew the answer. Maybe because she looked so helpless in that jail. Maybe he was sick of being alone. Maybe the thought of her going home with one of the farmers rubbed him the wrong way. "I don't know," he finally admitted. "Maybe I thought I was doing you a favor. I had this idea life with me might be a little easier than jail." He almost laughed.

"Well, I know." She paced in front of him with her hands locked behind her back like a tiny general before troops. "You wanted someone to nurse you through all your 'accidents.' You wanted a mother for your children. . . ."

"I haven't got any children," he reminded her.

She ignored him. "You wanted someone to keep your house, only you don't have a house. And cook your meals and sleep in your bed."

She looked like a top going faster and faster in the wind. "You wanted someone who would be at your beck and call but who wouldn't mind being dropped from a window or two if the need arose. Well, Sam Gatlin, I—"

"I never said I didn't have a house."

Sarah whirled around. "Yes, you did!"

"I said I didn't have a *cabin*. I have a house."

She looked confused. "Tell me true: Do you have a house the way you don't have children?"

He raised an eyebrow, having no idea how to answer her.

When he didn't say anything, she added, "Maybe I should hit you on the other side with my sewing box."

To his surprise, she drew closer. With him seated on the wagon's gate, they were eye to eye. "I forgot to check that bruise," she whispered as she brushed against his leg, leaning in to look at his forehead. "A bruise can be as bad as a cut sometimes."

Her face was so close he almost bumped noses with her. Her fingers shoved the hair away from his forehead, then remained in his hair to hold it away so she could finish her examination.

Sam remained perfectly still while her other hand brushed across his forehead.

"Does this hurt?" she asked as her fingers pushed against his tender skin.

Sam felt her words fan across his face. Her left breast pushed against his arm so slightly he wasn't even sure if they touched or he just felt the warmth of her body so close.

She moved between his knees to look closer. "Now, you tell me if I'm hurting you," she said as she tested the skin of his forehead.

She was killing him, Sam thought. With every breath he filled his lungs with the fresh honeysuckle smell of her. He fought the urge to pull her closer. He'd promised himself he wouldn't touch her until she asked him to, and if nothing else in this world he was a man of his word, no matter how she tempted him.

She treated him like a head of livestock she was examining for barbed-wire cuts, but he didn't care. He enjoyed it anyway. He liked the feel of her fist tugging at his hair and the way she leaned close.

"I have a house," he finally whispered when she didn't go away. "It's north of here on a small farm. I haven't been there in a long time, but I think I can still find it. It's got trees running along one side to hold the wind at bay and a well out back with the sweetest water in it."

Her laughter touched his cheek.

"I wish you did have a farm. I've always wanted a place to call home. My first husband promised me that dream. He told me he had a farm when we married, but I soon learned the bank owned most of it. I'll not fall into believing it a second time."

Sam frowned. He didn't want to hear about a first husband.

She returned to the study of his forehead. "I don't think you did any permanent damage except to my sewing box."

Moving away as fast as she'd stepped near, Sarah mumbled, "If you're able, I'd like to try and reach the children before dark. I don't want them thinking we just left them, as Tennessee Malone did."

Sam felt pain when he wrinkled his brow. "What children?"

"Your children. I don't care what you say, we're not leaving them to die in that clearing." She folded up the blanket.

"I've told you I don't . . ."

She was back an inch from his face again staring at him as if she planned to call him out for a gun battle. "How about we go to the clearing and get your real children, and then tomorrow we can start for your imaginary farm?"

Sam smiled. "Or pick up my imaginary children and go to my real house."

Sarah glared at him, not backing down an inch.

"I'll make you a deal. We'll spend the night at the clearing, but if there are no children by sunup, we load up and leave. I need to get you somewhere safe as fast as I can. Reed is determined to see me dead, and I'm in no hurry to give him another shot."

Worry brushed her eyes. "All right. One night in the clearing and then we lay low. Shake on it?"

He took her small hand in his but didn't shake. He only felt it for a long moment enjoying the softness.

Then she was gone, rounding the wagon and climbing up on the bench. "I'll call you when I reach the river. Until then why don't you try to sleep."

Sam leaned back against the blankets. "You know the way?"

Sarah lifted her chin. "I found it the first time, didn't I?"

He stared at the sky and figured out why *widow* was a

much more popular word than *widower*. She was determined to kill him. If she missed a single bump in the road, he would have been surprised.

He glanced over at the two bottles of whiskey he'd had Moon put in with the supplies. His leg still throbbed and his arm hurt like hell, but he wasn't sure he wanted to hear what she would have to say if he reached for one of the bottles. He downed the rest of the water in the canteen and tried to relax.

By the time they reached the river, the sky had grown cloudy. He slowly maneuvered up beside her on the bench. Using his unharmed leg, he braced himself and pulled her back against him as the horses splashed into the water. This time, with only one arm to hold her, he felt Sarah rocking on the bench more.

"Are you all right?" he asked as she bumped against him.

"No," she answered without looking at him. "I'll probably break my back any minute. I'm not strong, you know."

"You're doing fine," he encouraged as he slid his hand along her arm and braced her efforts as she managed the reins. "You made it down this river with me passed out last time. It can't be any harder now."

But they were both exhausted when they reached the clearing.

"How did you ever find this place?" Sarah asked as they unloaded.

"A friend told me about it." Sam didn't add that the friend had been an outlaw. "He said he could go up in the trees if he didn't want anyone coming to find him."

Sarah dropped the blanket she'd been unloading. "Up in the trees," she whispered as she hurried toward the edge of the cottonwoods.

Sam watched her moving along the tree line, staring into the branches.

"There!" she shouted. "There they are."

Sam limped over and looked up to where she pointed. The light played tricks on his vision, dancing between shadow and light, but after a few minutes he saw it. A shelf built between two huge branches about eight feet off the ground. A shelf floored wide enough to lay a blanket down and sturdy enough to hold two or three men.

"Well, I'll be." He moved closer. "All the times I've been here and I never noticed that."

Three small heads poked over the edge of the tree house. "Children!" he whispered in surprise.

Sarah poked him in the ribs. "Of course, children. Those are your kids."

They watched as the little ones climbed down from their nest. He thought of arguing with her one more time that he didn't have children, but with the proof in front of him, he didn't have much to stand on.

"Hello," K.C. said as she reached the ground and stared up at him. "We didn't think you would come back."

The two smaller ones stood at her side, looking up at Sam as if he were a giant.

Sarah touched each of them on the head. "Of course we came back, but this time you have to go with us. No more running away to hide."

K.C. shook her head. "The man, Malone, told us we would only be safe here. Nowhere else. He said our daddy would come for us."

"Well, now he has." Sarah smiled. "And we plan to take you somewhere warm to stay. Wait until you see the wool I bought to make you a dress."

If Sarah noticed that the children only stared at Sam, she did not comment.

K.C. only stared at her, obviously not believing a word.

Sarah hugged the two smaller children, then offered to make them something to eat. As the little ones began helping her collect wood for a fire, Sam's hand stopped K.C.

He waited until Sarah was far enough away not to hear, then motioned to K.C. to move farther along the tree line. The child looked frightened, but she obeyed.

After they were several feet away from the others, Sam lowered slowly to a downed tree trunk so he wouldn't seem so huge to her. When she didn't say anything, he whispered, "You know I'm not your father, don't you?"

K.C. nodded as she stared down at her fingers. "I thought you could be. I've never seen him in light, and I remember seeing you once talking to my mama. But you don't sound like he does. Back home he would always come late at night. I could hear him talking to my mama. She said he watched over us all the time, even when we didn't even know he was around. I would sometimes stay awake and listen to him talk. I liked the way he sounded."

Sam studied her. "What's your mother's name?"

"Molly," the girl answered. "But she's dead."

"And your father's name?"

"Mama would never tell me. She said it was best no one knew, not even me." Tears bubbled in the girl's eyes. "I don't know why she couldn't have told me. I wouldn't have said anything to anyone. I promise."

Sam thought of patting her on the shoulder, but he figured he might frighten the poor child to death if he did. "I know who your father is, K.C., and I know where to find him, but your mother was right, it's important we keep not only his name, but anything about him a secret until I can get the three of you to him."

He watched Sarah moving around the campfire, setting up a home like a mother hen. "K.C.," he whispered without looking at the girl. "Until we find your real dad, maybe you better keep telling folks I'm your father. It could be safest for both you and him."

The child nodded. "But when we find him, will he tell me?" She fought back tears. "Will he want us? Will he love us?"

Sam looked at her then, her blue eyes dancing with the fun of a lie. "I know for a fact he loves you. He'll want you." Sam grinned. "By the way, you have your true father's eyes. You'll know when you see him that he's the real one."

Before he could react, the child did the strangest thing. She wrapped her arms around his neck and hugged him.

TEN

"Don't even try to tell me those are not your kids," Sarah whispered an inch from Sam's nose. "I saw K.C. hugging you."

For a moment all he could manage was to breathe in the fresh honeysuckle aroma of the woman above him.

She'd crawled atop his blanket about the time his body relaxed enough to sleep. He barely had time to smile before he realized she only came to talk.

"They are not my children," he said calmly as she dug an elbow into his chest as though she leaned on a table and not flesh.

She touched his lips with her fingertips. "Quiet! They'll hear you."

He didn't care if the children heard him, but he did like the taste of her finger. The kids knew he wasn't their father. Frank Jackson's wife had taught them to lie to protect them; having an outlaw for an old man could be dangerous. She knew if they even said his name, it could place them in danger.

Couldn't Sarah notice they paid him little or no mind? Didn't she wonder why, if they were his kids, that they hadn't worried, or at least cared, if he lived or died?

Sarah had spent the entire evening referring to him as "Papa" in front of them but that didn't make it so.

Sam remembered meeting their mother once when he'd stopped at her place long enough to deliver a message from a man he owed a favor to. She greeted him with wide-eyed fear until she saw the letter in his hand. After that, Sam was pretty sure she never more than glanced at him again.

He tried to remember what Frank Jackson's wife had looked like. Thin. Not too tall. But taller than the lady propped against his rib cage.

"You cold?" he asked Sarah as she shivered.

"No," she lied as she pulled her blanket around her shoulders.

Sam guessed she had given away most of the covers to the children, who now slept soundly and warm by the fire.

"Come on, climb under mine." Sam lifted one side of his blanket. "If we use both our blankets, we might not freeze."

She hesitated.

"Don't look at me like that, Sarah. If I planned to attack you, I would have done so long before now."

She nodded and scooted beneath his blanket while spreading hers over them both.

"What are the rules?" she whispered, wiggling at his side.

"Rules?"

"You know, the rules for sleeping beside you. All men have them."

He let out a long breath, guessing the "all men" totaled one former husband. "I don't know," he answered honestly. "The few times I've had a woman in my bed, we didn't sleep."

Sarah leaned up and placed her elbow back on his chest as she stared down at him. "You never slept with a woman? Truly?"

For the first time in more years than he could remember, a blush warmed his weather-tanned cheeks. Sarah acted as if he'd just told her he was a virgin. In truth, for a man who spent most of his time alone, never staying one place long enough to get to know anyone, he probably was as close to a virgin as a man his age gets.

He watched firelight dance in her hair and tried to figure out how to explain. "The women I took to my bed worked nights and didn't have all that much time."

"Oh," she said. "Poor things. Granny Vee sometimes had to deliver a baby in the middle of the night. I always helped, and then it would take me days to get caught up on my sleep."

Sam fought to keep from laughing. "Well, I gave them a little extra money to help them out."

Sarah propped her chin on her hand. "That was nice of you. You see, Sam, about the time I think you are all bad, you surprise me and tell me something nice."

"Nobody's all bad or all good, Sarah." He couldn't see her eyes for the shadows, but he knew she studied him. The woman was always watching him as though she'd never seen the likes of him in her life.

He thought about telling her about the kids' father. About how Frank Jackson walked through a hail of bullets to help his friend out. About how a no-good member of a train-robbing gang had risked his life for another when the Bass gang had been ambushed at Round Rock a few years back.

Sam had been across the street when three members of the gang rode in to check out the bank. The sheriff and the Rangers had been tipped off, so they were ready for the outlaws. One was killed with a shot to the head by a young Ranger named Ware.

Sam figured the Bass gang would all be propped up in coffins within the hour. But Frank rode away that day, holding a wounded Bass in the saddle.

Later that night Sam accidentally stumbled into Frank's camp. The outlaw drew first and could have killed Sam, but he didn't. Maybe he'd seen enough killing for one day. But, whatever the reason, Sam never turned Frank Jackson in.

"I could tell you some of the rules if you like." Sarah pulled Sam from the past as she relaxed beside him. "I've been sleeping next to people all my life."

"All right." He put his head on his unbandaged arm and waited. He imagined the first rule would probably be that he'd never fall asleep with her wiggling next to him. He'd dreamed a few times of having a woman to sleep with, but there were always too many strings to make it seem practical or fair to her.

When he saw Sarah in jail, he'd thought, finally there was a woman who might consider being married to him an improvement on her status. The question that gnawed at him was why had he considered the idea this time?

"Well," she began, as if he were paying attention, "first, don't touch any more than necessary. And if your feet are cold, don't put them on the other person's leg."

"Are your feet cold?" he interrupted.

"My feet are always cold." She rose once more to her

perch on his chest. "And Granny Vee used to say never sleep with your face close to each other or you'll catch each other's breath. She told me once that she knew of a couple who slept nose to nose, and there wasn't enough air for them both. They were found dead in their bed one morning, their eyes wide open, staring at each other in surprise."

Sam couldn't stop the laughter that rumbled all the way from his gut. He almost knocked her off him.

When he calmed down, he asked, "Any other rules?"

Sarah leaned her head sideways, as if considering not telling him any more. "Just that there are some places you can accidentally touch and some places you can't."

"What are they?"

She rolled to her back and stared up at the stars. "Like our arms are touching now. That's all right."

"What's not all right?"

"I swear, Sam Gatlin, you must be seven or eight years older than me, you'd think you would have learned a few things in all that time."

"But you've been married," he commented, as if that somehow made her wiser. "You've been through this before."

"That's true. Marriage teaches you a great deal. But if you don't know some things, I'm not going to be the one to tell you."

Sam tried to sound serious, but he could never remember feeling so lighthearted. She was a shot of fine whiskey to his senses. "But if you don't tell me, how will I know?"

Sarah lay silent for so long, he didn't think she planned to answer him. Then finally she whispered, "I'll tell you if you break the rule. Otherwise, there is no need to talk about it."

"Fair enough," he agreed.

"And Sam?"

"Yes, Sarah?"

"I may have been married before, but it was nothing like this."

"You mean your husband wasn't stabbed and shot at or offered you the ground for a bed?"

"No, not that so much." She stared up. When she finally answered, he could barely hear her words. "My first husband never asked me if I was cold."

Sadness flowed liquid in her words, washing over Sam in the silence that stretched between them.

"Good night," she mumbled and turned her back to him.

"Good night," he answered, knowing sleep would be an elusive goal. The woman had a way of twisting feelings he thought long dead.

Fifteen minutes later he was convinced he'd be awake the rest of his life if she stayed by his side. "Be still," he grumbled after she'd changed from her back to her stomach for at least the tenth time. "Didn't *all* the other people you've slept with complain about your constant moving?"

"I can't get comfortable," she answered. "I'm not used to sleeping on a bed of rocks. And before you start trying to guess, I slept with Granny Vee because she was forever cold, my first husband because it's a rule, and Bailee and Lacy while we were on the trail because we usually didn't have the energy to search for firewood when we camped for the night."

She could have saved her list; he had already known the answer. "There's not much I can do about the rocks. Are you warm enough?"

"No," she admitted. "I think the blanket shrinks as we sleep."

He opened his arm and pulled her closer to him.

After a few tense minutes, her body relaxed and she pushed on his chest as if trying to fluff a pillow.

He ran his hand down her back and over the material covering her hips as he tucked her against him. "Warmer," he whispered against the velvet of her hair.

"That's one of the places you shouldn't touch me," she answered.

Sam removed his hand from her backside. "Oh." He tried to sound innocent. "Thank you for telling me. You'll remind me if I forget?"

"I will," she answered, already half asleep.

Sam closed his eyes. He never dreamed a woman could be so complex, so innocent, so hard to resist. The women he'd let himself get close enough to know had always been hard with callused souls and eyes void of any sparkle. They'd played a game, a game with many more rules than Sarah knew about.

He moved his hand along her shoulder, then down her arm, enjoying the way she swayed with his warm touch. She might insist their marriage be in name only, but he'd be willing to bet her body enjoyed the feel of him as much as he enjoyed the nearness of her.

When he reached her waist, he slid his hand ever so lightly up the front of her dress until her breast filled his palm. His wife was definitely all woman. The material of her dress did nothing to hide the fullness within his grasp.

She didn't move away, but only mumbled, "Sam. That's one of the places."

He smiled and took his time shifting his hand away. "Sorry, I'll try to remember."

She nodded and curled next to him. With her softness along his side, Sam didn't need his hands to know the pleasure of her.

"Sarah." He placed his mouth close to her ear.

"Yes," she mumbled.

"I've a rule."

"All right," she answered, as if she were too far into sleep and beyond listening.

"You have to sleep next to me like this every night. I like knowing you're safe. No matter what happens, promise?"

She didn't answer, so he shook her shoulder.

"I promise," she muttered, swatting at his hand as if he were no more than a bothersome fly. "Now let me sleep."

Sam thought about how good she felt in his arms. He could experience her nearness with the slight rise and fall of his chest, and her slow breathing brushed against his throat.

He didn't need her, he told himself. She was more trouble than anything. But maybe, for a short time, he could have another person in his life. He could pretend that there was a chance all the feelings inside him hadn't died.

They could live like regular people did and not think about the day he knew would come when he rode away. He'd disappear to keep her alive while going back to the death of feeling nothing once more.

ELEVEN

Sᴀʀᴀʜ ᴏᴘᴇɴᴇᴅ ʜᴇʀ ᴇʏᴇꜱ. ᴅᴀᴡɴ ꜰɪʟᴛᴇʀᴇᴅ ᴛʜʀᴏᴜɢʜ the branches of the cottonwood trees. Quickly she buried her head beneath the covers, hoping to push the day away and sleep another hour. She couldn't remember the last time she'd felt warm and protected all night long.

Sam's large hand rested atop her middle as if he were claiming something he owned. She blinked away the tears. In truth, he did own her. He'd bought and paid for her before he married her. She was his just like she belonged to Granny Vee that day Harriet Rainy traded her away. Harriet hadn't even said good-bye, she'd just shoved six-year-old Sarah toward the old woman's wagon and yelled, "Hope the girl is of more use to you than she's been to me. Her mother was probably no more than trash, but she unloaded the child on me and now I'm passing her on to you."

Granny had smiled when she'd yelled, "Climb up, girl," but she slapped the horse before Sarah was aboard. Sarah could still remember running to catch the wagon. Running to an unknown future, knowing only that it had to be better than the past.

Sarah rubbed her tears away on Sam's arm she used as a pillow. She was still running to catch a future, still hoping it would be better than the past. "I'll work hard," she whispered. "I'll make it better this time." She felt like a hand-me-down that had been passed along from one person to another all her life.

Glancing over at Sam, she was thankful he still slept. She hadn't meant to say the words out loud. He would find out soon enough that she talked to herself. The habit had always bothered Harriet, but Granny Vee found it funny. Mitchell, if he noticed, had never commented on the habit. He rarely talked to anyone much less himself. The week he had lost the farm, he'd simply told her to pack. Sarah had been in the wagon before he bothered to mention that they were going west.

The children moved around near the fire, pulling her back to the present. Sarah knew if she didn't get up fast, they would help themselves to whatever they could find for breakfast. She stretched and kissed Sam's whiskery cheek. "Good morning, husband." Forcing herself to be bright, she added, "I'm going to like you this day whether you deserve it or not."

She figured if she kept saying it, maybe one day she truly would. He might not have claimed the kids, but he had slept beside her without touching her, except for the few times he did so by accident. His good traits and bad ones were starting to even out. That was a beginning.

Staring at his sleeping face, she decided he wasn't a bad-looking man. If anything he looked cold, like he'd never had a reason to smile. Sarah grinned, remembering how she'd felt him laugh last night. It had been too dark to see his face and she remembered no sound, but something she'd said had made laughter rumble around in his chest.

In his sleep he looked younger. At first she'd thought him over thirty, but now she wasn't so sure. Without pain in his dark eyes or wrinkles across his forehead, he looked like a man midway through his twenties. How could a man become legend if he were truly so young?

She readied the pot of coffee and put it on the low fire. Stacking two cups close by, she then turned to pull bacon from the stash of food she'd stored in boxes in the wagon bed. She only unpacked what they needed, for she guessed Sam would want to leave as soon as they finished breakfast.

"Someone's coming!" K.C. yelled. "I hear splashing." All three children grabbed what they could carry and ran for the trees.

Sam sat up. He showed no sign of having been asleep as he reached for his rifle and stood. The cold gunman was back, she thought. No sign remained of the man who'd held her so gently in the shadows before dawn.

Sarah strained to hear something, but the morning fell silent except for the constant rush of river and the rustling of leaves.

"Go with the kids," Sam ordered as he circled the camp.

"But . . . ?"

He didn't wait for her to argue. With movements swift and deliberate, he pulled her to the base of one of the trees and swung her up to the hiding place they'd found earlier, as if she weighed no more than a pitchfork full of hay. The children climbed up the vine wrapping around the tree like it was a well-made ladder.

"Got enough room up there?" Sam tried to whisper, but anyone in the clearing could have heard him.

"Plenty," Sarah answered. "Are you coming up?"

"No, I'll greet our guest." Sam shoved two boxes of supplies up to Sarah. "No matter what, stay still and keep silent," he said. "The apples are in one of those boxes, in case it takes a while to talk our company into leaving."

Glancing at the children, Sam glared at them, silently warning them to also remain quiet. He returned a moment later with the rifle from the wagon and her shawl. "If our caller isn't friendly, can you back me up with this thing?"

Sarah stared at the rifle. "No," she answered honestly.

"Then you'd best stay hidden no matter what happens."

She lay down with the children so that anyone looking up toward the colorful leaves would see only branches. She raised her head just enough to watch Sam moving about the campfire, picking up blankets and tossing them into the wagon. He dragged the buffalo robe through the sand. For a moment she couldn't figure out what he was doing, then she knew. He removed all traces of any footprints besides his own.

As the splashing grew louder, she watched Sam throw the saddle from the buckboard over the horse he'd brought from town.

A rider rounded the bend and came into sight just as Sam pulled the cinch tight.

Sarah fought down a scream as she saw the newcomer pull his rifle from its sheath with lightning speed. He charged the clearing like a warrior.

Sam raised his arms to the back of the powerful black stallion and rested them against the saddle as if he saw no trouble riding toward him. He hadn't bothered to strap on his gun belt, but let it hang over the saddle horn as though it were no more than decoration.

The stranger pulled in his mount as he reached land, but did not lower his gun.

"Gatlin!" the man shouted. "Stand down!"

"I'm not armed, Dalton," Sam answered casually. "Come on in. I got a campfire burning and you're welcome."

The stranger rode up, his mount splashing water across the dry sand of the clearing. He was a big man, not quite as tall as Sam, but thicker. And several years younger, she guessed. A circled silver star sparkled on his chest.

Slowly, after looking around, the Texas Ranger lowered his Colt and climbed from his horse. "You alone?" he asked as his gaze swept the area.

"I am." Sam sat on a box near the coffeepot, doing his best to act as if nothing were wrong with his leg.

The caller didn't seem all that friendly as he stomped toward Sam. "Then how come you got two cups setting out by the fire, Gatlin?"

Sam didn't seem to be that interested in even talking to the man. "I heard you coming half an hour ago. I figured if you were wading through that cold water, you'd be wanting something hot. Of course, if you're not interested, I can put the other cup away."

The Ranger conceded, but didn't let his guard completely down as he neared. He had an easy air about him that made Sarah think he probably feared little. Like Sam, his clothes were dusty, but well made. They were not the clothes of a farmer.

The man squatted by the fire and waited while Sam passed him a cup of coffee.

Both men sipped the steaming liquid in silence.

Finally Sam had enough of the game. "Well, Jacob, you going to tell me why you're here, or have the Rangers simply run out of anything to do and started riding along river beds?"

The younger man ignored Sam's question. "Heard you

got married the other night in Cedar Point."

"Maybe." Sam crossed his ankles in front of him as if he were doing nothing more than passing time.

"They say you married a beauty of a woman. Said she looked like an angel. They even claim she might be too frail to make it out here in this rough country. Your life's not exactly easy being on the road all the time."

"They sure do a lot of talking," Sam commented as though he had no personal interest in what the Ranger said.

Jacob studied the clearing. "You have any idea where this wife of yours might be? Sheriff Riley would like to have a few words with her."

"I might," Sam answered. "What business is she of yours or the sheriff's? I paid her fine. She's free and clear." For the first time since the man arrived, Sam looked as if he might care why Jacob Dalton had taken the trouble to look him up.

The Ranger stood and faced Sam. "I've been trailing you for two days. Is she safe? Is she still alive? The storekeeper who calls himself Mr. Moon said you had a woman with you yesterday when you left town, but he didn't give out any information about you without a good bit of encouraging."

"Of course she's alive!" Sam shouted. "What do you think; I bought her out of jail so I could kill her and cut her up for jerky?"

Jacob looked as if he was considering the point. "I've heard some tales about you, Gatlin."

"You live another five years, Ranger, and I'll hear some tales about you as well." Sam smiled. "But thank you for your concern about my bride." His words left no doubt that he didn't appreciate the interest. "She is pretty as an angel. She's also mine. Which makes her none of your business."

The Ranger backed down ever so slightly. "Look, Gatlin, I don't believe most of what I hear in these parts about you or any other man, but I do need to talk to your wife."

"Tell Sheriff Riley he doesn't need to be checking up on me. My wife is fine."

"It's not that." Jacob took a deep breath as if making a decision. "I've been chasing a worthless old buffalo hunter by the name of Zeb Whitaker over half the state. It appears your wife and two other women ran into him before me, and they all confessed to killing the man." The Ranger laughed. "Which would have done me a favor if it were true."

Sam folded his arms over his chest and waited for the man to finish.

Jacob poured himself more coffee. "A few days before your wife killed him, he ambushed a rancher who supposedly carried a saddlebag full of gold coin."

"She doesn't have any coins," Sam answered.

"I figured that or she would have bought herself out of jail instead of getting bridled to the likes of you." Jacob grinned up at Sam. "I also figure you didn't make this coffee."

Sam growled. Jacob's laughter sounded nervous.

"I'm not here to cause her any harm, but to warn her. The day after you married her, we started hearing rumors that Zeb was still alive and looking for the three women who tried to kill him. Seems he believes they have his money. The sheriff warned the other two, but he asked me to track you down."

"What are you saying?"

"I'm saying Zeb Whitaker is coming after your woman, and if he doesn't get the right answer, he'll kill her. Word is he's got half a dozen men riding with him. He's promised them a cut of the gold and a turn at any one of the three women he finds."

"Over my dead body," Sam swore.

Jacob shrugged. "From what I hear you've been trying to make that a possibility. Picking up lead like it was on sale." He looked directly at Sam. "I didn't know how badly you were hurt. I needed to reach you and tell you I'm willing to help."

"I don't need any help. I'll take care of her."

The Ranger leaned close and added, "Zeb Whitaker is coming after your wife. You and I both know, if he makes it through you, she won't have a chance even if she's a crack shot. Much as you hate the idea, you need me to back you up this time, Sam."

"I don't even like you, Jacob Dalton," Sam admitted. "You are nothing but a snot-nosed kid who's been lucky enough to stay alive for a few years as a Ranger. Which is better than most, but it doesn't make you invincible. You're only interested in my wife because you see her as bait to catch Zeb Whitaker."

"Maybe," Jacob agreed. "But you'll take my help because you're not willing to risk her life on it. We're not dealing with some gunslinger or bank robber. Zeb's survived a long time out here in this wild country. He's tough as rawhide and smarter than most. I'd be willing to bet that the six or so men with him are cut from the same cloth."

"You think you're up to three-to-one odds?"

Jacob smiled. "Sounds about fair to me. When the shooting starts, you take the three on the left, I'll take care of the ones on the right."

Sam nodded as if the Ranger had a plan.

Jacob settled in. "Now, all we need is a safe place to

take her for a while. If Zeb thinks he can't get to your wife, he'll go after one of the other women. Riley and his deputy can worry about them."

"I've got a safe place."

"Here?" Jacob laughed. "Half the men who walk into Denver's bar know about this place. The only reason you weren't followed here is because it's so hard to get to. The multitudes who want to kill you are probably just waiting it out in town knowing you'll have to come in for supplies sooner or later."

"While you were getting all the answers, Ranger, what did you find out about the man who stabbed me, then brought his gang in to use me for target practice?"

"Levi Reed?" Jacob guessed. "He left town thinking you were dead, but it won't be long until someone tells him the truth. Rumor is he headed for the Fort Worth–Dallas area. As for his gang, I think they are all kin, so you can bet they're still together. Like a nest of rattlers, they claim the rocky land north of town. The body they left behind in your hotel room turned out to be Levi's youngest brother. He was mean, but more a pest than an outlaw."

"I'd seen the younger Reed's picture on a few posters. There wasn't enough money on him to make him worth my time to hunt, but since he was dead, I figured I might as well claim the reward." Sam laughed. "Just between you and me, I think he was shot by one of Levi's men when he turned and started to run. I wouldn't waste a bullet on him."

The Ranger grinned. "You didn't shoot him?"

Sam shook his head. "But I'm sure I'll get the credit."

Jacob poked at the fire. "Levi probably wants you dead more than Zeb Whitaker wants your wife. It might not be too healthy hanging around you two. I don't need to go out looking for the bad guys, I can just travel with you newlyweds. If I were guessing, I'd say there are likely twenty more such as Reed across the state. Men you tried to claim the bounty on or outlaws who know you put one of their relatives in the ground."

Sam saw no point in arguing with the truth.

Jacob finally looked straight at Sam. "So why don't you tell your bride to step out from wherever she's hiding. She might as well meet one of the few people in this state who are not trying to make her a widow."

TWELVE

Sam watched admiration parade across the Ranger's face as he shook hands with Sarah. Gatlin didn't know whether to be angry or proud. Jacob Dalton was closer to Sarah's age and Sam had heard more than one saloon girl refer to the young Ranger as handsome. But Jacob acted the fool, complimenting Sarah on the day, as if she had something to do with it, and waiting until she sat down on a box before he took the other seat, as if they were at some fine restaurant.

Groaning, Sam decided Jacob smiled way too much for a proper lawman.

He didn't know what to make of the man he once thought of as being able to handle himself. If Dalton grinned that way around an outlaw, he'd have those pearly whites knocked down his throat in no time. If fact, if Jacob didn't stop smiling soon, Sam might be tempted to perform the service.

Fighting the urge to grab Sarah and pull her behind

him, Sam stood like a statue while they talked. Sarah was full of questions about the other two women who had been in jail with her. Were they safe? Did Jacob know who they married? Were they happy?

The Ranger finally stopped her questions and told her about Zeb Whitaker.

To Sam's surprise, Sarah moved away from Dalton as the Ranger talked and inched closer to him, resting her hand on his arm just above where she'd bandaged it the day before. Sam covered her fingers with his hand and felt her tremble. He knew she needed to be warned about Whitaker and the danger she faced, but he didn't like the idea of her being frightened.

Sam growled; he didn't like much of anything happening this morning. If he had his way, he'd just as soon go back to bed and forget the Ranger ever rode up. And he knew that if he ever ran into Zeb Whitaker, he would make sure his killing lasted a bit longer.

Jacob finally stopped talking and walked close to the fire to pour himself more coffee.

Sarah looked up at Sam with those blue eyes he couldn't get enough of. "Whitaker aims to kill me?" she whispered.

Sam saw no reason to lie. He nodded. Fear widened her eyes. Before he realized what he was doing, he put an arm around her and pulled her close. "Don't worry about it, Sarah. I won't let him close enough to hurt you."

She pressed her cheek against his shoulder. "I don't want to have to kill him twice." She wrapped her arms around Sam's waist as though suddenly needing his warmth.

Sam felt the day going a bit better than it had started. He liked the way her head fit right under his chin and the way her hair smelled like fresh rain. She was a woman made to be held, he thought.

"Well, I'll be!" Jacob shouted from several feet away. "The lady really does appear to like you, Gatlin. Sheriff Riley told me, the night of your wedding, he gave her a chance to back out, but she stepped up beside you like you were the pick of the litter. Mr. Moon even said she must have been crazy about you the way she hung on you, but I didn't believe it possible. A walking, breathing woman actually likes the mighty Sam Gatlin."

"Walk softly." Sam glared at Jacob over Sarah's head. "I don't take lightly to any man questioning my wife's judgment."

Conflicting feelings bombarded Sam's mind. Normally, he thought of himself as void of emotions, but suddenly it was raining in the desert. He liked the idea of Sarah moving close, of her needing him, of her holding on to him now as if she might drown in trouble if she let go. Sam wasn't at all sure she liked him, but she trusted him and maybe that was more important in this country.

Sarah laughed as if unsure whether Sam's warning was only a joke. She patted his chest. "Stop trying to frighten the lawman, dear." She looked across to Jacob. "Of course I like my husband."

Jacob tilted his head, obviously trying to see Gatlin in a better light. "You ever hear any of the tales told about your husband, ma'am?"

"Yes," she answered. "Most I don't believe." She rubbed her hand across Sam's shirt. "All I know is he's never hurt me."

There she went again, Sam thought, patting on him like he was a pet. The woman had no idea who she was dealing with. Maybe Jacob was right, someone should question her judgment. He was not a man women hugged and touched, but now didn't seem like a good time to inform her of the fact.

Jacob looked from her to Sam. "I almost feel sorry for Whitaker. He thinks he's going after a helpless little woman. He has no idea he'll have to down a legend even to get near her."

"That's right." Sam looked straight at Jacob, silently making a promise.

An understanding passed between the two men as Sarah turned away. They talked while she made breakfast. Jacob voiced no doubt that Sam held Sarah's welfare as a top priority.

With Jacob's back to the trees, Sarah had little trouble delivering biscuits stuffed with bacon to the children. Her attempts at being sneaky kept Sam distracted as he talked with the Ranger.

About the time she finished packing the supplies, the men had formed a plan. Sam decided it would be better to take Sarah to a safe place than meet up with Jacob. They thought it made more sense to find Zeb than to wait around for him to storm across their lives. Jacob had a few leads. They'd try to locate the outlaw before he harmed one of the women. Jacob even made Sam promise to bring Zeb in alive. But first they had to make sure Sarah was safe.

"Want to tell me where you're taking her?"

"No," Sam answered. "The fewer who know the better. If you'll ride back to where the wagon turned into the river and wait a half hour to make sure we're not followed, I'll do the rest. Within the hour my wife and I will have disappeared completely. I'll see her out of harm's way and meet you back in Cedar Point in three days."

Jacob voiced his objections to the plan. He wanted to make sure Sarah was safe before he left, but Sam didn't think he needed help and there was a good chance Sheriff Riley in Cedar Point might. After all, he was trying to keep up with two women. Jacob might be needed in town more than here. The first week or so everyone would be on guard. But after a while they'd start to slip, and that would be when Whitaker struck.

The Ranger swung onto his saddle. "Three days, four at the most. I'll be looking for you!" he yelled to Sam then smiled and tipped his hat to Sarah. "And don't forget to stay out of Reed's way. Once we take care of Whitaker, I'll help you find Reed in Fort Worth."

"I don't remember asking for any help, Ranger. But Fort Worth is the last place I'd be heading right now."

Sam crossed his arms and watched the Ranger splash into the water and disappear around the bend in the river. He was a good man, despite his youth. Sam glanced at Sarah and grumbled, "If something should happen to me, find Dalton. He'll see you're safe."

She looked surprised. "I didn't think you liked him."

"What are we . . . in grammar school?" Sam frowned. "All of a sudden everyone seems worried about who likes who. It doesn't matter a damn if I like the man, he'll stand if trouble comes and not run."

Sarah shook her head as she packed the last of the supplies. "Well, I'm telling you right now that if trouble comes, I'm running." She moved toward him with her finger pointed. "And stop swearing in front of our children. I'll not have it." She poked him on the shoulder. "Do you hear me, Sam? I'll not have it."

For a woman who didn't like to be touched, she sure did her share of patting and poking, he thought. "I'll try to remember," he answered. "But the rules are starting to log-pile in my brain."

She didn't retreat, but continued to stare at him as if she meant business.

Sam grinned. "How about every time you come up with a new rule, one falls off the back of the list?"

She crossed her arms.

He fought the urge to toss her in the river. "Come on, we're wasting daylight. Grab the kids and get in the wagon."

"But Jacob will see them if we leave so soon."

"We're not headed in that direction." Sam didn't explain as he put out the fire. By the time she wrapped the children in blankets and tucked them into the back of the wagon, he'd erased any evidence that they'd stayed in the clearing. Without a word he lifted her onto the bench seat and climbed up beside her.

"Are you strong enough to drive?" she asked, remembering his wounds.

"I'll manage." He took the reins and grinned as she settled close to his side.

They turned upstream, the opposite way from where the Ranger disappeared. To Sarah's surprise, they traveled less than a half mile before Sam pulled the wagon onto dry land. He handed her the reins and slowly climbed down. "Head straight toward the sunset. I'll follow on horseback."

He swung up onto the black horse and rode along the river's edge. Before she lost sight of him, she saw him dragging a branch filled with dying leaves from the brush. He swept back and forth across the wagon's tracks, erasing the wagon ruts she had made.

Sarah kept moving, but it wasn't easy with no road to follow. Once she left the foliage near the river, the land spread out into an endless space of nothing but open land. She tried to maneuver around the rocks and groundhog holes, but found it impossible. The air was thick with the smell of sage and the dirt impatient to fly as the horses plodded forward.

Finally K.C. climbed up onto the bench beside Sarah and asked, "You ever drive one of these wagons before, lady? Cause you're not very good at it."

"I'm trying." Sarah laughed. "When I stare out over the land, it looks like prairie grass rolling along all the way to the horizon, but up close it's not quite that smooth. The horses seemed to be finding every rock for miles to stumble over." They crossed into a field of bleached bones where buffalo had fallen years before.

K.C. took up the job as scout, pointing out problems ahead before Sarah could even see them. The crackle of broken bones snapped along her nerves, but she didn't slow. Sam hadn't explained why she had to travel this direction without even a road to follow, but she trusted him.

The day aged. Sam didn't return. She followed his order and headed directly into the sunset. That morning she hadn't looked for him, figuring he was making it impossible for them to be followed. After noon she wondered where he was and guessed the ride across this prairie must be far easier on horseback. He might claim he was fine, but his wounds must still bother him. The sway of a saddle might be far easier to bear than the rattle of a wagon.

He's fine, she repeated in her mind every time she began to fret. But in the last few hours of daylight, worry won over hope. What if he fell off his horse? What if he met up with trouble? It seemed to follow the man closer than a shadow. What if he were no better at directions than he had been at remembering numbers back at the hotel? He might be halfway to the Oklahoma Territory before he realized he was going in the wrong direction.

As the sunlight faded, Sarah faced one of two possibilities. He must be somewhere behind them, hurt. He might have started bleeding again and lost too much blood to stay conscious. Or fallen from his horse and knocked himself out when he hit the rocky ground. If he was hurt, she wasn't sure she could find him. She wasn't even sure she could go back the way they came. The grassland played tricks, erasing wagon tracks as soon as they were made. Even if she could manage to make it back to the river, she'd never be able to follow a man on horseback with the wagon.

The second possibility loomed no brighter. Since he hadn't followed and if he wasn't hurt, then he had abandoned them. She refused to allow a single tear to fall. It made sense. She'd been nothing but trouble to him, and now he had an extra helping of worry with Zeb Whitaker out there looking for her. He obviously felt no attachment to his children, and he had never mentioned even being fond of her. Maybe he thought he'd been kind; after all, he'd given her a wagon filled with supplies and, she hoped, headed her in the direction of a town.

When not even the glow of a sun remained, she finally stopped. The children were too tired to eat more than an apple. The air turned frosty. They curled together on the old buffalo hide spread between the supplies in the wagon. She covered them with all but one of the blankets. Sarah thought of lighting a fire. Maybe Sam would see it and come in. But the light was as likely to attract bugs and unwanted guests as one lost husband.

Exhaustion ground like sand over her body. Her bones ached from being tossed around on the hard bench. She walked several feet from the children and spread out her blanket in the tall grass, then covered up with a section of the wool cloth Sam had bought her. She fell asleep even before she could get warm, figuring any dream was bound to be better than the nightmare she lived while awake.

After what seemed like only a minute, she felt an arm pull her against a solid body.

"Sarah?"

She jerked full awake, fighting to free herself from the form suddenly lying next to her.

"Sarah. It's me." Sam's voice filtered through her sleepy mind.

An inky darkness surrounded her, but she smelled his familiar masculine scent as his hand pulled her close to him once more.

"Sam." She wrapped her arms around him and held tightly. "Sam. You came back."

She felt the rumble of his laughter. "Well, of course I came back. I've been watching you all day making sure no one followed you. Once you stopped, I thought I'd wash up before I came into camp."

Sarah slammed her fist against his chest. "Why didn't you let me know you were near! I was so worried." She continued to pound, needing to release the panic that had hovered over her all day.

"So worried you fell asleep," he pointed out.

The thought that she must have worried over him finally registered on his brain, for he added, "It's all right. I didn't think about telling you. I thought you knew I wouldn't be far away."

Her hair brushed against his face as she rose to a sitting position and tried to see his face. In a sliver of moonlight she finally made out the outline of his jaw. "I thought you were hurt." She couldn't bring herself to say what else she felt, that she feared he might have left her. "I was afraid I would never be able to find you."

"I've never had anyone worry about me before." He cupped the side of her face with his hand. "There was no need." His hand threaded into her hair. He thought about the pieces of her past he knew about. "I'm not going anywhere, Sarah. I'm not leaving you. You're not something I just picked up along the trail and plan to toss away. You don't need to worry. When or if I ever leave you, I promise to take the time to say good-bye."

Before she could answer, he pulled her down to him and touched her lips with his. This time his kiss was not hard, but soft. He didn't take, but tasted her slowly. For a few moments she was too shocked to react. She'd never been kissed with tenderness, and Sam was the last man she expected to have any knowledge of such a skill.

He moved his mouth over hers as though hungry for a response. Requesting, but not demanding.

She didn't know what to do. The kiss before had been easy to resist, for it hurt her lips and pushed against her teeth. But this kiss was different. It caressed. It warmed. It welcomed her to a new world. How could a man who knew nothing of even being nice to people have such a talent?

Pushing away, she rolled from his chest and landed beside him on the blanket. For a long while they both stared up at the thin moon. Sarah tried to figure out what he'd done so different this time in kissing her and why she felt the way she did inside.

"If you're waiting for me to say I'm sorry again, Sarah, you'll wait till hell freezes over." His voice drifted on the wind.

"Don't swear," she corrected.

"The children can't hear me," he mumbled. "And I don't swear. We need to have a talk about which words are swearing and which are places."

He moved the wool she'd been using as cover over her and she jumped at his slight touch.

"Explain something to me." He moved toward her and his low words brushed her cheek. "You say you like me. I figure you married me of your own free will since Jacob told me the sheriff gave you a chance to back out even after you picked my name. You sleep with me and are always drawing near like there was barely enough room on this earth for us both to stand. But when we kiss you act like I've just attacked you."

She almost felt sorry for him. He sounded confused, as if he had just encountered an animal unlike any he'd ever seen or heard about.

He turned away. "Why'd you hug me just now if you weren't glad to see me?"

She closed her eyes as tightly as she could wishing his questions would go away. She always hated it when some fool asked a question she hadn't figured out the answer to yet.

"Good night," he said when she didn't answer.

"Good night," she answered in little more than a whisper.

"You still sleeping next to me, or do I get my bedroll?"

"I'm still sleeping next to you," she answered. "Everyone knows next to you is where I belong. I promised I'd sleep next to you. And I hugged you because I was worried about you."

For several minutes neither of them moved. She knew he wasn't any closer to sleep than she was. Finally she whispered, "Sam?"

"Hmmm," he answered.

"I've never been kissed before you."

For a while the words floated in the air between them. Finally he rolled back to face her. "Never?"

"Never. Not like you kiss me, not on the mouth. Mitchell kissed me on the cheek the morning we married. I don't think he knew much about things like kissing or maybe he just had no interest in kissing me. Even though he'd been married once before, he wasn't a man of the world like you."

Sam laughed. "In truth, I don't know much, either, but compared to you I guess I'm an expert."

She rolled until their faces were only a few inches apart. "Then, why do folks kiss, on the mouth like that I mean. It's not a necessary part of mating."

"Didn't you ever want to kiss Mitchell? After all, the man was your husband for a year. Surely once in that time you felt a fondness toward him."

"No," she answered honestly. "He was near forty when I married him. Like most folks that old, most of his teeth were missing. Just setting across the table watching him chew was as close as I ever wanted to get to his mouth."

She waited for an answer to her question, but instead, he asked another. "How old were you when you married him?"

"I was twenty. Which made me well into being an old maid. He lived on the farm next to Granny. His wife and kid had died a few years before. He would always talk to me when he came past our cabin on his way to town. Granny Vee wouldn't have allowed it if she'd known. She always thought some man would come along and take me away, then she'd have to die alone with no one to help her. But he didn't ever talk like he was interested in taking me, he just asked about our garden and such.

"When she died, the creditors came to get her things and he came over to get me. He said it wasn't right for me to just move in with him, so we went to the preacher at dawn the next day. He didn't want to miss many daylight hours of working. We were married and he went back to farming while I cleaned and moved in. Living with him wasn't all that different from living with Granny Vee."

"Did he love you?"

"I asked him once, and he said he loved his first wife and she died. He didn't plan on doing such a foolish thing again."

Sam didn't say anything.

Finally Sarah added, "The crops were bad last year and we lost almost everything. He sold the livestock for enough to buy a wagon and said he wanted to make a fresh start out West. I didn't want to go because I already knew the baby was coming, but I didn't have much choice."

"Did you love him?"

"Mitchell says a wife is supposed to love her husband. That's just the way it is. He said our ages didn't matter, he'd tell me the rules and we'd both do our jobs. But I think he thought I'd take care of him like I did Granny Vee when she got sick. Once in a while he'd remind me that he wanted to be buried next to his wife. But I couldn't do like he asked. We were on the trail when a fever took him, and I was too sick to have any say. Bailee told me when I asked that they buried him on a hill so he could see all the way back to where his wife was buried."

"So you love me now the way you loved Mitchell last year?"

Sarah didn't see his point. "I suppose. You're not going to start telling me where to bury you, are you?"

Sam returned to his back. "No, I'm not." He took a long breath and added, "I don't want you to bury me, and I sure don't want you to love me like you did Mitchell, Sarah."

"But that's the only way I know how to love a man."

"Then, I'd rather you didn't love me at all." He sounded tired. "Go to sleep. We've got a long way to travel tomorrow."

They lay in silence for a while. She tried to figure out what he meant by her not loving him. Finally she rose up and put her elbow on his chest. "Sam, are you asleep?"

"No," he answered.

"Would you tell me something?"

"What?"

"Does a couple have to be in love to do the kind of kissing you were doing to me?"

She felt his chest rumble. "No," he answered.

"Then, would you mind kissing me again? I want to see what it feels like when I know you are just doing it 'cause I asked."

He waited so long to answer she was sure he planned to deny her request.

"Lean down," he finally said without making any move to touch her.

"Closer," he ordered when she was an inch away.

Her lips touched his. There was freedom this time. He wasn't pulling her to him. He wasn't demanding. She could pull away any time she liked.

"Relax." His request brushed her mouth.

She melted against him, and his arm cradled her at his side as the kiss continued. At first she only wanted to see how he kissed, but slowly she found herself returning each movement. His tongue brushed across the top of her lip, her body tingled all the way to her toes. He parted her lips ever so gently, tasting her mouth with tender kisses.

Warmth spread through her and all her worries drifted away as he kissed her. She moved closer. The most wonderful part of the kiss lay in his nearness. Something about this strong man made her feel good whenever she touched him. Like all was safe with the world. She knew it didn't make sense, violence and danger rode shotgun with him, but that didn't change the way he made her feel. She cuddled nearer.

Suddenly Sam broke the kiss and turned his back to her. "Good night, Sarah." His voice sounded harsh.

She touched her fingertips to her lips. They felt newborn, soft.

"Sam?"

"What?"

"Would it be all right if I asked you to kiss me again sometime?"

"I'll think about it," he answered.

She didn't have to see his face to know he was smiling.

THIRTEEN

SAM MADE COFFEE ON A SMALL CAMPFIRE WHILE Sarah and the children still slept. Dawn melted across the prairie, carrying a cool breeze rich with sage, but he hardly noticed. Worry wrinkled his forehead in freshly plowed rows, for the day promised nothing but trouble.

If he'd been the one who'd made camp last night, he would have driven another hundred yards to a place where rocks and shrub trees blocked the wind and there was enough wood for a warming fire. And enough shelter for protection from a storm of bullets, he thought as he watched Sarah roll over in her sleep and reach for him. She'd have shivered all night if he hadn't held her close. He reminded himself that the cold was the only reason they'd slept wrapped up in each other.

She sat up and stretched, totally unaware of how beautiful she looked. "Morning."

"Morning," he poured her a cup of the steaming brew. She still wore her old dress that, by now, was dusty and wrinkled. Most of her hair had fought its way free of the thick braid she'd made yesterday morning. But she fascinated him with her beauty. Sam could not believe such a woman had asked him to kiss her.

The request had been so simple, almost innocent. But there was nothing innocent about the way he'd felt or about where his thoughts had wandered after he'd said good night. If he'd kissed her a moment longer he wasn't sure he could have turned away.

"There's a spring over by those rocks if you want to wash up." He tried to get his mind off the way she felt pressed close against him. The feel of her body along his lingered like a dream long after daylight.

Without a word she gathered up her bundle and went the direction he pointed. It seemed like half an hour before she returned. Her hair was wet and tied into a fresh braid. She smelled of spring water and honeysuckle.

"Thank you for the soap," she said as she accepted the coffee he offered. "I've never had so much."

He lifted the carpetbag Mr. Moon had added to their supplies and pitched it in her direction. "I thought you knew I bought you this as well to put your things in. If you think you have to go around with so many belongings, they might as well be in a bag."

She looked at the piece of luggage as though she'd never seen anything like it. "Thank you." She carefully pulled each of her treasures from her shawl bundle and placed them inside the bag. Then she folded the borrowed shawl and added it on top.

"You planning to wear that new dress we bought?" he asked.

Sarah shook her head. "Not on the road. I'm saving it."

Sam woke the children as Sarah started breakfast. When they were all fed and in the wagon, he tied the stallion to the back and climbed up beside his wife.

"You haven't said more than two words all morning." The thought crossed his mind that she might have regretted last night. "I'm starting to think the kids are rubbing off on you. I've never seen such silent children in my life."

"I've got a lot on my mind." She stared ahead. "And the children are just waiting, K.C. said, but she wouldn't tell me for what."

He glanced to see if they listened. They were sitting at the back of the wagon dangling sticks, as if fishing. Even in their game they whispered and used a kind of sign language, as though they'd been taught never to draw attention to themselves.

He didn't ask what was on Sarah's mind. Years ago Sam had given up losing sleep over who might be trying to hunt him down, but he could see Sarah's fear shining in her blue eyes. Trying to get her mind off Zeb Whitaker, he said, "Remember when Denver Delany told you to take me to Satan's Canyon?"

Sarah nodded.

"Well, the clearing you stopped at was only halfway there. Few know there's a back way out of that river area. For most folks, Satan's Canyon is just a place they talk about, but only a handful of folks know the way. I've even heard some say it's only a made-up place. Once in a while someone disappears and rumors start. Maybe he's gone to Satan's Canyon, they'll say, as if it were a magic place." He paused. "Before nightfall you're going to see it."

"Are you leaving me there?" Sarah's voice shook slightly. "Is that where you think I'd be safe?"

Sam laughed. "You'd be safe there, but no, I'm not leaving you. We're leaving the children on a farm in the canyon." Before Sarah could object, Sam added, "With their father."

"But you're their father."

"When Malone brought them to the clearing, he probably thought they belonged to me or maybe that's what their mother told him. She couldn't tell Malone, or anyone else, who or where their father is."

"I don't understand."

Sam shook his head. "It's not my secret to tell, Sarah. Not even to you. All I can say is that their father, their real father, will be mighty glad to see them. I never met a man named Tennessee Malone and I'd like to know how he guessed that I would be able to deliver them to their papa. He must have been a friend of their mother's, but he was taking a chance leaving them in the clearing."

Sam glanced back at the children. "What if I hadn't come along? Obviously, their father didn't even know to look for them there. He would have been risking his life to come so far away from Satan's Canyon, but I figure he would have made the trip if he even suspected they might have been in the clearing."

She watched him closely. "You're sure you are not their father?"

"Positive." He laughed. "But I'm afraid I can't tell you how I know who is. I've already said more than I should have. Anything else might put you in harm's way."

Sarah nodded. "You're telling me this much because you trust me, don't you, Sam?"

He stared out at the prairie. "I guess I trust you more than I have anyone in a long time." He glanced at her. "Hell, if I know why."

"You are supposed to trust your mate. That's a rule, I think."

"Only you're not my mate, Sarah. Right now all you

are is my wife." He didn't have to tell her where he drew the line between the two titles.

Sarah stared at her hands. "I know. I'll be one, but not the other. Not until I'm good and ready. You promised me that. You promised you wouldn't force me."

"I'm not going back on my word, Sarah." Sam frowned. "I told you that is not the way I want you. It will be with you willing or not at all." He knew that, for him, a mate might only come along once in this lifetime. Even then, a real marriage wouldn't be something that would last long if he stayed in his line of work. But if it came, he wanted the real thing. Not some duty she performed. Not a wife bought and bedded for the price of her fine.

Sam heard the children laughing and remembered what he'd heard it had been like between their parents. Their pa had been an outlaw traveling with the Bass gang, their ma a saloon girl moving from town to town, but when they came together there was no one else in the world but the two of them. He'd watched them one night from the shadows. The bar had been packed with cowhands and gamblers, yet all they saw was each other. Frank Jackson hadn't done more than touch her hand or brush her cheek, but Sam had turned away at the intimacy between them.

Sam wanted that kind of loving, not the kind that could be bought for a few coins or for the price of a fine. Maybe he wanted the impossible. He wanted a woman who wanted him.

There was nothing else to say to Sarah. She stood on one side and he on the other. As long as she could even think that he'd take her by force, she didn't know him well enough to care about him.

They fell into an uncomfortable silence. The day warmed and the hours passed without either of them thinking of anything more than that danger lay ahead. The ride was smoother than it had been because Sam knew the area well enough to know what parts to avoid. He stopped twice to allow them all to stretch their legs.

She followed him as he checked the horses. "The children are so quiet. I've never even heard the younger two say a word."

Sam didn't look at her. "They've been taught well. My guess is their lives depended on them remaining silent."

She moved closer to him and whispered, "Sam, I'm afraid for them. We are probably the worst two people in the state to be close to right now. What if trouble comes before we reach their father, assuming what you say about there being a real father is true? I don't even know how to fire a rifle. How can I protect them?"

"I understand. That's why I'm getting them somewhere safe as fast as I can. In a few hours they will be with their father, and all I'll have to worry about is you."

She leaned against him as though needing his warmth. Sam didn't bother to ask what was wrong, he just held her gently. The woman had no idea how she made him feel when she touched him so casually.

"I'm not brave," she whispered against his chest. "I never have been."

"Yes, you are." His words brushed against her hair. "You married me, didn't you?"

When she pulled away, he didn't try to hold her. As she walked toward the wagon, she laughed. "I married you because you looked like you owned a razor, which was more than I could say for most of the men at the raffle." She glanced back at him and lifted an eyebrow. "However, I haven't seen much use of one since we married."

Sam followed and lifted her into the wagon. Before she

pulled away, he moved his short beard against her cheek. "You will, soon as I find hot water."

Sarah's small hand glided along his jaw, playing with the short beard.

The action was small, no more than a touch, but Sam thought about it for an hour. He even wondered what she would do if he asked her to touch him like that again. This "in name only" marriage grew more difficult by the minute. The problem, to his way of thinking, was where to draw the line between the marriage and mating. She wanted to sleep next to him, seemed to need him near, even asked him to kiss her, but she had made it plain she would not participate in any lovemaking.

It occurred to him that to Sarah the bedding was an act, but to him it was far more than that. Or at least, he wanted it to be. He'd had the other, the act, and he guessed she had, also. He'd caught glimpses of loving between couples. So why couldn't it be that way for him? Almost like a secret they sheltered from the world. A private language they spoke to each other that no one else understood. He wasn't sure he could even explain it to Sarah. In his mind, he'd always thought the loving came with a marriage, but Sarah had been married and knew nothing of it.

By mid-afternoon the rolling land turned rocky, with rough roads that crisscrossed the prairie. Small farms and ranches were fenced off now and then, but no signposts or names marked the way.

"What is this place?" she finally asked. "I can't say exactly what's wrong, but something is."

"Back before the war, a gambler won this valley during a horse race. He bet on a horse by the name of Satan, so he called this place Satan's Canyon. From time to time the gambler sells off small farms to folks who want to live a quiet life. People who want to disappear. They change their names and move here. As a bounty hunter, it wouldn't be wise for me to go into town, but there's a place I can stop where someone will meet me."

"How do you know all this?"

"I've helped a few men vanish. I even told them to shoot me if I was ever fool enough to come looking for them. I only hope they'll ask questions before I get within range."

Sarah caught the reflection of a rifle from the cliff above. "Someone's watching us," she whispered.

"I know. They have been for about an hour. They're allowing us to make it to the trees without trouble. That's as far as strangers can go."

Sarah scooted a few inches closer and slipped her hand around his arm.

He didn't lie and tell her not to be frightened.

A thin fog set in by the time they reached a huddling of trees. It whirled around them, chilling the air and making distance hard to judge. Sam made camp while she combed the children's hair, then wrapped each one in a warm blanket. To her surprise, they asked no questions.

She tried to feed them, but no one seemed interested in eating. They waited as darkness settled around them, black and cold. As the hours passed, the children crawled into the back of the wagon and went to sleep.

Sarah could stand the silence no longer. She paced around the fire. When she circled Sam for the third time, she asked, "Are we going to wait all night? If there is someone out there, surely they've figured out who we are by now. If they thought we planned to do them any harm, they could have killed us ten times over by now."

"Don't leave the light of the campfire," Sam said, as though he hadn't heard her questions.

Sarah continued to circle. She wanted to scream that

she couldn't stand to do nothing, to simply wait. Whoever had been watching had more than enough time to show himself and meet with them. Maybe no one was coming. Did Sam plan to stay out in this clearing forever? She decided she'd talk to him again. They should journey on into town. As they'd discussed earlier, if someone wanted to kill them they could have done it long before now. He might be hesitant to go farther, but she grew tired of waiting. Patience was never her style. No one, even some retired outlaw, would see her and three children as a threat.

Just as Sarah realized she'd gone beyond the ring of firelight, an arm circled her shoulders and pulled her backward. She opened her mouth to scream a warning to Sam. Before sound could escape her throat, she tasted the cotton of a gag being shoved into her mouth.

Panic shot through her veins as she fought for her life in the blackness. She swung wide, encountering only air, than kicked into the fog. Firm hands pulled her arms behind her, tied her as if he were unaware that she objected. "I mean you no harm," a low southern voice whispered as a rope bound her skirt at the knees.

For a moment she didn't know if she was angrier at the attacker or at Sam for letting such a thing happen. He was supposed to be watching her, guarding her. Where was Sam now? Probably sitting by the fire, downing more coffee and wondering when she'd walk back into the light.

Her attacker lifted her over his shoulder and moved beneath the trees. He lay her down among the leaves and vanished.

Sarah struggled with her bonds, but made no progress. The more she wiggled, the more she sank into the leaves beneath her. If she kept moving she would be completely covered and no one, not even in daylight, would ever find her. She would die without a sound. And Sam would probably stay by the fire and mumble about how he told her not to go outside the firelight.

She forced herself to be still as voices sounded from the direction of the campsite.

"Gatlin? Is that you?" a southern drawl called out.

"It is," Sam answered calmly. "Step into the light."

"I can't do that," came the Reb's answer. "Put your weapon down."

"I can't do that," Sam echoed. "You've got my wife." It was more a statement than a question. "You hurt her and you're a dead man, Frank."

"I didn't hurt her," the stranger answered. "She's tied up over by the trees." He paused a long moment. "You know I wouldn't hurt her, Gatlin."

Sam made a sound. Sarah couldn't tell if it was agreement or growl.

The stranger continued, "She's not very big, Gatlin. You might want to think about throwing her back in and hoping for a bigger one next time."

"You haven't seen her in the light," Sam answered. "She's a beauty."

"I'll have to take your word for it, Gatlin. I don't plan on staying around until daylight. I just came to see what your business is in Satan's Canyon and to tell you, if you're not gone by daybreak, you and your lovely bride will be buried here in this clearing."

"I figured as much. I came with news."

The southerner's voice grew even lower. "I already know my Molly is dead. They said she was shot by stray bullets during the Fourth of July celebration. No one's fault. I heard about it a month ago."

He fell silent for a long time, then whispered, "I wish I could have said good-bye. We were married for almost ten years and never got to live together more than a few days at a time. I always thought it would be too dangerous for her to be here. Thanks, though, for coming to tell me."

"I didn't," Sam answered. "I brought you something. Come take a look."

"No, thanks," the stranger answered. "I remember the last time we met, you promised me that if our paths ever crossed again you would be the bounty hunter and I'd still have a price on my head."

"That was my plan, but three blue-eyed surprises showed up in my life. They're asleep in the back of the wagon." Sam reached and lifted Sarah's carpetbag from the supplies. "In fact, you're welcome to the wagon if you're interested in taking them off my hands. My job is done. I got them to you."

"Drop your weapons!" The southern voice sounded suddenly angry. "I want to see them."

Sam lowered the rifle. "I won't shoot you, but I'll not stand in Satan's Canyon unarmed. For all I know you're not the only outlaw hiding in the fog."

Sarah twisted, trying to get free. She saw the outline of the stranger between her and the fire. He had a gun pointed right at Sam's heart.

Leaves scratched her cheeks as she tried to see what was happening.

Sam's voice sounded calm once more. "I wouldn't have brought my wife with me to deliver the children if I planned to gun their father down. Is she all right? I've never noticed her being quiet for so long before."

The stranger cradled his weapon and relaxed. "She's fine. I can hear her wiggling in that pile of leaves I dumped her in. Remind her I used a clean handkerchief when she's swearing at me later."

Sam stepped away from the wagon, pulling the reins

of his horse free of the back bar. "I'll do that. Now, you'd best be on your way. Kids need to be home in bed by this hour."

Leaves blocked some of Sarah's vision. She only saw the stranger's back as he neared the wagon. K.C. unfolded from the blanket as her father drew near. Without a sound she moved into his arms and the outlaw lifted her from the wagon.

"Daddy," she whispered in a sleepy voice as her thin arms held on tightly. "Can we go home now?"

Without loosening his hold on his daughter, the man reached in and touched the other two sleeping bundles. For a moment his head lowered as if in prayer.

"Daddy?" K.C. patted his hair. "I knew it was you the minute I heard your voice."

He raised his head and kissed the child. "Yes, let's go home."

He climbed onto the seat and picked up the reins. When he glanced back at Sam, he nodded once. "I'll repay you for this, Gatlin. I swear."

"No need. Just point me in the direction of my wife."

The stranger motioned with his head as he flicked the reins.

Sam watched them go before turning in Sarah's direction.

She wiggled, letting him know where she was. Leaves completely covered her. Trying to scream was useless, but she kept kicking her feet to let him know where to search.

For ten minutes she listened to Sam sifting through the dried leaves in the blackness before his hand finally touched her body. With a mighty tug he pulled her from the foliage. "Come out of there," he said, as if she'd been playing some game and he'd finally caught her.

Sarah jerked as he wrapped his arms around her and

began untying her hands. She mumbled through the gag and rubbed against his face.

Sam laughed. "All right. I can't do everything at once." He slid his hands up her body to where the gag was tied in her hair and pulled it free with a tug.

Sarah spit cotton from her mouth. "Who was that man?" she demanded.

"What man?" Sam pressed her against him as he worked on freeing her bound hands.

"The man who tied me up. The man who said he was the father of your children."

"What children?"

She could feel laughter rumble in his chest even though his words sounded serious.

"How many times do I have to tell you I don't have any children? And, though it's dark, I think we are the only two people standing here. I guess your invisible children were finally claimed by their invisible father."

Sarah leaned away. "You're not going to explain, are you Sam?"

He pulled the rope from her hands. "No," he said, as if that were all the answer she needed.

Sarah didn't have to ask, she had figured most of it out from the conversation between the two men. The stranger was obviously a wanted man whom Sam had let go for some reason. The children were his, but he hadn't been able to live with their mother, or even go after them when she died. But they knew him, or at least K.C. did.

Sam worked on the rope tied around her knees as she tried to decide whether to push for an answer. Sarah didn't think she would get one. His silence suddenly added character to a man she thought void of any.

"I can untie that one." She twisted, trying to reach the knot.

He shifted his shoulder into her hip, attempting to move out of her way.

With a sudden gasp Sarah tumbled backward. She grabbed his arm as she fell, pulling him off balance.

She landed atop the leaves and he landed atop her.

For a moment they remained perfectly still. His body pressed against her from her shoulder to her knees.

He pushed away. Without a word he moved his hands down her skirt to the rope. The warmth of his fingers seeped through the layers of her clothing.

"Don't touch me like that, Sam," she said, embarrassed at the way he'd handled her in the darkness. "And don't land on me. I'm fragile. You could have broken every bone in my body."

He stood. "I should have left you tied up and gagged. Maybe I can get the invisible father to come back and hide you better next time."

"You didn't have to feel my whole body, or tumble atop me." Embarrassment, more than anger, forged her words.

"I had to find the rope." He walked toward the firelight. "How else was I going to untie you in the dark?"

He whirled so suddenly Sarah almost ran into him. "And another thing. I didn't touch your whole body. When I do, you'll know it."

"There is no *when*, there is not even an *if*."

She was only an inch away, poking her finger into his chest.

"You said once that I could touch you. You said there were touches that were all right. Well, that's what I was doing." He turned around and resumed his track back to camp.

"Well, I've changed my mind. Just because I asked you to kiss me doesn't mean I'm ready to be bedded. Maybe

I'll just go back to being a virgin and stay an old maid all my life. Your flattening me when you fell atop me isn't that much different than what my first husband did in mating. Seems to me it's something I can do without."

He turned again, only this time she sidestepped him. "I wasn't bedding you out there, Sarah. I slipped and fell. You just happened to be beneath me." He shook his head. "Maybe I should be the one getting mad for you being in the very spot where I tumbled."

"Then how come you said the same thing Mitchell used to say every time he mated with me?"

"What was that?"

"I'm sorry." She didn't look at him. "He always said I'm sorry like it was something dirty that he was doing."

Sam opened his mouth to argue, than closed it again. Now was not the time to have this discussion. He had to think of her safety first, then he'd think about strangling her for driving him crazy.

She picked up her bag and checked to make sure she had all her things.

"We can't stay here," he said, as if they hadn't been yelling at each other. "I'll get you to a safe place, if the weather holds." He swung up into his saddle and held his hand down to her. "This may not be as comfortable as the wagon, but it'll be faster."

She took his hand and he lifted her up behind him. She hung on for dear life as he rode with speed and skill through the black night.

The weather didn't hold. Within an hour rain drizzled down on them. Without a word he slowed and pulled her in front of him, opening his coat around her. She melted into his chest and held tightly across his heart.

It was almost midnight when they reached a small settlement built around a train station. Sam lowered her in front of a café that faced the tracks and told her to order him coffee while he saw about getting tickets and his horse shipped on the next train.

Sarah nodded as if she understood and forced herself to open the door to the café. She wasn't about to admit to Sam that she'd never been on a train, or in a café. She had about decided never to talk to him again. The man made no sense.

Tables were scattered around a room layered in dust and neglect. Several men, all travelers, she'd guess from the amount of luggage piled around them, played cards and drank near one corner. A mother had put chairs together for her sleeping children in another corner. She glanced up at Sarah and smiled. Three soldiers huddled close to a stove, passing a jug around and laughing among themselves. They had no luggage. She remembered seeing a supply wagon pulled near the tracks. If she were guessing, she'd say they were waiting for something, or someone, to arrive.

She'd seen cafés like this in small towns. When she and Mitchell passed through settlements, the idea of stopping to eat seemed a foolish one as long as they had supplies stored in the wagon.

"You want anything?" a bald man shouted from a doorway leading to the back of the café. "We close as soon as the train comes. With the rain, it's bound to be late, so you got time to order something."

"Coffee," Sarah answered. "Two coffees."

The man disappeared. Sarah took a seat close to the mother and children and unwrapped her wet shawl. The air in the room was warm and smelled of stew, but tiny drafts, where the poorly made walls didn't fit together, chilled her. She curled into herself, hoping to get a bit warmer.

She was almost asleep when the bald man sat two coffee mugs in front of her. "You want some soup?" he asked. "We got enough left for a couple of bowls, but you have to pay for it up front. That way if the train pulls up and you run for it, I still got my money."

"Two bowls," Sarah said. "And bread if you have it."

The café owner stared at her. "It'll cost you two bits extra."

Sarah fished for the coins in her bag and paid him for the meal.

When he brought the soup, she almost asked if she could have her money back. As far as she could see there was no meat in the stew. Odd bits of vegetables floated like tiny roots on the top. She drank her coffee and tore off a piece of bread.

The door slammed against the wall as Sam entered. He carried his saddle draped over one shoulder and his rifle in his free hand. She watched him scan the room carefully, then move toward her.

He didn't say a word as he downed half the coffee in one draw and stared at his soup.

Sarah giggled. "Stew," she whispered.

Sam raised an eyebrow. "You're sure? Looks more like the dishwater."

"That's what the man said."

"Can you cook better than this?"

"If I can't, you can always come here for a meal," she answered.

"I'd rather starve."

She saw Sam's smile die as he watched something behind her. Before she could even turn, she heard his Colt clear leather beneath the table.

"It is!" one of the young soldiers shouted loud as a carnival barker with a full crowd. "It's Sam Gatlin!"

The noise woke one of the woman's babies, and he began to cry.

Sam lifted his weapon onto the table, but didn't pull his fingers from the handle. "I'm just waiting for the train, soldier." His deadly calmness frightened Sarah far more than the man's yelling. "I'm not looking for any trouble."

Another soldier joined the first. They were now only a few feet from her back. Sarah could feel them near. She didn't need to turn around. "We're not trouble," the young man said again. "But from what I hear of you, trouble follows you like thunder follows lightning." He slapped his silent companion on the back. "I heard one time down in San Antonio—"

"If you will excuse me, gentlemen, my wife and I were about to have a meal, and we're not really interested in any story."

Sarah shifted so that she could see the men. They were young, very young. One pulled back, heeding Sam's warning, but the other leaned closer. His eyes were wide with excitement and adventure.

"I didn't know you had a wife." He smiled at Sarah. "And a beautiful one at that." His forehead wrinkled. "Now, what would an angel like you, honey, be doing with a killer like Sam Gatlin?"

Sam raised the Colt to the table. "Did you hear that once down in San Antonio," Sam began in almost a whisper, "I shot a man in the leg for beating a homeless dog?"

The soldier's eyes widened. "Actually, I heard you killed him."

"Most stories get exaggerated with the telling. Only one I can think of that doesn't." Sam moved the barrel of the Colt slightly.

"And that would be?" The soldier's voice sounded higher.

"That would be the one about where I shot the man who insulted my wife." Sam's aim held steady just below the soldier's belt.

The soldier took a step backward. "I meant no disrespect, ma'am. I call my own mother honey, I swear I do."

He hurried back to his friends. For a few minutes the café was silent, but before Sarah finished her coffee, the group of gamblers began mumbling about how it wasn't right for a man like Sam Gatlin to be around polite folks. She couldn't hear most of what they said, but the talk grew louder, faster, harder.

Sam sat his coffee down and lifted his saddle as the train's arrival sounded. "We'd better go, Sarah," he said, pulling her along. "Before cowards drink themselves full of bravery."

FOURTEEN

Sam hurried Sarah through the foggy night toward the train. With his saddle over one shoulder, he swung her onto the platform with his free arm, thinking she weighed less than his gear. Three short toots of the whistle warned them to hurry.

"What's happening?" she whispered. "I don't understand. All we were doing was having a meal. That's what people do in cafés." She said the words as if she had suddenly became a great authority. "Those men had no right to bother us."

"It doesn't matter." He held her close as they moved along the corridor. "We'll be out of here in a few minutes." Sam pushed her into the private car and locked the door behind them.

The seats were worn and tattered. Cigar smoke hung in the air. Sam frowned; at least they were safe. A soot-covered lantern cast a flickering light around the room that neither of them seemed in a hurry to move farther into.

The train jerked. Sam widened his stance so that Sarah could brace against him.

"No," she finished her thought. "It does matter." She dropped her bag onto the nearest seat without letting go of the fistful of shirt at his waist. "Why did those people look at you that way?" The tiny compartment was forgotten as she stared up at him. "Why did we leave? What's wrong with us, Sam? We had money. We paid for our food."

Sam stared at her as the train rattled, gaining speed. "It's not you, Sarah. Those people were not angry at you. They were mad at me." He closed his eyes, dreading the questions to follow. Where would he begin to tell her all he'd done over the years? He had been a soldier, a Texas Ranger, a frontier fighter, and now a bounty hunter. Not yet thirty, he felt he had fought his way through several lifetimes.

"How often?" she whispered still holding to his shirt.

"How often what?"

"How often do people treat you like that?"

The sway of the train moved her against him in an action that warmed his blood. Leaning closer, he let the aroma of her honeysuckle skin calm his tired nerves. He rested his hand over her fist, which still gripped his clothing. "Most all the time. Now and then. Never. What does it matter?"

Closing his eyes, he enjoyed the feel of her skirts brushing around his legs. He didn't really care how others treated him as long as she was near, but he knew she needed to know the truth. "Once in a while someone doesn't know who I am. This is a big state. There are still a few places to hide. Sometimes I'm in a small town for a week or so, then a drifter, or a gambler, or a stagecoach driver remembers me. From then on I'm no longer a person. I'm just a hired gun they've heard stories about."

He waited for her to react. He'd been a fool to think she'd go on talking to him, arguing with him like he was just a man. How many days would it take before she realized how living with him was going to be?

He decided he must be a coward because he didn't want to look down and see the fear reflecting in her face. He didn't want to hear the questions. *How many showdowns? How many battles? How many men have you killed? What stories are true about you?* They were basically all true, changing only by degree.

To his surprise, she remained silent. When he finally looked down at her, she had turned to watch night rushing by outside the window as if he hadn't said a word.

"Sarah?"

She glanced at him and he saw no fear in the ocean of her eyes. "I'm sorry, Sam. I'm so tired. Can we talk tomorrow? I'd really like to go to bed."

He folded down the top berth and pulled out the bottom bench, turning the small space from sitting area to sleeping quarters. She combed out her long hair. Even in the shadowy light, she looked more angel than woman. He couldn't help but wonder what he'd done by giving her his name. For one moment, when he'd first married her, he'd thought he saved her, but now that he saw his life through her eyes, he wasn't so sure. They'd been married over a week, and all she'd known was danger.

Sarah laughed as she pulled off her shoes, then slipped her dress over her head. "Next time I'm in a store, remind me to buy a real nightgown." She yawned like an exhausted child. "A married lady should have a gown to wear and not just have to sleep in her undergarments."

Sam watched her, thinking he would never complain about her lack of a gown. He liked the way she looked in her undergarments. Pulling off his jacket and gun belt, he spread out on the bottom bed. He couldn't remember when his body had ached in so many places. It was time to take a few days to rest.

Sarah curled up beside him on the bottom bunk. She stretched out, trying to make room to sleep on the few inches he'd left.

"Sarah." He scooted over. "There's a top bunk if you'd be more comfortable."

"No," she answered. "I'm fine."

He wondered if she really wanted to be next to him or if she just followed one of her rules.

"Good night," she whispered, sounding as if she were half asleep.

"Good night," he answered, pulling the blanket over them both. She'd left her hair free for once. Sam couldn't help but smile as he bundled a handful and tugged it out from beneath the covers. "Sarah, are you afraid of me?"

"No, Sam," she answered with another yawn. "Are you afraid of me?"

Sam thought about it while her breathing grew slow and steady. He kissed her cheek and chuckled. "You know, Sarah, I think I am."

They were pulling into Dallas by the time he awoke. He ran his hand along Sarah's back and smiled as she melted against him. He knew her body by the way she rested against him each night in sleep. "Wake up, wife. We're in Dallas."

Her hair curtained most of her face as she sat up and stretched. She looked more like a rag doll than a woman. The strap of the loose chemise she wore had slipped off one shoulder and pulled a few buttons loose. He saw the swell of her left breast revealed before she absently re-buttoned her undergarment.

Sam forced his gaze to rise to her face. She wasn't looking at him. She'd almost stopped his heart with her beauty, and she was not even aware of it.

Closing his eyes, Sam swore to himself that he'd be dead in no time if he didn't get out of such cramped quarters with her.

"If you can manage to comb that hair, I know a hotel where you can take a real bath and they'll bring breakfast right to your room."

"That would be nice," she answered as she reached for the new dress Sam had bought her at Mr. Moon's place.

Sam couldn't help but laugh as she slipped it over her head and disappeared. When she finally pushed her head up through the opening, her arms were flapping like long wings made of fabric.

"You can't wear that," he said as he pulled on his coat. "Two of you could fit inside."

Sarah looked disappointed. "I can fix it." She raised her arms silently asking for his help. "But not before the train stops."

He pulled the dress over her head, careful not to touch her. He'd learned his lesson back in the woods when he'd untied her. She was a woman who wanted to be touched on her terms.

Ten minutes later she was wide-eyed when they stepped into the Windsor Hotel. The door handles were gold, and huge chandeliers hung above them, sparkling like stars. The floors were covered with thick oriental rugs in places and polished like no shoes ever walked across them in others.

Sarah walked three steps into the lobby and froze. "I can't go in there." Alarm almost choked her words. "I've never been in a place like this. I've never even seen a place like this." She looked up for help. "I don't think regular folks are supposed to be in here, Sam."

"It's all right. I've stayed here before, and I promise you they'll let us in. When I want to disappear, one of the best places I've found is in the middle of people. With so many around, no one ever looks at anyone." He handed over his saddle to a man in a red jacket. "Stow this for me, would you, Dan?"

"Yes, sir, Mr. Garrett. Nice to have you back." Dan carried the saddle away.

Sarah wasn't convinced. "He called you the wrong name." She held her carpetbag to her with both arms, as if someone might take it away from her by force.

Sam half encouraged, half shoved her into the nearest chair. "Stay right there. I'll check in."

When she stared up at him, he added, "I'm only going to the desk. I'll never be out of your sight. Nothing bad will happen to you here." Sam placed his holstered Colts over her bag. "Here, you can have my guns." He smiled. "If anyone bothers you in the next few minutes, feel free to shoot them."

She frowned, not seeing anything funny in her fear. It occurred to Sam that he was probably the most likely person in the room she'd want to catch within her gun sight.

He sensed her watching him as a man smiled from behind a long desk and offered him a pen. "Welcome back, Mr. Garrett. Will you be staying long?"

"A few days," Sam answered. "Can you send a man to pick up my horse at the station and have him delivered to the hotel stable?"

"Of course, sir. I'll also have your trunk sent up from the basement."

"And ask someone from the dress shop across the street to stop by this afternoon. My wife would like to order a few things." Sam glanced at Sarah. "Her belongings were destroyed." The hotel employee didn't need to know that it had been weeks ago since Sarah's things burned on the wagon train.

If the man behind the counter noticed Sarah or her ragged dress, he was too professional to comment. "Will there be anything else, Mr. Garrett? I've put you in the usual suite."

"Yes." Sam shifted. "I'd like two tubs delivered, one set up in each room. the fireplaces built high, and breakfast within the hour." Sam smiled at Sarah. "We've been cold, dirty, and hungry far too long."

Without another word Sam walked over to Sarah, strapped back on his gun belt, and lifted her bag. Offering his arm, he waited. "Ready, Mrs. Garrett?"

Sarah looked as if she had a few questions, but he guessed the bath sounded so good she would play Mrs. Garrett for a while, if that's what he wanted. She might not be a woman of the world, but she was a fast learner.

They walked the length of the hotel and climbed a staircase to the second floor. He unlocked the door to a two-room suite and watched her circle the rooms. Though he'd stayed in the room many times, now he saw the place through her eyes. He had planned to bring her here the morning after their marriage, but Reed had stabbed him in the back and changed the agenda. Sam couldn't help but ponder how different things might be between them if she'd have been able to see this side of him before she saw the dark side. Would she have thought him a gentleman, or at least been willing to accept him as a man?

Sarah remained silent as men hurried around them delivering huge bathtubs and lighting fireplaces in both rooms. The clerk from the front desk brought an armful of mail and stacked it neatly on the desk in the drawing room. When his assistant carried in a trunk, Sam directed it be left beside the desk in the first room.

"We'll return as soon as the water heats," the last man said as he left the room.

Sam gave a few extra instructions, then closed the door.

"Is this your house?" she asked with a worried look.

"No." Sometimes she looked so young. She might think she knew all about doctoring and cooking over a campfire, but she was suddenly out of her element. He could read the uncertainty in her eyes. "I just stay here when I'm in town. They're used to cattlemen coming in covered in dust." He glanced at the door leading to the bedroom. "I'll be working in this room most of the time, so you can have a little privacy in the bedroom."

Sarah followed him through an open doorway. He walked around the bed and tossed her bag on an overstuffed sofa bed by the window. "You've got good light with the drapes open, if you want to stitch up that dress." He began removing his gun belt.

She stopped him with her hand over his.

Sam grinned. "I can do this myself, Sarah." She couldn't have missed the laughter in his words.

"We can't get comfortable, Sam. You've made a mistake. This can't be where we're supposed to stay."

"Yes, it is—at least for the next few nights."

"But it must be expensive. How will we ever afford such a place?"

"It is expensive and I can afford it," he answered. "And I plan to enjoy it. I hope you will, too. Not all of life has to be sleeping on the ground or crammed into smoky trains."

Sarah backed away, glancing around at all the fine things. "But the rugs, the drapes, even the little objects sitting on tables are finer than I've ever seen before.

Surely no one in his right mind would put such things in a room for rent."

"Sarah." He tried to keep his voice kind. "It's all right. This is our room. No one will kick us out. Unpack your bag."

"But they don't even know your name."

"Here, my name is Garrett. And you are Mrs. Garrett. I find it far easier to move in town without questions if I use Garrett."

"But that's not your real name."

"Maybe it's as much my name as Gatlin," he answered.

She lifted first her knife, then her sewing basket from her bag and placed them on a writing desk. "So I married a man who can't remember his name," she mumbled as her fingers slid over the soft material of the half-chair, half-bed. "That's not all bad. At least he's not the drunk I thought or the shiftless father I feared he was. He's improving by degree."

"Sarah?" He waited for her to stop her rambling. "You're talking to yourself again."

She faced him, her cheeks red with anger. "My short-comings seem a far lesser problem in this marriage than yours, if you don't mind me saying, Sam whatever-your-name-is."

"I wasn't criticizing, I was only commenting." He shoved his hands into his pockets and reminded himself he was not to touch her. "It doesn't matter about the name. You're still my wife."

A light tapping at the door made her jump and reach for the knife.

Sam crossed into the drawing room and opened the door. A line of men in red jackets filed in as Sarah hid the blade within the folds of her skirt.

The men filled both tubs with steaming water, left an

assortment of soaps and lotions, and disappeared without a word. Sam collected a towel from the washstand and moved to the door. "There is a lock on this door if you'd feel more comfortable while taking your bath. No one will disturb you. I'll be in the next room. We can argue after we're both clean."

She hurried to the door, and for a moment he thought she might not want to end their discussion, but she only asked, "Would it be all right with you if we left the door open between the rooms?"

Raising one eyebrow, Sam fought down a smile. "I guess. There is a robe in the wardrobe for you to put on after your bath."

"Who does it belong to?"

"The hotel. They leave it there in case you forgot yours."

"How nice." She turned toward the tub, unbuttoning her clothes as she moved toward the steaming tub.

Sam forced himself to go into the other room. He would have liked nothing better than to stay and watch, but at some point she was bound to notice and object. He opened the trunk he kept stored at the hotel and pulled out clean clothes that had been made to fit him. It always felt good staying here . . . he heard Sarah splash into the tub . . . but never as good as it did right now.

She let out a slight sound.

"You all right?" he yelled, fighting the urge to step around the door and make sure all was well.

"It's wonderful," she answered with a laugh. "Oh, Sam, it's so warm. So very warm and wonderful. And the soaps. They brought my favorite. I've never seen such a huge bar."

Glancing through the stack of mail, he tried to get his mind off the sound of her bathing. He'd ordered the honeysuckle soap delivered because he knew how much she treasured the slim piece of it she carried wrapped inside her bag. He could hear her humming, and from the splashing, she must be washing her hair. He opened another letter, then another, not caring that his bath was getting cold. Anything warmer than the river would be fine.

Finally he undressed. The bandages on his arm and leg were spotted with dried blood and dirty from the trail. Working at the knots was useless. He glanced around, but she had his knife. "Sarah!" he yelled, frustrated.

"Yes?"

"I can't get the bandages off. Could I borrow your knife?" He was almost at the door when he remembered to wrap a towel around his waist.

"I'll bring it to you," she answered as he crossed into the bedroom.

The sight before him stopped his heart. She must have just stood, for water shimmered down her body like liquid silver in the firelight. Her waist and hips were smaller than he'd thought, but her breasts were larger. The beauty of her shook him to his very core.

Without looking up, she reached for her towel and stepped from the tub. When she'd retrieved the knife and turned from the windows, she glanced up and noticed him for the first time.

"Oh, there you are," she said, as if he'd watched her bathe a hundred times. "I wouldn't have minded bringing it to you. I need to get out of that water before I wrinkle." She tucked the corner of the towel around her.

Sam couldn't have moved if a buffalo herd headed full speed toward him. He stood as she walked closer with the knife.

A foot away she knelt and lifted his towel enough to cut the bandage from his leg. As before, her fingers brushed the skin around his wound as if she somehow thought she could make all the pain go away. And in truth, she could, for he didn't feel anything at the moment but the touch of her hand along the inside of his leg.

"You're healing nicely," she said as she stepped away to toss the bandage in a small trash can by the dainty Victorian writing desk.

Sam knew if he didn't move fast, she was sure to see how much he wanted her. His body gave away his need for her all too plainly.

He darted out of the room and made it into the tub before he heard her say, "Sam?"

When she walked around the bedroom door, he'd managed to cover himself with a section of the towel that had followed him into the bath.

"Sam." She smiled. "You forgot the bandage on your arm."

Sam looked at the wound and decided being a fool was preferable to being embarrassed. "Oh, I did, didn't I?" He couldn't remember the last time he'd thought about being embarrassed.

She knelt by the tub and cut the bandage across his arm. Her towel pulled dangerously low over her breasts.

"This wound looks like it may leave a scar." She brushed her fingers along his arm.

"Sarah," he managed to whisper. "It will be all right. I think you need to get dressed." He thought about adding, "before I pull you into this tub with me," but didn't. She had no hint of the effect she had on him.

She stood. "Of course, the woman from the dress shop will be here to help me pick out a few new things."

The top of her breasts were so close he could have easily touched them with his arm. Her skin looked flawless and pink from her bath. Sam closed his eyes and smelled the warm, clean fragrance that always filled his lungs when she was near. Honeysuckle.

He swore he'd buy a case of the soap before they left Dallas. He looked up, enjoying watching her walk to the door.

She glanced back and smiled. And in that smile he saw the truth.

Sarah knew exactly what she was doing. She was slowly torturing him to death.

FIFTEEN

SARAH CLOSED THE DOOR BETWEEN THE TWO ROOMS and leaned against it. She'd never done anything, in her life so brazen, and she wasn't sure why she'd done it now. Since Sam had kissed her and turned away two nights ago, he'd been acting like he hardly noticed she was a woman. Even when he'd fallen on her in the leaves, he had done nothing improper. She'd been angrier at what he hadn't tried than at what he'd done.

She didn't want to be his true wife. She didn't want to be anyone's true wife. But a part of her needed him to see her as a woman. Since he had kissed her that night, he acted as though he wasn't still attracted to her. He held her. Slept next to her. But he didn't try to kiss her.

The first man in her life to look at her with hungry eyes didn't seem to want her anymore. Sarah's pride could not take the blow without fighting back.

Sam's body hit the door with such force, she jumped away in panic.

He stood in the opening glaring at her. "I thought it would be locked," he offered in explanation.

Clutching her towel around her, Sarah backed away. She'd gone too far, she thought. She hadn't meant to tease him to the point of madness. "I wouldn't have closed it," she stammered, "if I'd known you wanted it open. This is your room, after all."

"And you are my wife." His voice was low as he moved into the room. "After all."

She reminded herself that she wasn't afraid of him, but a naked man, angry and staring at her, was more than her limit of bravery.

He took a step toward her, flinging water off his wet body as he moved. He reminded her of a wild animal. Powerful, strong, sure of his movements.

Sarah closed her eyes, hoping he would vanish.

When she opened them once more, he was still moving closer. She backed up a step and turned away.

"Sarah? Look at me."

She shook her head. She didn't want to look at him, even though a part of her found his strong body fascinating. There was nothing soft in the make of him. He seemed all muscle and bone. Like a magnificent animal standing proud and tall before her.

"Sarah." He lowered his voice. "Look at me."

"No." She hiccupped. "You don't have any clothes on."

"You've seen me undressed before. I don't think it would be anything new to you. After all, besides the doctoring you must have helped with, you've been married twice now and you're not a child bride."

She forced herself to meet his stare. "I never saw Mitchell, not naked, not once in the year we were married." She wanted to scream that her first husband had nothing to do with how she felt when she looked at Sam, but she wasn't sure she had enough words to make him understand.

Sam let out a long sigh. "I had no idea you found nudity so repulsive. After all, you are not fully dressed yourself." He reached for the thick wool man's dressing gown in the open wardrobe and pulled it on. Then he retrieved a white robe with rosebuds embroidered across the collar for her. After wrapping it around her shoulders, he stepped back a few feet and folded his arms. "There, we're both dressed. Will you answer a question for me now?"

Sarah wiggled into the sleeves of her garment and let her towel fall to the floor. "All right." She wanted to tell him he looked strange in the robe far too small for his frame, but she was afraid he might take it off again. "What would you like to talk about?" She faced him.

He smiled. "Were you teasing me just now?"

She lifted her head, but didn't bother to lie. "Maybe. A little. Sometimes you act like you forget I'm a woman."

Closing the distance between them, he stood near. "I may forget a lot of things, Mrs. Garrett, but the fact that you are a woman is not one of them."

He didn't reach for her, or bend to kiss her. He simply stood near. Very, very near.

"I thought my name was Mrs. Gatlin?" she whispered, breathing in the fresh smell of him. Tiny droplets of water clung to the hair on his chest not covered by the robe.

"What do you want of me?" he asked so quietly no one could have heard his words even if they had been in the room. "If I come too close, you push me away. If I stay away, you tease me to come closer."

Sarah looked up at him, feeling the warmth of his gaze on her face. "I don't want anything."

"Answer me, Sarah. I don't want to play a game."

She lifted her chin. He was right. But admitting what she wanted might be far more dangerous than playing any game. "I want you to hold me. Just hold me," she corrected. She hated admitting her weakness to him. Everything about him was strong. Sarah couldn't imagine him ever admitting to needing anyone.

"All my life I've felt like I've been begging for someone to hold me." She wanted no lie, no pretence between them. "No one ever has. I just thought that you might if you found me desirable."

Gently he moved one arm around her waist and the other against the back of her knees. He lifted her into his arms and cradled her there as if what he carried were priceless.

"I'll hold you, Sarah, if that's what you want. But I can only hold you as a man holds a woman. Don't ask me to do this as just your friend."

Sarah's heart pounded in rapid fire against her chest. She nodded once. He had a right to set a few of the rules. He'd honored hers.

"And when I'm finished"—his words brushed against her ear—"you'll have no doubts about my finding you desirable."

He walked past the bed to an overstuffed chair placed near the fire. He brought her into the folds of the velvet chair as he sat down.

For a long while, neither said a word. She leaned her head against his shoulder, and his strong arms wrapped around her.

Finally he kissed the top of her head and asked, "Is this what you wanted, Sarah?"

"Yes," she answered. "Thank you."

She stretched slightly and brushed her mouth across his

lips. "I'm sorry about the other night," she whispered. "I know you weren't attacking me."

He didn't move as she continued to brush light kisses across his lips as she talked.

"I was frightened and angry and a little hurt."

His hesitance excited her far more than any advance he could have made. She moved her fingers through the course straight strands of his hair while her bottom lip brushed across his cheek. She loved the feel of this man, the taste of him, the smell of him.

"I'm not afraid of you," she whispered against his ear. "Just let me be a woman around you, Sam."

He closed his eyes and leaned his head back.

Sarah took his silence as agreement. She spread her hand out at the base of his neck and pushed the robe open. "I don't find you repulsive. Shocking maybe, but never repulsive. I guess because I doctored you, I feel like, in a small way, you belong to me."

When he didn't answer, she let her fingers comb through the hair of his chest. She saw Mitchell a few times in his longhandles and once without a shirt, but he dressed in the darkness before dawn and expected his privacy at his bath. He considered bare flesh not only indecent, but unhealthy. She had never even wanted to know what he looked like without clothes, and he had shown no interest in seeing her.

Sam was different. She'd seen his body and wondered what it would feel like to touch him. And with each touch her curiosity grew.

She liked the way Sam's muscles tightened as her palm spread across his chest. Mitchell had been someone who came along when she needed a home. He'd never cared enough about her to talk to her more then necessary, much less argue with her. He placed little value in her. Sarah would stake her life on the fact that if Mitchell had been standing in the rain the night the sheriff raffled her off, he wouldn't have bothered to bid. He'd got her for free when Granny died, and that had been her worth to him.

But Sam never treated her as though she were worthless. He might have been the one who paid the money, but in a small way he belonged to her. She'd patched him up, helped him escape more than once, and argued with him across half the state. He might claim to be the meanest man in Texas, but he protected her. She knew without a doubt that this scarred, powerful man would put himself between a bullet and her.

Sam's hand covered hers, putting an end to her exploring.

She looked up into his dark eyes as he raised her hand and kissed her palm. Her fingers trembled when his lips moved to her wrist. She felt his kiss on her skin with each pounding of her pulse. The gentle action by the hard man surprised her.

He opened his mouth and traced across her wrist with his tongue. His head was down. Dark hair covered his face, but she knew he enjoyed himself. When she shuddered, he pulled her closer against his chest and continued.

"Sam," she said out of breath.

He looked at her without letting go of her hand. "Do you want me to stop?"

"No," she answered. "Please don't."

"Close your eyes," he whispered. "Let go of the fear, Sarah. I'm not going to hurt you. I swear. I only want to touch you."

The warmth from her bath and the heat from his body relaxed her into the softness of the chair.

She floated as his hand moved along her thigh, creating

a longing for more with each stroke. The dampness of his hair brushed against her throat as he kissed just below her ear. A delicious warmth spread through her as his hand skimmed across the soft robe.

She felt as if he were treasuring the feel of her, worshipping the fact that she was so near, so soft in his embrace.

Sarah dug her fingers into his hair as his hands moved up to her shoulders. He pulled her closer, pressing her breasts against his chest as his fingers slid over her back. She wanted to purr like a cat and stretch to his touch. Each time she moved, even slightly, Sam stroked her once more, gently molding her body.

The moments passed by with the ticking of an old clock on the mantel. Minute by minute, touch by touch, she grew accustomed to him until finally she did as he'd asked and floated into a peaceful paradise. There was danger in trusting him, compared to the starvation of loneliness if she did not.

He pulled her close suddenly, as though he had to hold her tight. She rested against the pounding of his heart as his hands moved slowly down her back. She smiled and buried her face into his throat so that he could feel as well as hear her soft cries of pleasure.

She didn't stir when his kiss lowered to her throat. The clean smell of his hair filled her lungs as he crossed beneath her chin to continue his journey. Now the slightest pressure of his hand or nudge of his head moved her as though they were dancers knowing each other's steps. She felt liquid in his arms, flowing in waves to the rhythm of his heartbeat.

His hand cradled her head and raised her lips to his mouth. His kiss teased her until she smiled. This was what she'd longed for and hadn't known how to describe. Sarah felt cherished, loved, and desirable.

His kiss deepened. His caress grew bolder across the thin fabric of her robe. The reminder to stop him from touching her intimately passed as no more than a fleeting thought amid the shower of sensations washing over her.

She shifted, allowing his hand to move from her waist to cup her hip. His breath grew suddenly ragged against her throat as his fingers tightened over her flesh.

"Is this what you wanted?" he asked.

His mouth tickled along her skin and his warm breath spread down her throat. "Do you feel like a woman now?"

"Yes," she answered thinking that she'd spent a lifetime longing for such closeness. "Thank you."

She felt his laughter more than heard it. "You're welcome," he mumbled as he nibbled on her throat.

He pressed her against him and held her so close she matched her breathing with his. She drifted to sleep feeling safe, cherished.

Sam watched her in the firelight. Her robe gapped open and the light clearly defined her breasts. He studied the shadows dancing across her skin. Without a doubt she was the most beautiful creature God ever made. He moved his hand along the flesh at her waist and slowly upward to just below her breast. The soft mound pushed against his finger, daring him to journey further.

She was his, he reminded himself. She was his in the eyes of man and God. He could touch her anywhere he pleased. He had every right, and right now he had more desire for her than he'd ever felt for a woman.

But he wanted her willing in his arms. Not asleep. Never forced or tricked, or worse, out of duty. He wanted her wanting him. He wanted to build a need within her so great for him that she cried out his name in longing.

He didn't want to be only a husband or a man for Sarah. He wanted to be the only man Sarah would ever want.

He lowered his hand and pulled the robe over her breasts. Then he leaned and kissed her gently. Her mouth opened to his request even in her sleep. Her lips were full and ripe from their earlier explorations. She sighed as he tasted her one last time before he carried her to her bed and covered her.

At the doorway to the drawing room, he turned and watched her sleep for a while. She brought a peace to his life. A peace he'd never known.

Hours later Sarah opened one eye. He was gone. The tub remained, the fire cold in the hearth.

She grinned and cuddled deep into the covers, thinking she'd like to sleep the day away. But then, just as she drifted back into sleep, she smelled something.

Coffee.

Sarah rolled over and noticed that the table by the window had been covered with a white cloth. Huge dishes with shiny lids were stacked atop it.

Bacon?

She managed to crawl from the covers and tiptoe closer. Carefully she opened one lid. Biscuits.

She opened another. Bacon and eggs.

Another. Jams.

"Sam!" she yelled as she opened more with baked fruit and tiny sweets like she'd never seen. "Sam!"

"What?" he asked as he hurried around the door from the drawing room. "Is something the matter?"

Sarah glanced at him tucking a crisp white shirt into dark pants. "Sam. You'll never believe this. Someone has left all this food in our room."

His shoulders relaxed. "I know. I ordered breakfast

hours ago but wanted to wait until you woke."

She pulled a chair to the tiny table. "I'm starving."

"So am I," he answered, but when she glanced up he was looking at her and not the food.

SIXTEEN

SAM WALKED THE STREETS OF DALLAS, NOW EMPTY IN midnight's silence. Unlike Fort Worth, where bars and drinking lasted until dawn, Dallas operated on an invisible timetable. If Fort Worth was a wild kid, Dallas was a matronly aunt. Though both lay along the Trinity River, Dallas was a trading-post settlement, with mostly only scares of Indian attacks, while Fort Worth was born as a fort with an Indian raid happening as recently as thirty years ago.

A part of Sam wished he was in Fort Worth. The town had always suited him better. Until recently, Dallas provided more of a haven from danger than a place he went to look for trouble. He could change his clothes and move about among the businessmen and shopkeepers without worry of being recognized. He would have guessed that here also lay a safer place for Sarah. Only after tonight, he knew better.

The young Ranger had been right about Reed heading

south. But it had been Dallas, not Fort Worth, the outlaw rode toward. Sam planned to be waiting for Reed when he arrived. He had no time to wonder if Reed was gunning for him. Sam needed this problem solved so he could get on with the business of finding Zeb Whitaker before the old buffalo hunter found Sarah.

Sam stopped by a streetlight and lit a thin cigar as he thought of the woman who waited for him a few blocks away. He couldn't decide if marrying her had been the dumbest thing he'd ever done, or the smartest. He'd been a walking dead man for years, and somehow she'd shaken him awake. Now he seemed to have his full load of worries. But then again, there were a few benefits he hadn't planned on.

He smiled to himself. She'd surprised him this morning with her request. It took all his concentration to touch her and hold her without taking her to bed. Years of holding back all emotion taught him well, but he wasn't sure how long he could play her simple game of touching, nothing more. She wanted him near. She wanted him to see her as a woman. She wanted to be held. But she didn't want him in her bed.

He took a long draw on the cigar and released the smoke. Not yet, he thought with a grin. He'd never courted a woman, but he thought he'd give courting his wife a try.

Sam would hold to his word. He'd wait until she said she was ready. She'd be the one to come to him and beg for a marriage in more than name only. Then he'd love her as he'd never loved a woman and leave her someplace safe. She'd have her home and enough money to live, and he'd have a memory that would last him the rest of his life.

Sarah didn't know it yet, but she would give him the

one thing he thought he'd never have. Men like him didn't have a chance at anything more than a quick roll in the hay with a woman who charged by the hour. Sarah would give him a glimpse of what life could have been like with a wife. And that glimpse would be enough. It would have to be.

Sam pushed away from the post and moved toward the back alley. He had work to do.

An hour later he stood in a place where his boots stuck to the floor and the smell of filth burned his nostrils. He'd already tried three saloons, and this one looked no more promising than the others. He stood at the corner of a bar nursing a beer, watching those around him. Several men were well into a mean drunk and growing louder. A chubby barmaid, well past thirty, had rubbed against him several times, silently offering more than drinks as she passed. Her blouse lowered with each encounter and the lingering possibility that she would be going home alone obviously bothered her more than anyone else in the bar.

"Ready for another one, mister?" Her ample hip bumped his leg.

She smelled of old potatoes, Sam thought, and found himself longing for the scent of honeysuckle near.

"No, thanks." He didn't meet her eyes. He'd learned a long time ago folks seldom remember details about people they don't face directly. "I'm fine. Just waiting for someone."

"Name's Norma, mister." She winked. "Buy me a drink and I can be your someone."

"I'll buy you that drink if you need one, but I'm leaving alone." Sam didn't want to give the woman any hope of making future sales. He'd seen women of the night turn crazy mad in a blink when they thought they'd been lead to believe they'd found a man for the night.

She poured herself a drink from the bottle in front of Sam. "Suit yourself. You don't know what you're missing."

He eyed her carefully and thought that he knew exactly what he was missing. A filthy bed, a woman who'd been handled so much she started sighing before the buttons of her blouse were undone, and a hollowness afterward that made him ache inside. He'd rather starve than dine at the likes of her table again.

"Wanna tell me your friend's name?" She leaned on the bar and crossed her arms just below her breasts. "I might know him. I know most of the men who come in here on a regular basis. I've been here for more than ten years."

"His name's Reed," Sam answered, thinking he would have guessed she'd survived in this smoky air for more like twenty years. Her wrinkles were from hard times, not the sun. "A thin fellow with gray salted into his black hair. He's missing the trigger finger on his right hand."

Her eyes widened before she shook her head. "Ain't never heard of a man fitting that description. Lots of men come in here missing body parts since the war. Fingers. Arms. Legs. I'm probably not going to notice a finger gone."

He thought he heard the hint of fear in her voice. She knew Reed. Sam would bet his life on it. "He's not my friend, but I need to find him."

She looked around the bar, hugging herself tighter and straining the material across the back of her blouse. "Look, mister, I ain't looking for trouble."

Now he knew she recognized Reed's name. She might not be the type of woman Reed liked. Too old. Too rounded. But she'd heard about the man. Maybe even seen him.

Sam scanned the room once more. A willowy girl, little more than a child, cleaned off a table in the back. She ran more to Reed's tastes. "Mind if I ask the other barmaid? Maybe she has a better memory."

The woman's hand shot out and gripped his arm, then turned away in fear when she looked into his eyes. "Don't ask her," she stuttered. "She don't want to remember that man. Leave her be, mister. She ain't done nobody no harm on this earth."

Sam didn't have to ask for the story; he'd heard it in other towns. Reed liked to buy the young ones for the entire night, and the next morning they were lucky if they were still alive. He might only have four fingers left on his right hand, but he could wheel a blade with the best of them.

The thin maid turned as if sensing she was being talked about. For a second her light frame reminded him of Sarah. Then Sam saw the scar that crisscrossed along her cheek.

Sam turned back to the woman who'd called herself Norma. "If I offered you money . . ." he began.

"It ain't worth the price," she answered.

"If I told you I'm looking to kill Reed?" Sam tried again. "He's the one who scarred your friend. I've seen his work before. I'd like to see that he doesn't do it again to some other woman."

She looked at him long and hard, sizing him up as a man. As a gunman. They both knew if she passed information along and Sam didn't kill Reed, Reed would find out and come after her.

"Where can I find you?" Norma whispered as she leaned too close.

Now it was Sam's turn. If he told her where he was staying, she could as easily tell Reed as let Sam know

Reed was in town. The question was, did she hate Reed more than she feared him? If he'd been alone, Sam might have bet on her hatred, but he couldn't risk Sarah's safety on a hunch.

"I'll be in one of the bars along this street. If you need me, leave word at the Irishman's place three doors down." Sam passed her twice the money she would have earned for the night. "Just let him know you're looking for me. I'll know why."

She smiled down at the coins. "And who are you, mister? I didn't catch your name."

"I'm Sam," he risked. "Just Sam."

She looked up. "I haven't done anything yet." She glanced at the thin girl once more. "But I'll help if I can." When she turned back, she smiled her flirty grin once more. "Want to come home with me just for some fun? No extra charge."

Sam shook his head.

"Married, are you?" She giggled. "I'll never tell."

Sam declined once more, not even tempted by her offer.

She shrugged. "No harm in asking. I've seen men like you before. Married to the core, I call them, till death do them part. Not sure if it's a blessing or a curse."

Sam winked at her. "I'll let you know when this lifetime's over."

SEVENTEEN

Sarah awoke trying to decide which part of her thoughts were dreams and which were realities. They'd spent the first afternoon at the hotel eating and choosing clothes she liked from the dozens brought over by two ladies who ran a small dress shop across from the hotel. She didn't tell Sam that this was the first time in her life she had gotten new dresses never belonging to anyone else.

As soon as the ladies from the dress shop knew her size, boxes of undergarments, shoes, and hats arrived along with the freshly pressed dresses she'd selected. Sam worked on a stack of papers in the drawing room, but she knew he watched her through the open doorway.

When the third wave of boxes arrived, Sarah hurried to his side as soon as the delivery men left.

She knelt by his chair and whispered, "Stop them, Sam."

He offered his knee as a chair for her. "Why?"

"I can't keep all these things. I've never had so much. I can't carry everything." Sarah plopped down on the bed and said, "When I was little, I bundled my belongings each night in case I had to move at dawn. Harriet Rainy used to say, 'I've a mind to kick you out, child. You ain't worth feeding.' Later, when I went to live with Granny Vee, she'd always warn me that I might have to leave 'if times got worse.' Even Mitchell used to yell when he didn't like the supper, 'You're out of here if you don't cook a better meal next time!' I kept trying because I didn't have anywhere else to go if he didn't want me."

Sam's big hand brushed a tear from her cheek, pushing memories aside, as well. "You can own more than you can carry, Sarah."

"I've never had so much." She leaned against his shoulder, liking the easy way she could touch him. Since he'd held her that morning, a peace had settled between them.

"Me, either," he whispered against the top of her hair.

He lifted her off his leg and ordered her to try on everything that had been delivered. He said he planned to watch, but a knock at the door called him away.

When he returned, wrinkles crossed his forehead. "I'll be back in a few hours," he mumbled as he grabbed his hat. "Stay here. You'll be safe." Then he disappeared, saying something about business to take care of without delay.

A few hours later a huge trunk arrived with a note declaring she should fill it and be ready to travel.

Sarah carefully selected each item and packed the trunk. She had no idea where his place was, so she selected warm clothes as well as cool ones. By dark everything was ready if he should return and demand they leave.

Only he didn't return and Sarah finally dressed in one

of her new nightgowns and crawled into bed. She'd wanted him to hold her once more as he had after they'd taken their baths. But twice in one day was probably too much to ask. No wonder he stayed away, she thought. She was definitely a demanding woman.

He didn't return the next day, but meals were delivered, and the two ladies from the dress shop came to make alterations which Sarah could have done herself. She spent her time resting and eating her fill. On the afternoon of the third day she opened the windows and watched the street below. Roses arrived with her lunch along with a card from Sam. "Wait" was all it said.

By nightfall she'd remade the dress he'd bought her at Mr. Moon's store and then fell asleep alone once more.

The next morning Sarah smiled in the dawn light, remembering falling asleep listening for the door. This strange man was becoming a part of her life even when he wasn't around. The memory of the morning he'd held her drifted in her mind.

Her eyes adjusted to the light. As usual, Sam wasn't beside her. He had not slept in their bed for three nights.

Pulling on her wrapper, she moved to the doorway and looked into the shadowy drawing room. Panic tiptoed along her spine. Something was different.

In the early light she noticed Sam's reading chair placed a few feet from the hallway door. She hadn't moved the chair there when she'd checked the lock and gone to bed.

Sarah tiptoed into the drawing room. When she rounded the chair, Sam's form took shape in the shadowy dawn.

His muddy boots were propped next to his trunk and his arms were folded tightly over his chest.

Sarah silently moved closer and stood beside him. She reached her hand out to wake him, then realized a rifle rested across his legs and another stood within easy reach against the trunk. He hadn't just fallen asleep in the chair; he stood guard.

Fear gripped her heart. If she touched him unexpectedly, he might counter before he recognized her. He was a man trained to kill and hadn't stayed alive so many years by not reacting quickly.

She sat down on the floor next to him, watching him sleep. He couldn't be comfortable, she mused, but how many hours had he been there waiting for trouble to come knocking?

She didn't make a sound as dawn spread light into the room.

Finally, with a sudden jerk, he woke. He stood, checked the lock at both the door and the window, then relaxed as he set the rifle aside. He stretched, working cramped muscles.

Sarah didn't say a word or move. Eventually, his eyes came to rest on her with her legs curled beneath her nightgown. A slow smile spread across his face. "Morning, Angel." Sam reached down and lifted her to her feet.

"What's wrong?" She didn't want to waste time. She wasn't sure how much they had left.

"Nothing," he said, but the lie reflected in his eyes.

Sarah gripped his wrinkled shirt in frustration. She'd known the peace of the past few days could not last, but she'd hoped it might linger just a bit longer. "Sam, tell me. What's kept you away? Have you word about Zeb Whitaker?"

"No."

"Then what?"

"All right. You need to know." He nodded toward a chair, but she didn't sit down. "I think Reed and his men rode into town last night. I make it my business to know an outlaw's habits. Reed likes to visit houses of . . ." He hesitated, choosing his words. ". . . a group of ladies when he's in town. I got word a few days ago that he's worn his welcome out in Fort Worth, so I guessed he'd move on to look for his entertainment in the alley bars of Dallas. His needs are such that not every place can satisfy him, so it's relatively easy to guess where he'll go. I've spent the past few days stopping by and offering a few dollars for information."

Worry replaced anger in Sarah's veins. "What else? I need to know the rest."

"One of the women who offered to help me watch for Reed disappeared last night. Her boss said it wasn't unusual for her to vanish for a few days, but it worries me. I had no way of tracking her down, but I felt a need to keep an eye on the other women who said they knew Reed. I waited until the saloon closed last night before I headed back here."

Sam touched her hair, then watched a loose strand curl around his finger. "I'd planned to return sooner, but thought you might be safer alone." He sighed. "I tried to send word so you'd know I was near."

"I felt you were close," she admitted. "I knew you hadn't just left me."

Sam walked over and pulled a rope in the corner of the room. "They'll bring breakfast up," he said. "I don't think it would be safe for us to go out together. Folks might not notice me milling around, but they're bound to remember a beauty like you."

Sarah shook her head. "No one has ever noticed me except you, Sam. I'm just a pale—"

"Stop." He faced her. "Stop believing a lie."

She met his stare. "You're blind," she answered, sud-

denly angry that he would keep claiming she was something she knew she wasn't.

"Then let me stay blind, Sarah." He pulled her to him.
"You are the closest I'll probably get to heaven."

He held her tightly for a long while, as if he was unsure
what to do with her. Slowly her body softened and she
molded to him.

He smiled. There was no need for words. They both
knew this nearness was what they wanted. What they
needed.

She wrapped her arms around his waist and felt his
sharp intake of air.

"You're hurt," she tried to pull away.

He didn't loosen his grip. "It's nothing. I was just backing up a young deputy last night in a street fight."

"Sam Gatlin, you can not even leave me for a few days
without getting yourself hurt. I swear to goodness, how
did you manage to stay alive without me near?"

Sam laughed. "I'm not sure I was alive. Before you, I
didn't have anything to worry about. I didn't have anything to protect."

"You didn't have anyone who cared if you lived or
died."

"And do you care?"

"Of course I care, Sam, you're my husband. I'm supposed to care."

Sam's arms dropped to his sides. "I almost forgot. The
rules."

She felt him go even though he hadn't taken a step
away from her. "What makes you so mad when I say
that?"

He plowed his fingers through hair that was already
disheveled from sleep. "I don't know. Maybe I just want

you to care if I live or die for some other reason than it's a rule the wife is supposed to abide by."

"I told you I didn't want to care about a man who's got the life span of a moth." She wanted to tell him that every time she even thought about caring for someone they up and died on her or kicked her out without a thought. She was sick to the core of trying to care. Couldn't he understand that? Surely he didn't think he got undying love for the price of bail.

Sam picked up his Colt and checked to make sure the chamber was full. "You're right, Sarah. I may not live out the winter, but one thing I promise you, I'll get you settled somewhere safe before I wander off and get myself killed. You deserve that much for marrying me."

His smile never reached his eyes when he added, "I have a feeling my luck can't hold much longer. When it goes, at least I'll have the best-looking widow this state has ever seen."

"What do you mean, your luck can't hold? Do you call getting stabbed, shot at, and beat up lucky?"

"No." He laughed. "I call lucky finding you."

He leaned down and touched his lips to hers, then laughed when she wrapped her arms around his neck and held him there.

When he finally broke free, he whispered, "I take it you have no objection to my kiss this morning?" His hands circled her waist and lifted her off her feet so that she was eye level with him.

"No," she answered when he lifted her higher so he could kiss her throat. "I've no objection. In fact, I'd like to be held for a while, if you don't mind. I like the way you make me feel."

"Are you saying you missed me?"

Sarah looked down at him. "I missed your touch. Please hold me again, Sam."

"You're a demanding wife," he mumbled as he kissed her. "But dear God, how I missed you."

"It's not that I'm demanding. I've been waiting for a long time."

"Then kiss me back," he ordered, "and I'll do as you ask."

She placed her mouth on his as he lowered her level to him.

As before, the kiss grew bolder. He explored her mouth and taught her to respond. Fire melted down her body, making her ache to be closer. She starved for a feeling she never knew existed. A hunger to be near him. A longing to give him as much pleasure as he gave her.

She dug her fingers into his hair and held on as desire stampeded across her senses.

His hand slid into the collar of her nightgown and pulled several buttons free. As his mouth moved lower down her throat, she fought to remember to breathe.

"I've been thinking about you, Angel." His words touched the hollow of her throat. "Thinking of kissing you like this." His mouth moved against her as he spoke. "I wouldn't have thought it possible, but I missed the taste of you as dearly as a man dying of thirst misses water."

She leaned her head back as he pulled another button free.

The last time he touched her had been slow and gentle; now there was a hunger in his kiss that made her pulse race.

He lowered her on the settee, leaning her over his arm so that her back arched as he knelt beside her. With another tug, several more buttons gave way and his mouth moved lower.

Gasping for air, the rise and fall of her breasts moved against the sides of his face as he continued to taste her flesh. The stubble of Sam's beard rubbed against the inside of each mound, contrasting with the softness of his lips and tongue. The cotton gown barely covered her, leaving her rounded flesh exposed.

It was only a matter of time before his mouth found the soft skin and gently kissed each in turn.

"I'm so hungry," he mumbled. "So hungry for you, Sarah."

When he raised to her lips, her mouth was already open. She trembled beneath him. Without breaking the kiss, he pressed his hand over her waist and tenderly stroked her. His fingertips moved along her waist, then slid to the small of her back, journeying downward to cup her hip in his large hand.

His hand returned to her back. "I missed the feel of you. Not some woman, or just a wife, but you, Sarah. You."

The second time his hand ventured down, his touch was bolder, feeling fully of the supple body beneath her gown.

She welcomed the warmth of his hand spreading across her, loving the way he suddenly needed her.

As he became familiar with the curves of her body, she reveled in his caress. She rolled to her back and let him stroke her, needing the fire of his embrace over more of her flesh. When he twisted her back to face him so he could kiss her once more, there was an urgency in both his kiss and his touch.

Sam stared down at her with smoky desire reflecting in his dark eyes. "Open your nightgown, Sarah. Let me see you."

With shaking hands, she pulled the gown down to her waist and pressed her eyes closed as tightly as she could.

"Sarah, look at me."

She didn't move.

"Sarah, did Mitchell ever see you like this?"

"No," she whispered.

"Then look at me."

She wanted him to know that she might be shy, but what they now did would never be an embarrassment to her. "He never asked. I never wanted to show him." She fought the need to tell Sam that Mitchell had never seen her as anything but useful.

As their eyes locked, she realized the beauty of herself reflected in his eyes. He couldn't have pretended. In some small way, and maybe only to this one man, she was beautiful. She truly was.

"Touch me, Sam," she whispered, longing for the feel of his hands on her flesh.

His caress moved along her shoulder.

"No." She laughed. "*Touch* me."

Hesitantly he moved his palm over her breast. When his thumb crossed, she arched her back, begging for more. She closed her eyes, enjoying the feel of his hand moving over her tender skin. He explored every curve, returning again and again to cross her peak, then chuckled softly as she moaned in pleasure.

He was like an artist, warming clay as he molded it in his hand.

When she opened her eyes, she found him studying her. He shoved away part of her gown that had lingered as if he could not stand anything to touch her except his hand.

When he noticed she watched him, he asked, "Are you cold?"

"No," she answered, wanting to thank him for asking.

"Does this embarrass you?" He gazed into her eyes as his hand tightened over her breast.

Her eyelids closed and her lips parted as a sigh of pure joy escaped. "No," she answered again, marveling that she didn't feel the least embarrassed. "Would you mind if I ask you to do it again sometime?" she whispered when the pleasure allowed her to talk once more.

A smile lifted the corner of his mouth. "I wouldn't mind."

He leaned forward and touched his lips to hers. Then, like warm water trickling down her throat, his mouth moved down, only this time he didn't stay at the valley between her breasts, but claimed her with his mouth.

Sarah bolted upward with a bliss that coursed through her every pore. By the time he'd finished tasting first one and then the other, desire drugged her completely. He returned to her mouth and drew her very soul out with the depth of his kiss.

His fingers moved across her, touching her boldly now as he kissed her. She drifted in heaven. When he covered one breast with his mouth and the other firmly within his hand, she thought she'd die of pleasure. She arched her back and cried his name.

Sam stopped and buried his face in her tangled hair. "Are you all right?" he whispered, out of breath. "Did I hurt you?" He sounded unsure, as though he'd never done this before. "I'm afraid I got carried away."

She moved her cheek against his. "No, you didn't hurt me." Low in his ear, she whispered, "Get carried away again, please."

Sam raised hungry eyes to meet hers. Without breaking the stare, his hand moved to her bare skin once more.

She smiled as he memorized her with his touch. Desire fired in his gaze, warming her, telling her she'd not have to beg for his touch. She silently said his name, leaving her lips parted as he lowered his mouth to grant her unspoken request.

She didn't respond when a light tapping sounded at the door, but Sam swept her into his arms and carried her to her bed. By the time he'd reached the bedroom, the man holding her had turned to stone. He dropped her onto the bed in haste.

"It's too early for them to be bringing breakfast." His words were cold, factual.

She caught a glimpse of Sam's eyes, now hard as the steel of the Colts he strapped around his waist.

He pulled the door so that anyone in the hallway could not see her, then lifted his rifle before answering the tapping sound.

"Who is it!" All tenderness had vanished from his voice.

The tapping came again. More urgent this time.

Sam moved beside the door.

Sarah forgot to breathe. Her first thought was to hide under the covers, but if Sam thought bullets might permeate the door, they'd surely reach her.

"Step away," Sam ordered through the door.

Sarah could no longer stay still. She clutched the covers around her and hurried to stand behind the opening to her bedroom. From there, through the sliver in the crack, she could see Sam. Something he'd said to the Ranger days ago flashed through her mind. *They'll have to get through me to harm Sarah.*

She wanted to scream, "No! Don't kill Sam! Not because of me!" But fear held her, packing ice water around her senses until she knew she could do nothing but wait.

"I said step away from the door!" Sam's voice rattled through the two rooms.

He raised his rifle to his shoulder and slid his foot a

few inches in front of the door. With lightning movements he turned the knob and raised his fingers to the trigger as the wood tapped against the barrier of his boot.

He looked into the hallway through the sight on his rifle.

Sarah forced herself to watch. Slow, endless seconds ticked by.

Sam didn't lower the rifle as four bloody fingers twisted their way around the door and brushed his white shirt.

EIGHTEEN

Sᴀᴍ sᴛᴇᴘᴘᴇᴅ ᴀᴡᴀʏ ғʀᴏᴍ ᴛʜᴇ ᴅᴏᴏʀ, ʜɪs sʜɪʀᴛ streaked with blood as a woman stumbled across the threshold and into his drawing room. Her gray wool cape slipped off her rounded shoulders, and he recognized the barmaid who'd told him a few nights ago that her name was Norma.

She staggered forward, revealing long crimson lines sliced along her throat.

"Help me!" she cried with the terror of a death cry. "Please, help me!"

Sam caught her as she fainted, a bloody mass of rags and wool.

"Sarah!" His shout bore the order of a general in battle. There was no time for discussion. "Sarah, I need you."

His wife rushed to his side before her name died in the air. She didn't say a word, just stood ready. If he'd had the time, Sam would have complimented her. But there was work to do, and fast. Trouble had come to call.

He shoved the rifle into Sarah's hands and heaved the barmaid off the rug. "Bolt the door."

She followed his command as Sam tried to find a place to put the woman. She was easily twice as heavy as Sarah, maybe more. And unlike his wife, Norma knew no silence. She mumbled and cried, still fighting demons.

With no help from the barmaid, Sam made it to the settee, where only moments before he had been loving Sarah. He deposited the woman on the upholstery, struggling to free himself from her fleshy arms. In her hour of need he seemed to be the shore she clung to as she regained a measure of strength.

"Help me," she begged, holding his shirt in a vise grip. "Please, help me, mister. I'm a dead woman if you don't."

Sam stared down at her as she fought to catch her breath. He wasn't sure what he could do. She very likely put both his and Sarah's life in danger by coming here.

"Of course we'll help you," came Sarah's voice from somewhere behind him. She shoved Sam out of the way as if he weren't a mountain standing in her path. "Now lie back and relax, dear."

Sam stared as Sarah knelt between him and the woman bleeding on the couch. She carried a basin of water and several towels draped over her arm. It crossed his mind that she never called him dear when he was wounded. She was usually too busy calling him other names.

"Just lie still and let me have a look at those cuts." Sarah dropped a small towel into the water. "We'll deal with the one on your arm as soon as we clean the ones at your throat."

The woman stared at the angel before her in total fright. She stopped crying, or begging, or screaming. She just lay there while Sarah worked, as though sensing she was somehow in good hands.

Slowly the snow of the towel spotted with blood, and the basin of water turned crimson.

Sam hadn't even noticed the cut running atop her forearm, but he knew how the barmaid felt. He'd reacted the same way when Sarah doctored him. Like heaven had let one of its angels free for a moment. His wife hadn't lied when she said she knew how to handle the wounded. She worked with skill and speed.

"Now, this is a little cold," Sarah whispered as though talking to a child. "It will help stop the blood's flow along your throat."

Sarah wet a clean towel and pressed it over the woman's throat. As she lifted the barmaid's hand to hold the cloth in place, she asked as calmly as if she'd been at tea. "Now, what did you say your name was, dear?"

"Norma," she answered. "Just Norma, ma'am. If I had a last name once, I've forgotten it."

"Well, don't you worry, Norma. You're going to be just fine." Sarah wrapped the wound across the woman's arm as she spoke. "I've tended many a cut, and the first thing we have to do is stop the bleeding. As far as I know, two things will help do that. One is cold water and the other one is a good tight bandage."

To Sam's surprise the barmaid leaned back and closed her eyes, allowing Sarah to tend to her wounds. He couldn't move as Sarah worked her magic, talking all the while of how much better she would feel in a few minutes.

Finally, when all but a thin line of blood was gone from the woman's throat, Sarah glanced up at Sam. "It's going to be all right," she whispered. "Whoever did this may have meant to frighten, not kill. Another quarter inch and she would have died."

Sam frowned at the barmaid. If it was Reed's work, he'd gotten sloppy or careless. With two slashes he had probably meant to kill. One slash would have frightened her plenty.

Sam wished she'd never found his door, but curiosity got the better of him. "How'd you know where to find me?" he snapped with more anger than he'd meant to show.

Norma looked frightened as she glanced past Sarah to him. "When you left the other night, I ran across the street to my place and got my boy to follow you. For all I knew, you was one of Reed's men come to make sure none of us ever talked about the man or what he did to Ellie."

"I didn't come back here to the hotel that night." Sam shot the words at her in rapid fire.

"I know," she answered. "But my boy's smart. He said you circled the place a couple of times, and with each passing, you stared up at a window on the second floor like you was searching for gold."

Sam swore to himself. He'd always been so careful about covering his tracks, but the old hag was right. He might not have returned to the hotel room, but he couldn't resist looking up at the windows in hopes of seeing Sarah pass. He'd let his fascination with his wife put her in danger. He should slit his own throat.

With Sarah's help, the woman sat up. "I wouldn't have come if it weren't important, mister. I would have told the Irishman I was looking for you and waited like you told me to do." Her eyes brimmed with tears. "But Ellie ain't got the time. I had to find you."

"Ellie?"

"The girl you saw in the bar that night you came in to ask me to look for Reed," Norma whispered as if someone might overhear them. "The one with the scar running across her face."

"I remember," Sam answered. "What about her?"

Norma closed her eyes and forced words out. "The man you were looking for—Reed—came back late last night. I didn't notice him until well after time for the bar to close. Me and Ellie was cleaning up when I saw him standing in the shadows. He was twirling a thin silver knife between his fingers like it was no more than a toy."

She made no effort to block the tears running down her face and dripping off her chin. "I told Ellie to hide in the back, and I turned to face Reed." She smiled. "But I ain't no fool, I keep a big old bowie knife handy just in case there's trouble. I pulled it out from behind the corner of the bar before I walks toward the thin snake of a man."

Sam glanced at Sarah. Her eyes were huge with both interest and fright. He fought the urge to pull her beneath his arm.

Norma straightened, remembering. " 'What'a you want, Mr. Reed?' I yelled before I got so near him that he could reach out and tickle me with that silver blade. 'We're closed for the night,' I says real official. He looked at me like I was spilled whiskey, then pointed toward the door where Ellie Girl had gone with his hand, like I wouldn't notice he was missing a finger."

The barmaid's eyes grew wild as she continued. " 'You ain't the one I want, woman,' he says and moves toward me like he planned to walk right through me if he had to. 'The one I want already has my mark on her,' he says. 'She knows the game I like to play.'

"Well, I starts yelling and show him my big knife. I was the one who held Ellie after he left her bleeding, and I didn't plan on doing it again."

Norma looked up at Sarah. "I don't know much about doctoring. I was real worried I would do the wrong thing. We couldn't pay no doctor, but I put the soot from the fire on the openings so they'd stop bleeding and not swell up. I don't know if I done right. It left a bad scar."

Sam watched Sarah. His wife's eyes sparkled with unshed tears. If he thought she'd leave, he'd order her from the room. There was no need for her to hear this. Reed wasn't after Sarah. The man was gunning for him. But Sam didn't bother even to ask; he figured Sarah would never leave.

"What happened?" He knew the rest of the story would be no better than the first.

The barmaid touched her throat gingerly. "He came at me all of a sudden, like a changing in the wind that takes your breath away. I fought him, swinging my knife. But he was too fast. Before I could cut him once, he hit me up the side of my head so hard the room started to whirl. Next thing I know I'm lying in the grime of the floor. He had his knee pressed so hard against my chest I couldn't get no air. I heard him laugh just a moment before I felt the knife slice along my throat."

Norma reached for Sam's hand, but he pulled away. He needed to be ready if trouble broke into the room. A part of him strained to hear footsteps coming toward the door. Reed may have known nothing about Sam being in town. The outlaw may have only stepped into the bar to find the girl. But if Reed saw the old woman run to tell someone, it was a sure bet that he'd follow.

"What happened next?" Sam noticed Sarah took the woman's outstretched hand.

"Reed grabbed my hair and started slamming my head against the floor. I guess I wasn't dying quick enough for him." She blew her nose on the corner of one of the towels. "I don't know how many times he did it. After a few hits I could hear the thuds more than feel them. I must have blacked out, 'cause the next thing I knew I was staring at the ceiling and feeling something warm trickling down my neck. I got up and looked around, but Ellie and Reed were gone."

Norma wiped her nose on the bandage Sarah had just tied around her arm. "He got her, mister. I just know he got her, and this time he'll kill her for sure."

Sam reached for his rifle.

Norma cried, "You got to go after them, Mr. Sam! You got the look of a man who wears a gun easy. Like a real gunfighter. I don't know of nobody else who might have a chance with a killer like Reed. I'll pay you. I got twenty dollars saved this month. It's yours if you can find Ellie and bring her back."

Sam knelt on one knee beside the sobbing barmaid. He finally understood. "She's your daughter, isn't she?"

Norma nodded. "I don't tell folks. Don't want them to think I'm that old. But I'm her ma and I love her more than I love my own life. I done the best I could for her and my boy. They ain't had much, but we never went hungry. Most women in my line of work give their youn-guns up, but I couldn't."

Sarah put her arm around the woman's shoulder. "Sam will help," she whispered. "He'll find Ellie and bring her back."

Sam looked from the barmaid to Sarah. "I can't." How could Sarah make such a promise?

"You have to," she answered, as though her request were a simple one.

"I can't leave you here!" Sam stormed. The idea that he might leave Sarah to face Reed frightened Sam more than any gun pointed in his direction ever had. "Half the town might have followed her to the hotel. I have to think of your safety, Sarah. I can't go after Ellie and leave you in harm's way."

Sarah stood and placed both fists on her hips. "You

have to go, Sam. You have to try to save her daughter while there may still be time."

"Why?" Couldn't she see that risking her life wouldn't be worth trying to save some young saloon girl who was probably dead already? Reed usually took his time with the women he tortured. He liked to frighten them with talk before he made terrified believers out of them with his knife. But tonight Reed might figure someone would come after him for taking the girl a second time. He might hurry or decide to leave no witnesses to complain. Sam had to make Sarah understand. He needed to be here with her. To protect her.

Sarah looked at him with sadness in her beautiful pale blue eyes and whispered, "Because her daughter could have been me."

NINETEEN

It took a while before Sarah convinced Sam that she and Norma would be safe in the hotel room. After all, if someone *had* followed Norma from the back alley saloon, he would have burst the door down by now. If Reed took Ellie, he couldn't have followed Norma, and the old barmaid was certain there was no one else in the place after closing time.

Norma finally ended the argument by swearing she could handle a rifle better than she could a knife. Sam made her promise to keep the gun across her lap and plant at least three bullets in anyone who entered.

When a tap sounded at the door, they jumped, but with the call of a breakfast delivery, they all let out a breath at once. The women hurried into the bedroom while Sam answered the door. He questioned the two delivery men in red jackets, and they both claimed that the lobby had been quiet since long before dawn. One said he noticed a woman wearing a cape run up the stairs, and another said he'd seen two businessmen leaving earlier. Other than that, one man swore, no one had entered the hotel. They both claimed it would be another hour, maybe more, before most folks ventured from their rooms.

Sam didn't like his choices, but he grabbed his jacket and checked his Colts.

"We'll be all right, Sam," Sarah whispered from just behind him. "You have to at least try and save the girl."

Sam closed his eyes. Seeing Sarah's beauty would only make it harder to leave. The memory of her leaning back with her gown open still lingered thick in his mind.

Her fingers moved along his back as if she had every right to touch him. As if he belonged to her. "I'll be waiting when you get back," she promised.

He wouldn't turn around, he told himself. How could he leave her if he looked into her eyes?

"Come back safe," she whispered.

He wanted to ask her if she cared, but he didn't think he could bear to hear her say that it was a wife's duty to care about her husband.

He felt her head rest against his back between his shoulder blades. She craved the feel of him as dearly as he craved watching her.

"I have to go." He walked toward the door wishing that someone, anyone, even that bothersome Texas Ranger was near enough to protect Sarah this morning. Grabbing the handle, he said, "Lock the door behind me." He didn't look back as he slipped through and waited on the other side until he heard the lock click into place. The small lock wouldn't save Sarah if Reed came after her. Sam's only choice was to find Reed before he found Sarah.

He stormed down the steps past a surprised bell captain who had never seen Mr. Garrett wearing a twin set of polished Colts.

"Morning, sir," the man mumbled as he hurried to open the door for Sam. "Is something wrong, sir?"

"No," Sam masked his worry. "I'm just going hunting."

He stormed out of the hotel, scanned the street for anyone out of place, anyone watching. If Reed waited, even in the shadows, Sam would have seen the movement when he pulled back, out of sight.

Nothing.

Sam took a deep breath and headed toward the saloon where Norma and Ellie worked. Norma said her room was across the street from the bar. Reed would need a place to have his way with Ellie, and Sam guessed the man had little fear that Norma would follow. He probably figured the older woman was dead, or at least too frightened to come near him again.

The apartment building across the street was Sam's best bet. With luck, he'd find Ellie still alive. Reed always took his time, loving the look of fear in his victim. That's why he returned again and again to the same woman, Sam figured. That's why he always found women who were alone in the world without anyone to protect them. If they had been too frightened to turn him in to the sheriff the first time he called, he felt free to return, knowing he'd see the terror in their eyes the moment they saw him.

Sam knew Norma came to him because if she'd gone to anyone else probably no action would have been taken. Most of the law in Dallas wouldn't bother to get in fights between what they called the cockroaches in the back alleys. The few men who might come would wait until they knew a crime had been committed. By then, it would be too late for Ellie.

Clouds blocked the morning sun, making the back streets dark and damp. Sam hated the way the air thickened with moisture and made the stench of garbage and filth heavier. As he entered the boardinghouse across from the bar, he tried not to breathe in deep of the smell of unwashed bodies and rotting food.

A rat the size of a cat ran across the toe of his boot, and Sam had to fight the urge to pull his Colt.

He moved down a dim hallway where papers were stacked in nests for those who didn't even have the few dollars a month for a room. Most of the doors were opened for circulation. These boarders had little to steal.

Sam listened at each door. Only snoring and an occasional cough. He moved up the stairs to the second floor. At the far end of the hall he saw a small boy curled into a ball. Soft sobs drifted in the air.

Sam walked silently until he stood a few feet from the boy. He knelt down and touched hair the same color as Ellie's. "How are you doing, son?"

The boy jerked as if Sam had struck him, then crawled farther into the blackness.

"I'm not here to hurt you. You're Norma's boy?"

The child nodded.

"I'm here to help your sister. You know where she is?"

The boy pointed toward the last door at the end of the hallway.

"She alone?" Sam stood slowly.

The child nodded. "For now," he mumbled. "But the man who came here with her said he'd be back and no one was to go into that room." His eyes were so round in fear they seemed to cover half his small face. "He told me my sister would die if anyone opened that door."

"There any other way into that room?"

"Nope. There's a window, but it's too small and too high up for even me to climb through."

Sam took a step, turning his head slightly, listening.

"Stay here," he said, glancing briefly at the kid. "No matter what you hear, stay here."

The child curled tightly into his ball, making him almost invisible amid the trash and shadows.

Sam stood at the doorway. Something wasn't right, but if he hesitated long, the girl might be dead.

Grabbing the top of the doorframe above him, he swung, feet first into the flimsy wood. The door shattered, splintering in every direction as his body passed through. Sam's Colts seemed to fly from their holsters to his hands before his feet hit the floor inside the apartment.

Sam blinked, letting his eyes adjust to the sudden bright light of a lantern only inches from were he'd landed. Several tenants along the hallway yelled at the sudden noise, but none opened their doors to investigate.

Taking a step forward, Sam let the barrel of his guns follow his gaze around the room. Broken furniture, clothing strewn across the floor. The odor of kerosene thick in the air.

He stepped around the lantern and moved farther into the room.

Tomblike silence greeted him. Ragged drapes looked as if they had been pulled down from the window and circled around a pile of papers and clothes, almost like a nest or a campfire.

Sam circled, keeping his back to the wall, his body away from the window. He tried to make sense of the odd odor filling the room.

Then something moved in the mass of clothing.

Watching closely, Sam neared. The bundle moved again.

He knelt, lifting a blanket aside with the tip of his gun. Whatever lay beneath the trash remained still. Glancing at the lantern placed so near the front of the door, Sam suddenly understood.

He lay one gun aside and quickly pulled the material away. The thin frightened girl lay gagged and tied to the floor.

Lifting the last bit of quilt that had covered her head, Sam met her stare. He motioned for her to remain still.

The scattered clothes. The kerosene. The lantern close to the door.

Someone had left her here, knowing that when the door was opened, it would hit against the lantern. Fire would spill across the already soaked clothes. The girl, and probably whoever tried to save her, would be covered in flames within seconds. Only luck had kept a piece of the door from tumbling hard enough against the lantern to topple it onto the trash.

Sam shoved the clutter away from the girl and untied the gag around her mouth.

"I'm here to help," he whispered, pulling at her ropes. "Are you hurt?"

She stared with wide, frightened eyes and showed no sign of understanding a word he'd said.

Sam ran his hands over her, expecting to encounter blood or broken bones. "Are you hurt?"

She didn't answer. Whatever had happened in this room before he got here had terrified her beyond caring. Sam lifted her up. She was like straw in his arms. He knew he was putting himself in great danger. Reed could be waiting on the street to gun him down. For some reason Reed had left the girl, but obviously planned to return.

He'd think about what had drawn the outlaw away later. Right now he had to get the girl and her brother as far away from this place as possible.

When Sam passed the boy in the hallway, he motioned

with his head for the child to follow. The minute the boy saw his sister, he hurried to catch up. His oversize clothes made a flapping sound along the passageway.

"Where we going?" he asked as they hurried down the stairs. "What if that man comes back? He's not going to be happy if Ellie's gone."

Sam didn't look down at the boy as he asked, "Do you want Ellie to wait for him?"

"No," the kid answered. "I didn't like him. He made Ellie cry, I could hear it through the door. I couldn't hear what he told her, but I heard her say she wasn't going to do it, and then he swore and said yes she would when he got back."

They were at the landing. Sam's gaze searched every corner for movement, but the town was still silent. Only the sun streamed in early brightness along the streets.

"What's your name, son?"

"Luther."

"Would you trust me, Luther?"

"Sure. I followed you for two days. I don't know what you are, mister, but you ain't no outlaw. Ma said you might be a hired gun, or a Texas Ranger not letting nobody know."

"This place have a back way out?"

Luther pointed, then followed.

At the far end of the alley the boy hesitated. "I need to say something before you take me any farther." He kicked at the ground without looking up. "I was standing in the shadows when that deputy got himself into trouble the other night. I saw what you did."

Sam frowned. He must be slipping if a boy could follow him for two days and watch his every move. He also didn't like the idea of someone seeing him do a good deed. It would be hard on his reputation if it got out.

"Does this mean you don't want to come?"

The boy looked up at Sam for the first time. "They planned to ambush the lawman. If you hadn't left them both bleeding in the gutter, the deputy would be dead right now."

Sam turned down a street to the left, charting his course. "So, Luther, are you coming or not? If you're afraid of me and want to stay here, I'd suggest you stay out of sight." He hated that the boy had watched the fight, but he guessed Luther had seen a great deal in his life already.

Luther hurried to his side and tried to match Sam's long strides. "I ain't afraid of you, I was just wondering why you didn't stay around and let the deputy know what you did."

"No need," Sam grumbled. After all his efforts over the years suddenly everyone he came across was deciding not to be afraid of him. First Sarah, then Frank's kid, and now this alley brat.

They moved through the shadows between the buildings. Sam had spent enough time in Dallas to know he was headed in the general direction he wanted to go. Few people moved about, and those who did paid no notice of Sam.

When they turned onto a dusty road leading out of town, Sam needed to explain a few things to Luther. "The man who was with your sister is the one who cut her face. I'd like to take you and Ellie where you'll be safe for a while. I'll let your mother know where you are. The ladies in this place will help you all find a safe place to live."

The boy looked as if he was chewing the decision over. "You ain't taking us to jail, are you?"

"No. I'm taking you someplace where your sister can

get help." He glanced at the girl bundled in his arms. She was more child than woman.

Sam turned down a path leading to a mission he'd visited many times before. The path wound around for half a mile. By the time he saw the small church, he had the feeling he was far from town. The sisters rose before dawn to begin their prayers.

Sam glanced at the boy. "Now, you be on your best behavior in here. No swearing, or stealing, or spitting."

"Aw, hell." The boy spit on the side of the road, getting it out of his system. "I'll do it for my sister, but I don't need no help. I've been taking care of myself since the day after I was born."

"Thanks." Sam knocked on the door. "She'll need you."

A tall woman in a habit answered his pounding. She smiled up at Sam as she stepped aside and allowed him to enter.

"Morning, Sister," he said as he sat Ellie down on the bench by the fire. She looked so weak, as if even her spirit to live had been frightened out of her. "I brought you a couple of souls in need. Have you room for them?"

"Is she hurt?" The sister knelt in front of Ellie and took the girl's hand.

"Just frightened," he answered. "They need food and a place to rest for a few days. I'll figure out some way to get them out of town so they can get a fresh start somewhere else if you can see to their immediate needs."

"We can take care of that." The nun stood and held her hand out to Luther. "If you'll come with me, I'll show you a place where you can eat all the oatmeal and cinnamon bread you want."

Luther looked at Sam and whispered, "Spittin' and stealin' might be worth oatmeal, but I'll have to think about givin' up swearing."

"Do the best you can," Sam offered. "Maybe they'll give you two meals a day for trying."

The boy seemed to see the logic. He followed the nun.

Sam stayed with Ellie as two old nuns came in and gently helped her to stand. Their soft voices and kindness drew her through another door with promises of a warm bath and rest.

Pulling off his hat, Sam dug his fingers through his hair. They were safe for the time being, but Reed would be looking for them soon. The only good thing would be that hunting for Ellie might keep Reed from coming after Sam. All Sam needed was a little time to get ahead and become the hunter instead of the hunted.

He crammed his hat on and headed for the door, planning to drop by and let Sarah know Ellie and the boy were safe, then start looking for Reed. There was no time to waste.

Sam was almost at the door when a soft voice called his name.

Turning, he faced the tall nun. For a moment they just looked at each other, and he knew she did the same thing as he. They remembered.

"I've worried about you," she whispered.

"I'm fine," he answered as he took her hand in his and held on tight. "Thanks for the shirts."

She didn't look as if she believed he was fine. "I had a dream, Sam. In my dream you were walking with an angel with hair so blond it was almost white."

Sam grinned. "Ruthie, you always did have an instinct about things, even when you were a kid, but this time you're seeing me still alive, and the angel at my side is my wife."

Suddenly a little girl shone through all the clothes of a proper nun. "Oh, Sam! You married! You really married."

He laughed. No matter how bad things had been when they were little, Ruthie always made him feel good inside. He always tried to protect her, and she always tried to understand him.

"I could be an aunt." She tried to keep her joy to a whisper, but Sam saw the sparkle of his mother's eyes in Ruthie's.

Sam almost said "doubtful," but he wasn't about to go into details of his marriage with his kid sister. "Can Sisters of the Church be aunts?"

"Of course we can." She slapped his shoulder. "I'd love to meet her. I can't believe you found someone who actually likes you. She must be a truly wonderful person if she saw through that tough shell of yours."

Sam couldn't resist. "She even thinks I'm handsome." He knew he was pushing it. Sarah hadn't exactly said he was handsome, more like that he wasn't repulsive, but he saw no harm in the small lie.

"No!" Ruth's mouth dropped open. "I'll pray for her sight to return, for she must be blind as a bat. Tell me more."

"Well, she looks like an angel and worries about me whenever I'm out of her sight. She thinks I need her around." He smiled, deciding he was starting to wonder how he had made it through life without Sarah.

"More," Ruth insisted. "Tell me more."

He took a breath and debated how much to tell his sister. "I met her in prison where she was a confessed murderer."

Sister Ruth laughed. "Stop it, Sam. Though I've often wondered where you would meet a nice woman traveling around chasing outlaws. Tell me more and stick to the truth."

"She's young. Years younger than me. Maybe five or

six. She looks frail, but she's not. And bossy. I'm afraid I've married a very bossy woman."

Sister Ruth smiled. "I love her already. Will you bring her to see me?"

"When I can," he promised. They both knew how careful they had to be about even knowing each other. Ruth's life would be in danger if anyone knew she was related to him. There were men in the state who wanted to do him harm, and if they thought they could get to him through her, they would.

"I know." She squeezed his hand one last time and then let go. "I'll be patient. One Sunday I'll look out over mass, and there you'll be with an angel sitting next to you. And, of course, she'll already be rounded with child."

"One Sunday," he answered in promise.

TWENTY

SARAH DRESSED IN ONE OF HER NEW FROCKS WITH lace at the collar and cuffs. Standing in front of the mirror, she could do nothing but stare. Before her stood a woman she had never seen before. Her hair. Her eyes. But that couldn't be her looking back from the glass. She'd seen herself in the mirror at Granny's almost two years ago. Since then there had been no time for more than a glance of how she appeared in window reflections and in water.

She moved closer to the glass. Somehow, when she hadn't been looking, a woman had replaced the girl. Sarah straightened. "It's time for me to stop allowing others to run my life," she said to her reflection. "I'm a grown woman." She pushed her hair back on each side with small ivory combs the shop ladies had said matched perfectly with her dress.

When she returned to the drawing room, sunlight sparkled through the windows as though all was well with the day. True to her word, Norma kept the rifle close and watched the door. But Sarah noticed she still managed to eat two platefuls of breakfast and drink half the pot of coffee while maintaining her guard. They had spent the morning talking while Norma grew more restless by the hour.

"I can't just wait," Norma whined for the tenth time. "Not when my babies are out there somewhere, maybe hurt, maybe dead. I got to go see. I should have gone with him to find my Ellie."

Sarah tried to calm her, but in truth she agreed. When Sam had left them here hours ago, it had seemed like a good idea at the time, but now she wished she'd gone with him as well. Maybe she didn't know how to use a gun and she might be near worthless in a fight, but she still needed to know he was all right. Thinking back over their short married life, she realized he always got hurt, and she needed to get him out before he fell. Who would help him walk away if she wasn't there?

"You shouldn't go out," Sarah tried to explain to the barmaid whose dress was torn and bloody. "But no one knows me. I could go for a walk and see if I hear anything. If there has been trouble near your street, people will be talking about it."

Norma pulled her cape around her. "You're not going without me. I know the way and I know who to ask."

Without another word, the women nodded at each other, silently agreeing to their pact. Ten minutes later they turned a corner a few blocks from the hotel and entered another world. Odors floated around Sarah, bombarding her senses. Too many cook fires. Too many bodies.

Sarah picked up her pace, trying to keep up with Norma's long strides. Sam had been right, this was not the place for her. A drunk tumbled out of the doorway from one of the saloons. He bumped into Norma, who slammed into Sarah. Both women struggled to keep their footing as Norma yelled at the drunk. A beggar followed them for half a block, claiming one need for coin after the other. Children brushed Sarah's skirts as they played a game of dodging wagons in the road. Work wagons filled with supplies and coal labored along the uneven streets, stirring up a cloud of dust almost as high as Sarah was tall.

They should have stayed in the hotel. At least there, trouble would have to come through the door. Here, in the alleyway, it might come from any direction. Sarah wished she had thought to bring her knife. At least then she'd have some protection. Or maybe she should carry one of Sam's Colts. After all, he had two. Surely he wouldn't feel a need to shoot more than six outlaws at one time.

"This is where I live," Norma mumbled at Sarah's side. "You stay here, miss. I'll go see if anyone is upstairs."

Sarah nodded, thankful she didn't have to go inside the building. The street held all kinds of danger, but the dark hallway looked even more frightening. A baby's cry blended with an argument and a mother yelling at her kids, making the very house moan with life.

Norma disappeared.

Sarah waited.

She could hear her own heart pounding. Except for the few times she'd been at the meetings on the wagon train, Sarah had never been around more than a few dozen people at one time. Now she felt as if she stood in the center of a hive. She could hear them talking, coughing, walking. Their smells surrounded her. They seemed to be moving closer. As she waited their very breath warmed the air about her.

Sarah stepped back, wanting to lean against the brick of the building so that at least one side would not be bombarded by running children and drunks staggering on the street.

"Watch it, lady!" A young man, barely more than a boy, hauling coal pushed against her.

Sarah twirled and jumped away from him. He reminded her of a human mole, for days of dust from his job layered his skin and clothes.

Another's hands stopped her movements as she backed away from the boy.

She twisted and stared into the dirty face of an older man. He held a shovel in one hand and touched the sleeve of her dress with the other. If possible he was even filthier than the first. Most of the man's teeth were missing, and the only spot on his body not black with dirt was a place above his upper lip where his nose had been running.

The smell of coal dust filled her lungs as she drew in air to scream. The man leaned on his shovel and smiled with an almost toothless grin.

"Pardon me." He didn't look the least bit sorry. "I didn't mean to get dirt on your fine dress." He brushed his hands over her arms, causing more damage than cleaning. "I'm sure glad you bumped into me, though. Ain't she something, Charlie?"

The boy with the bucket spit slightly as he giggled.

Sarah backed up until her shoulders struck the building. Trash piled half her height blocked her left and the shadowy alley lay to her right. She tried to look past the men to where Norma had disappeared, but she couldn't see beyond the bulk of dirty clothes before her.

They were harmless, she tried to convince herself. After all, it was the middle of the morning and they were standing on a public street.

"You out here by yourself?" the leader asked. "Don't seem like you're in the right neighborhood. You lost?" He didn't wait for her to answer. "Don't see many around here that look so untouched. You got the prettiest hair I ever seen."

Sarah cringed as both men stared at her as though they'd found a treasure amid the trash.

The man raised his blackened fingers to stroke her head, but an inch from touching her, he froze.

Sarah looked up and saw that a fist held the toothless man's arm in place. Then she heard a familiar voice, low and deadly, say, "If I were you, I'd think twice about touching her."

Sarah looked past the little man to see the broad shoulders of Jacob Dalton. Even in the shadowy alley the sun caught on the star he wore pinned to his chest.

"Who do you think you . . ." The toothless man turned.

"Morning, Mrs. Gatlin," Jacob said, still holding the other man's arm in midair.

"Good morning, Ranger Dalton." Sarah tried not to laugh as the dirty hand tried to wither out of Jacob's grip. "It's nice to see you again."

The Ranger seemed to remember the man dangling from his fist. He let go of the man's wrist and tipped his hat to Sarah. "Mind if I walk with you, ma'am?"

The two coal workers hurried to their wagon and moved on down the street without looking back.

"Actually, I'm waiting for someone," Sarah answered. "But you could wait with me."

Jacob glanced up and down the street. "Gatlin didn't leave you out here by yourself. If he did, I'll have to have a talk with him and knock some sense into that thick head of his."

Sarah smiled. "No, he doesn't even know I'm out."

Jacob relaxed and Sarah couldn't help but think that the Ranger must feel that dealing with a careless wife would be far easier than calling Sam Gatlin a fool.

"If you don't mind my saying, Mrs. Gatlin, that's a mighty pretty dress you're wearing."

Sarah blushed. "I don't mind, but please call me Sarah." She'd never been called anything but her first name.

"All right, but you have to call me Jacob." The Ranger looked years younger than he had a minute ago when he'd threatened a man with simply the tone in his voice. "And, Sarah, you really shouldn't be in this part of town without protection."

The Ranger, who'd stayed alive by always being ready to fight, was unexpectedly blindsided by a huge bundle of clothes.

Before either of them could react, Norma stormed at him in full sail. "Get away from the lady, cowboy!"

Jacob lifted his arm to block the rain of fists flying his direction. He reached for his gun, but never cleared leather as the barmaid protected Sarah.

"She don't want nothing to do with nobody." Norma continued to hit Jacob. "Didn't your mama teach you not to bother fine ladies?"

Sarah tried to introduce Jacob to Norma, but the young Ranger looked so laughable trying to dance out of range.

"Sarah! Help me out here," the young Ranger begged.

Norma pulled her next swing and looked at Sarah.

Sarah did her best to sober. "Jacob Dalton, I'd like you to meet my protection."

He shoved his hair away from his handsome face and tried his best to give a slight bow to Norma. "Pleased to meet you, ma'am." When he was sure Norma didn't plan another attack, he turned his attention to Sarah. "I was wrong. Maybe I'm the one who shouldn't travel outside Main Street without protection."

Norma folded her arms beneath her breasts and glared at him. "You know this cowboy, Sarah?"

"He's a friend of Sam's and harmless." Jacob looked offended at the comment, but Sarah continued talking to Norma. "Thank you for your efforts to assist me." She leaned closer to the barmaid. "Did you find your daughter?"

Norma shook her head. "Good news I'm thinking."

Sarah agreed. She had feared they would find Ellie dead.

Norma lifted the bundle she'd tossed at Jacob. "I talked with a man who sleeps off most of his drunks in the hallway. He said some big fellow came by early this morning and kicked the door down, but he didn't remember hearing shots fired."

"Sam," Sarah whispered.

Norma nodded. "The bum was too far into drunk to think, but he remembers seeing my boy following the big man out the back door. I looked around where we live. The place had been trashed, but I didn't notice any blood."

"Blood?" Jacob stepped closer. "What's going on here?"

Sarah linked her arm in his. "I'll tell you while you see us back to the hotel." When Norma didn't budge, she added, "If Sam left, he's probably not coming back here. We'll be safer waiting at the hotel until Sam gets in touch with us."

Norma followed as Sarah explained everything she knew. Jacob left them at the steps of the hotel and said he'd check out any word about Reed that the local law might have.

Jacob was two steps away when he turned and rushed back. He caught Sarah's arm as she moved up the second step. "I almost forgot. I heard a rumor that Zeb Whitaker is in jail. I'm headed that way to make sure as soon as I can saddle up." He smiled at Sarah. "With luck, you won't have to worry about him anymore."

Sarah jumped with joy, reaching one arm out to hug the young Ranger's neck. "Thank heaven! I can't sleep at night thinking he's out there somewhere looking for me."

Just as he set her back on the step, Sam came into view from behind Jacob. Before Sarah could tell Sam the great news, her husband stormed up the hotel steps two at a time and disappeared through the wide door.

"Lordy, Lordy," Norma mumbled in the stillness that followed. "That's one angry man."

"Want me to go up with you and explain?" Jacob's forehead wrinkled as he touched the handle of his Colt.

Sarah shook her head. "Of course not. He'll be delighted when he learns we don't have to worry about Zeb anymore."

Jacob raised an eyebrow. "Sam Gatlin don't appear to be a man who has spent much time in his life being delighted about anything. I can see him more getting angry."

"Or maybe getting even," Norma added.

TWENTY-ONE

SARAH HELD HER HEAD HIGH AND FORCED HERSELF to climb the steps. She'd sent Norma across the street to buy thread so they could mend the barmaid's blouse, assuring the woman that there was not anything to worry about. She had nothing to fear from her husband, Sarah reminded herself. She only wanted a moment alone with him to explain what he'd seen on the street.

In truth, Sarah swallowed down panic as she reached the door. She had never seen Sam so angry. She'd heard people say that they knew someone who would get angry enough to spit nails, but until today she'd never thought the expression might be true.

Opening the door as quietly as possible, Sarah half expected him to start shouting at her before she could get into the room.

Only silence greeted her.

She closed the door behind her and waited. Nothing. Maybe he hadn't been as mad as she thought. Maybe he'd had time to think it over, and he realized that she wasn't doing anything improper.

Before she made up her mind, he stormed from the bedroom, his hands filled with shaving gear and the clothes he'd worn the day before. "Get packed," he ordered. "We're leaving." He tossed his clothes into the trunk he'd left in the drawing room for days and crammed his shaving supplies into his saddlebags.

"Sam, what is it?" Any joy she felt at knowing Zeb Whitaker was in jail vanished when she realized Reed was still out there looking for Sam. What if Reed knew they were in Dallas? Were they running? Hiding? Or going after Reed?

She reached out and touched his sleeve as he passed. "What's wrong?" Her imagination was quickly coming up with all that might have happened.

He jerked away, making her stumble forward with his sudden action.

She watched him walk away. He hadn't even noticed she'd tripped. He simply continued his packing. She moved closer. "Sam?"

He turned so quickly, she stepped back, feeling almost as if she'd been hit by a blow. "What's wrong? What's wrong?" His voice grew in volume as he closed the distance between them. "I see my wife hugging a man on the street, and you ask me what's wrong?"

She stood her ground. "Sam, let me—"

"No! I know what I saw."

"But . . ."

He wasn't listening. "Tell me, Sarah, did you ask him to hold you, too? Did you melt against him like warm butter so he could feel—"

Her slap hit his face with all the force she could muster. "How dare you?"

He didn't move as the side of his jaw turned red with the imprint of her hand. "How dare I what? How dare I pretend I'm your husband when we both know I'm not?"

"You are my husband."

"In name only, Sarah."

"So that's what you're so mad about. The fact that I won't sleep with you."

"No, I'm mad as hell about you standing on the street wrapped up in another man arms."

Sarah raised her hand.

"You hit me again, woman, and I swear you'll regret it."

"Then hit me, Sam!" she yelled. "I always knew you were a wife-beater. Hit me hard so my whole face will turn purple if it will make you feel better. I'm not changing my mind about mating with you until I'm good and ready, and I'm not apologizing for hugging a friend for bringing good news."

She balled her fist and lifted her chin, daring him. She'd take the blow if that's what it took, but she was tired of backing down.

Sam lowered his voice. "I'm not going to hit you, Sarah. Get ready. We leave within the hour." He turned back to his packing.

Sarah knew he was still angry at her, but she didn't know what to do. Her pride wouldn't let her defend herself because she hadn't done anything wrong. He didn't look as if he would listen anyway.

She tried to help him pack, folding clothes he'd thrown into his trunk. The silence thickened between them even though they were only inches apart. When Norma tapped on the door, they both jumped.

"Is it all right to come in?" she whispered to Sarah.

"Of course it's all right. Everything is fine," Sarah lied.

Norma approached Sam slowly. "Mr. Sam? Did you find my girl?"

Only Sarah noticed Sam was fighting to keep his voice calm. "I found her. She's scared pretty bad, but not hurt. I've got her and the boy at a safe place. It would probably be best if we wait until dark before I take you and Sarah."

Norma nodded. "Thank you, but I need to see her soon." She sat down in the chair by Sam's desk, relief washing over her. "I can't tell you how grateful I am to know they're safe. I may not have been the best of mothers, but there ain't nobody can say I wasn't a caring one."

She didn't seem to notice that she was the only one participating in the conversation. "This has been quite a day. I don't know if I can live through many more like this. My heart can't take it." She wiped her brow on her blouse sleeve. "But it all turned out good in the end. My kids are safe and that man Sarah killed ain't going to bother her anymore." She patted her chest. "I could use a drink."

"There's a bottle in the bedroom on the dresser," Sam said. "Help yourself."

When Norma left the room, Sam placed his hand over Sarah's as she spread the wrinkles out of his jacket. He wasn't caressing, he only meant to draw her attention. "What do you know of Whitaker?"

For a moment she didn't want to tell him. "Jacob said he got word Zeb is in jail. That's what Jacob came to tell us. I don't have to worry about him."

She raised her gaze to Sam's dark stare. The anger had left them both, but the wounds were still there. He hadn't trusted her. He'd been jealous of nothing. No apology would take the hurt away even if he offered.

And she'd slapped him, Sarah thought. She'd slapped hard, wanting to hurt him.

Sam pulled his hand away as Norma came back into the room carrying two glasses. "Anyone want to join me?"

"No," they both answered at once.

She shrugged. "Well then, I'll have to do the best I can to finish this bottle all by myself."

"Enjoy it. Where you're going there will be no drinking."

"What?"

"You'll be safe, but there's no drinking or swearing and no men allowed."

Norma swallowed her first gulp of sin. "I'll be in hell."

"You'll be out of Reed's reach, and that's what you want." Sam set a rifle by her chair and walked toward the door. "Stand guard while Sarah packs. I have to go downstairs and arrange a few things." He turned and glared at them both. "We leave as soon as I get back, and both of you better be here when I return."

Norma looked frightened, but Sarah walked past him no longer afraid of him. "Then you'd better hurry," she whispered.

Sam's knuckles whitened, but he didn't follow her.

Instead, he forced his body to turn and walk out the door. He was halfway through the lobby before he allowed his fists to relax. He thought of finding Jacob Dalton and beating him to a pulp, but Sarah would probably be mad about that, too. Not to mention how the Ranger would feel. Plus Jacob Dalton was big enough that the fight would be an even one, which would take some time. With his luck he'd return late and find his wife out in the streets hugging someone else.

He slammed his fist on the desktop. Why did she have to look so damn beautiful? She'd taken his breath away when he'd seen her on the steps. Then she'd hugged Dalton and he'd felt as if someone had shot a cannon into his gut.

"May I help you, Mr. Garrett?" a frightened desk clerk asked.

Sam coughed. "Sorry," he mumbled. "Something in my throat. Didn't mean to startle you."

The clerk remained out of reach.

"I need to have trunks delivered to this address north of here." Sam scribbled on a piece of paper. "And would you ask someone to let the livery know I'll be picking up my horse within the hour?" Sam tried to think. "Oh, and have a buggy waiting outside. My wife will be down in a few minutes."

The clerk nodded and promised to have everything done.

Sam walked into the café and took the first table. He needed both time and space between his bride and his temper. He thought about ordering whiskey, but wasn't sure he could stand to face both Sarah and Ruthie with liquor on his breath.

"Coffee," he mumbled as the waiter neared. "Hot and black."

"Make that two," a familiar voice said from behind Sam.

He didn't turn around. The Ranger was popping up more than locoweed after a rain lately.

Dalton turned a chair around and took the seat across from Sam. He shoved his hat back and smiled that all-too-bright grin Sam was starting to hate. "You don't deserve her, you know," Dalton opened.

Sam saw no point in arguing the obvious. "I know." He frowned at the Ranger. "But neither do you."

Jacob raised his hands in surrender. "I make it a point

to stay away from married women." His steel gaze leveled with Sam. "But if you ever hurt her . . ."

"Don't waste a threat." Sam leaned back as the waiter placed two steaming cups on the table and hurried away.

Jacob nodded once as though he'd said what he came to say. He started to rise, then remembered the coffee and relaxed back in the chair. "Sarah's a beauty, she truly is, but I've got my eye on this young thing up in Clarendon. I'm just waiting for her to finish growing up. Then I plan to marry her before she becomes a professional."

Sam raised his cup to his lips thinking he would settle things with the Ranger if that's what Sarah wanted. "What's she planning to be?"

"A whore."

Sam gulped boiling coffee. When the pain subsided enough for him to speak, he asked, "I thought you said—"

"I did." Jacob shrugged. "She wants to be a lady of the night." The young man winked at Sam. "I guess you and I are just meant to marry criminals. Sarah confessed to murdering Zeb, and my girl dreams of being the highest-paid hooker in Texas."

Sam smiled. "Only Sarah didn't kill Zeb Whitaker."

Jacob nodded. "I thought of that. If she's not a murderer, then she shouldn't have been fined. And if she didn't owe a fine, she didn't have to marry you to get out of jail."

Sam didn't like the Ranger's logic.

"So I'm thinking that, unless there's a baby on the way, Sheriff Riley might consider calling the whole thing off."

When Sam frowned, Jacob added, "Don't worry. I bet he'll even give you your money back.

TWENTY-TWO

SARAH PACKED ALL HER NEW CLOTHES IN THE TRUNK, but she placed her personal belongings in the carpetbag so that she could hang on to them. Part of her still feared owning more than she could carry.

Norma talked continuously from the drawing room. Now that she knew her children were safe, she had found a reason to celebrate. The bottle provided by the hotel gave her the means. "I'm going to get my babies and get out of this town. Go somewhere and make a new start. Maybe I could be a cook. Back years ago I was fair at the job. Wasn't much excitement to it, though."

Sarah tried to pay enough attention to her chatter now and then, but Sam filled her thoughts. She just couldn't understand why he went into such a rage over her hugging Jacob. Surely he didn't think that touching Jacob was anything like touching him. Sam was her husband, after all.

"He's the man I want to touch. Something about him draws me." She shook her head. "I'm making no sense.

It's like wanting to pet a porcupine because no one else has ever touched him."

"Did you say something?" Norma yelled. "I didn't hear you real clear." Her words slurred together. "I'd come in there to talk while you pack, but I'm suppose to be keeping an eye on this door."

"Nothing!" Sarah shouted back. "I was just mumbling something about my husband."

Norma laughed. "Talking about that man of yours, huh? I don't blame you. He's one fine man, that's for sure."

"He's one foolish man," Sarah said, more to herself than Norma. "Getting all mad and jealous of me hugging the Ranger, like I was the only woman he'd ever known."

Her words sank in slowly. *The only woman.* Could it be possible that what he'd told her was true, he'd never cared about another? If he thought he was losing her to Jacob, no wonder he was so angry. No, that couldn't be right. He was almost thirty. He must have cared about at least a few other women. Hadn't he called a woman's name when he'd had the fever? Sarah could not be the only woman Sam Gatlin had ever called his own.

". . . he is for sure." Norma's words reached Sarah.

She stepped to the door and looked at the now rosy-cheeked Norma. "I'm sorry, what did you just say?"

Norma's whole face wrinkled in thought as if she'd just been asked to take some kind of test. "I was saying"—she pointed one chubby finger at Sarah—"that your husband might be one fine man and all, but he's married to the core. I knew that the night I met him. There ain't many a man who'll turn down a free ride between the sheets, but he did without hesitating."

Now it was Sarah's turn to look confused. "You offered him . . ." She wasn't sure she knew the right words to say what she needed to ask.

Norma waved her hands in front of her. "I didn't know he was married to a fine lady like you. I thought he was just a man looking to get a little relief from the urges all men have. It's a service I provide. It don't mean nothing."

Sarah nodded. Now she was on ground she understood. Granny Vee told her all about how a man has a need sometimes and he's got to satisfy it. She said that if you are his wife, it is your duty to lie still and let it happen. Sarah had been in Norma's shoes once: She'd provided a service for Mitchell and it hadn't meant anything. She had made up her mind when Mitchell died that she would never do it that way again. Not even for a second husband. If it didn't mean anything to her, it wasn't happening.

She turned her attention back to Norma. "You offered to bed Sam?"

Norma grinned. "I guess you could call it that, ma'am. But he wasn't interested." She winked. "My guess is he's getting what he wants at home."

"But he's not," Sarah admitted before she realized she'd said the words out loud. "I asked him to wait."

Norma wiggled her eyebrows as though she'd just come to the discovery that they were loose. "Does he want to? I've heard of men who ain't all that interested in any woman."

"He's interested. He touches me sometimes in a way that makes me melt inside. And he looks at me with such hunger, like he might die for the need of me."

Norma snorted. "If he's interested, but he's waiting just because you asked him to, I hate to be the one to have to tell you, but your man must have that terrible illness called love."

Sarah didn't see how that could be possible. They'd only known each other a matter of days and most of the time he'd been wounded or fighting with her. Didn't people who love act differently? If Sam was acting like he was in love, yelling and screaming at her about nothing, she wasn't sure she wanted to know what he'd be like if he didn't love her. She loved him, of course. She had to. It was a rule.

"I don't think it's love," she finally said. "Maybe, like you said, it's just because he's a man and has needs."

Norma laughed. "I could have taken care of him if all he had was a need. My guess is he's got a hunger for far more than I can offer him."

Sam opened the door before Sarah could ask more. He didn't look as angry as when he'd left. He checked that Norma still had the rifle in her lap and frowned at the half-empty bottle of whiskey.

When he looked at Sarah, his dark eyes seemed to be searching for something. "You ready? I've got a buggy waiting, and the men will be up for the trunks soon. I've talked with Dalton, and our plans have changed a bit."

"Yes, all packed," she answered. "But could I have a word with you in here for a minute before we leave?"

He followed her into the bedroom and closed the door. "We don't have much time. If you're planning to yell at me, it may have to wait until I get you two to safety."

Sarah turned and wasn't surprised to find him glaring at her. She wouldn't have been surprised if he'd reached for one of his Colts. Their argument still lingered in the air, like the words were floating above them, too high to pull back, too low to forget.

Before she changed her mind, she closed the distance between them and wrapped her arms around his neck.

He didn't bend down, so she had to stand on her toes to kiss him. Her lips pressed hard against his.

He didn't respond.

She leaned closer, allowing his body the feel of her

from hip to shoulder, then she pressed her mouth to his once more.

The hard line of his lips softened slightly as her mouth continued to tease, but he did not kiss her back.

"We don't have time for this, Sarah."

"Then stop me," she whispered against his lips. "Push me away."

"Sarah, we can't."

"Push me away, Sam. Turn me down." She spread her fingers over the cotton of his shirt, loving the feel of his solid chest. "I'm not stopping unless you push me away."

"Not likely!" His strong arms circled her and locked her against him. His kiss was wild with need.

Sarah felt him lift her off the ground and moan as she opened her mouth. She knocked his hat off as her fingers moved into his hair. He wanted her, she almost laughed. This strong, powerful, maddening man wanted *her*.

They kissed until Sarah felt weak with a need for more. When he finally broke the kiss, he moved to taste her throat as though he couldn't get his fill of her.

She whispered in his ear. "There's a world of difference between hugging a friend as a thank-you and holding my husband, Sam. It's not the same at all."

He didn't answer, he just continued planting light kisses along her throat as his hand moved up to tighten around her breast.

"I'm your wife, Sam," she whispered as she kissed his ear. "I'm your woman and no one else's."

He raised his head and stared down at her. "But what if . . ." he asked, as though he knew of some reason her words might change.

"There is no *what if*. I want no other man to hold me and touch me. And when I'm ready, I want no other to bed me."

"Now seems like a good time." Sam smiled, but she couldn't miss the hunger smoldering in his eyes.

She laughed, moving her cheek against the hard line of his jaw. "I thought you said we have to hurry. If we don't get Norma out of here soon, she'll be too drunk to walk."

Sarah pulled away and turned toward the door.

Closing his hands around her shoulders, Sam drew her back against him as if he couldn't bring himself to share her with the world.

Leaning her back against his chest, she circled her hands around his neck. As she knew he would, Sam let his fingers roam the front of her dress.

"I want to touch you without all these clothes in the way."

She sighed, agreeing as his hands warmed her through the material.

"I want to taste your whole body, Sarah." He lowered his mouth to the side of her neck. "Dear God, how I want you."

Before she could answer, a loud *thud* sounded from the drawing room.

Sam reacted first. He shoved Sarah behind him and drew his Colt as he reached for the doorknob. "Stay here!" he ordered.

Sarah followed him into the drawing room. All was silent. The door was still locked. Not even the air seemed to have stirred.

Except Norma. The chubby barmaid lay flat out on the floor, the whiskey bottle still in her hand.

Sam glanced back at Sarah. A smile lifted his mouth, but she could still see the embers from the fire they had started a few minutes earlier in the bedroom smoldering in his eyes. "Next time I'm ordering you to come along. Maybe I'll have a better chance at getting you to stay put."

Sarah shoved her way around him. "Something's wrong with Norma."

"Yeah, she's out cold. Probably not used to whiskey that hasn't been watered down."

"What do we do?"

Sam heaved the woman over one shoulder. "If you can hand me my saddlebags, I think I can carry her to the buggy. You'll have to get that bunch of clothes behind her chair. When she wakes up, she'll probably want her things."

Sarah did as he asked, then ran to get her carpetbag.

"Maybe if we walk out slow and easy no one will notice I've got an old barmaid on my shoulder."

Sarah giggled. "It's worth a try."

Unfortunately, they only made it halfway down the stairs before Norma woke up. She moaned and groaned about being carried out of a fine hotel like a sack of potatoes. Then, when Sam refused to stop and put her down, she started waving at everyone and yelling "hello" as if she were riding in the Fourth of July parade. To Sarah's surprise she seemed to be on a first-name basis with a few of the gentlemen in the lobby. Several more ducked their heads and hid behind hats as Norma passed.

Sam dumped her into the back of the buggy.

Sarah calmly handed him his hat and smiled. "I guess we won't be going back there again."

"Too bad," Sam whispered. "I had a real nice time there."

He lifted her into the buggy and took the reins. Neither of them seemed to hear Norma mumbling about being treated like freight.

Within minutes they pulled up to a mission just outside of Dallas. The aged adobe walls covered with ivy made the place seem like the most peaceful setting on earth. A solid wood door, six inches thick, waited for them at the end of a garden path that could have been a painting.

Sarah helped Norma down as Sam grabbed her bundle of clothes.

"I'm giving up drinking." Norma hiccupped. "It feels good going down, but it always wants to come back up."

Sam rapped on the door when the women finally caught up to him.

The whiskey must have reached Norma's tear ducts, for she began to cry and confess all her sins. By the time the heavy wood door creaked open, she'd made it through the first twenty or so years of her life, but Sarah guessed she was just getting started.

When Norma saw the robes of a nun before her, she knelt down and kissed the woman's hand.

Sarah watched as the slender nun cradled the woman beneath her arm and welcomed her with kind words as though Norma were coming home.

"Now, there will be no more drinking, dear," the Sister said. "But you and your children will be safe here for as long as you need to stay."

Norma cried softly as they moved through a small room and into a hallway. "I never started out to make such a mess of this life. I meant to be a good mother, I swear I did."

"You're a fine mother. All you need is a little help, and that's what we specialize in, a little help." The Sister spoke to Norma, but her dark eyes watched Sarah.

Sarah wondered if she looked as if she needed help and didn't know it, for the nun continued to stare at her.

"I'll show you to a room where you can rest," the nun told Norma. "Your Ellie is sleeping just down the hall, and last time I looked your boy was eating in the kitchen. We'll see that no harm comes to them while you rest."

Norma let the Sister lead her into a room almost devoid of furnishings. Without a word the old barmaid crawled into the small bed. The kind nun covered her and whispered, "I'll wake you if Ellie needs you."

Sarah looked up at Sam and smiled. He'd found the perfect place. She couldn't help but wonder how many other times he'd brought lost souls here. Sam wasn't quite the ruthless bounty hunter he claimed to be.

As they moved back into the hallway, Sarah noticed the nun still stared at her, but couldn't figure out why.

"Have you room for one more, Ruthie?" Sam broke the silence. "I'd like my wife to stay here for a few days while I take care of some business."

The Sister smiled at Sarah. "I'd love to have her stay. I'd like a few days to get to know the mother of my future nieces and nephews."

Before Sarah could ask what was going on, the Sister hugged her. Sarah had no intention of staying behind, but the Sister's welcome felt so sincere.

When Ruthie pulled away, Sam put his arm around the tall nun and said with pride. "Sarah, I'd like you to meet my baby sister."

Sarah couldn't believe it. A hundred questions came to mind. As she looked at them side by side, she saw the same dark eyes, the same strong chin. All at once they were all talking. Ruthie wanted to know everything about how they met. Sarah wanted to hear about how she became a nun and how she kept up with Sam. If he'd been ten when their father died, she must have been two, for Sam had said once that his mother died in childbirth two years before his father had been killed in the war.

They moved into a large kitchen and circled a table. Ruthie brought hot tea and pumpkin bread. While they ate, Sam's sister packed a five-pound cloth sack with basic supplies.

Sarah thought of how strange it was to think of Sam having family. She'd guessed that he was all alone like she was. But he wasn't like her. He had someone who cared about him and loved him. From the way they talked, their parents had loved each other.

Sarah had had none of that. He had a base to grow from and she didn't. She could say she loved him if she wanted to, but in truth she knew nothing of the feeling. She realized how wrong she'd been to believe there was a rule that could make someone love another.

Sam and Ruthie talked of their childhood, of growing up being passed around from family to family. They talked of having each other, of how when things got bad they would stand by each other.

When Sam enlisted to fight along the frontier, Ruthie moved into a mission, and there she found her home.

As they talked, Sam slipped money into the large pocket of Ruthie's apron.

"You don't have to, Sam," Ruthie whispered.

"For Norma and her children. It'll get them a fresh start."

"I'll see to it," Ruthie said.

Sarah was surprised by the exchange, but acted as if she hadn't noticed it. She thought Sam didn't even like Norma, yet he'd helped her and her children, and done so in a way the woman would never know about.

When Sam stood and mumbled something about needing to get on with the plan, Ruthie touched Sarah's hand. "It will be grand having you stay with me for a few days. I have my duties here, but we'll have lots of time for long talks. And don't worry about Sam. It's always hard for him to say good-bye, even when he knows he'll be back in a matter of days. You'll see him again before you know it."

Sarah looked around for Sam as Ruthie's words sank in. He'd been gone more than a few minutes.

She glanced over to where Ruthie had set the supply bag. It was gone. He was gone.

"I'd love to stay, but I can't." Sarah almost knocked the chair over in her haste. "I have to go with Sam." Dread drifted through her thoughts. What if she missed him? "Excuse me."

She was at a full run when she reached the garden door they'd entered an hour before. Her carpetbag sat just inside on a table. He'd left it for her. He'd left her.

Sarah grabbed her belongings and opened the door.

Sam had one foot in the buggy.

"What are you doing?" She grabbed his shirt. "You were going to leave without even saying good-bye."

"I told you I have something I have to do. I'll be back in a few days. There is no sense putting off what I have to do. You'll be safe here."

"You weren't going to say good-bye."

He turned around and faced her. "How could I look in your eyes and say good-bye to you, Sarah, without holding you? I don't think they allow that kind of thing in the mission. At least not in the way I want to hold you. I thought it was better if I just kind of slipped away."

Sarah tossed her bag into the buggy. "Well, you don't have to worry about being proper with your farewells, because I'm going with you."

"You are not."

She climbed into the buggy. "This is where I belong, next to you." She crossed her arms and leaned back, staring straight ahead. "You even made me promise to sleep next to you every night."

Sam figured it was a losing battle, but he tried logic. "It may be rough, Sarah. There may even be trouble."

She looked at him. "Then we have no time to waste. You'd better teach me to shoot before dark."

The mission door opened and Ruthie stepped out. She looked at first her brother and then Sarah already in the buggy.

Sarah tried to smile. "Thank you for the offer to stay, but I'm needed here with Sam. He can't go without me."

Ruthie nodded and winked at her big brother. "It's about time he needed someone. I'll see you both again."

Sam swung into the buggy. "One of these days, wife, I'm going to win an argument with you." Part of him wanted to pick Sarah up and toss her back where she'd be safe. He hated the idea that she might be in danger. But he couldn't call her a liar. He did need her.

TWENTY-THREE

VALUABLE TIME TICKED AWAY, AND THERE WAS NOTH-
ing Sam could do about it. Since he'd had word that Reed
and his men were camped near Fort Worth, he'd wanted
to finish the trouble between them once and for all.
Ranger Dalton rode out after they'd had coffee before
dawn. He was now three hours ahead of Sam. Jacob
planned to check things out, then backtrack to meet up
with Sam. But Sam couldn't even seem to get on the road.

First, Norma had to be taken to the mission, then his
sister always thought they had to talk. Now Sarah insisted
on going with him, and of course, shopping had to happen
before they could leave town. At this rate he'd be an old
man before he ever caught another outlaw. He was beginning to believe there was a reason why he'd never
known a bounty hunter to marry.

The only good thing about the direction they were riding was that once Sam settled things with Reed, they
would be near his place. Sam wanted to take Sarah home.

It was the one thing he had to offer her. A place she could call her own. He wasn't sure she believed he was telling the truth when he talked about it, but she'd see the farm soon enough.

Glancing in her direction, he did have to admit Sarah was quite a sight riding beside him. While he'd found her a horse and gathered supplies, she'd insisted on switching into a pair of trousers and a shirt she picked up at the saddle shop. Both were far too big and of poor quality, but she hadn't complained. Even the hat she bought looked like a hand-me-down. But the small leather moccasins he'd insisted she wear fit her feet like gloves. They laced to the knee so she would have extra protection against scrapes along the trail.

She'd told the truth when she said she could ride. He enjoyed watching her long gold braid bounce from side to side as they galloped out of town. In truth, he enjoyed watching every part of her swaying in the saddle. He might never use a buggy again.

"You handle a horse like a top hand, Mrs. Gatlin," he offered when they finally slowed to allow the horses to walk.

"I used to take care of Granny Vee's old nag. I'd ride whenever I had my chores done. I've always loved animals." She glanced at him. "That's probably what attracted me to you."

"You like this over a buggy?" He couldn't help but wonder if she had any idea of how much of an animal he was. She was so sure she could tame him, but Sam knew she had little chance.

"Oh, yes." She leaned forward and patted the gray mare's neck. "I can't believe you found such a fine horse to rent."

"I didn't rent the animal. I bought her. If you want, she's yours."

Sarah looked at him in surprise. "Mine? Just mine?"

"If you want. I know you can't fit her in that bag, but she's yours just the same. I've got plenty of room in the barn on our place, and there's a pasture with a creek that runs through it. I'd have to do some work on the fence, but it wouldn't take me more than a few days."

Sarah pulled her reins. Sam did the same.

"You mean she's mine to ride." Sarah pushed her hat back and looked at him.

"I mean she's yours to keep, Sarah. If I'd have known you liked to ride, I'd have gotten you a mount earlier."

"She's mine to keep, forever?"

Sam was starting to feel as if he were talking to an echo.

"Forever." He didn't know what more to say, but he had to talk to her. He had to let her know where she stood, with him, the horse, with everything. "If you ride away from me one day, at least I'll know you're on a good horse."

"Thank you for the horse." She patted the animal once more. "But I'm not leaving you, Sam. I don't know why you think I might. You're my husband."

He watched her, surprised she'd read him so clearly. The Ranger's words haunted his thoughts. How had he put it exactly? "If Sarah isn't already with child, Sheriff Riley might call the whole thing off." She might say she wasn't leaving, but Sam wondered how she would react if she knew it could be possible.

"To my way of thinking, when we married, we made a deal," Sam said. "I'd bail you out and take care of you. That means a home for you to stay and that you'd never go hungry. In exchange, you'd be my wife. Cook my meals when I'm home, keep house, and share my bed when you're ready."

"It is a fair bargain. More than I could have hoped for."

She didn't say anything else, but Sam saw it in her eyes. She wanted more. The problem was he had no idea what the more could be.

"We'd better stop here and let me teach you how to use a gun," he said, changing the subject. "If you're going to ride with me, you'd better know a few things."

They directed the horses into a wooded area half a mile from the road. Sam took his time showing her how his .45-caliber Colt worked. For Sam the weapon had been almost an extension of his hand for years. He found it hard to believe anyone would not know how to use a six-shooter.

At first he had been in a hurry to finish the lesson and ride on, but as they sat close, their heads together, looking at how to load the weapon, Sam decided he didn't care if it took days.

When she was ready to pull the trigger, Sam propped a branch up with rocks about thirty feet away and stood behind her. The weapon looked huge in her hands as she raised it and fired.

She jumped and almost dropped the gun.

Sam laughed. When she tried again, he was prepared. He made her stand on a rock so that she was almost as tall as him, then he braced her, circling his arms around her, talking low in her ear.

When she fired again, she rocked against him.

For almost an hour she aimed at the branch and fired. Each time he patiently went over his instructions once more, touching her gently as he talked, loving the way she leaned into him as she grew tired. Fascinated by how she took his slight caresses as though they were as natural as breathing. At sundown the branch still stood, but neither of them seemed to care.

They camped beneath the live oaks and feasted on food Ruthie had packed in an old flour sack. There were times when silence stretched between them, but neither seemed to mind. The air grew cold as the sounds of the night whispered around them.

Sam built up the fire, wondering if Jacob would see it from the road when he backtracked looking for them. They were on the same road, they'd catch up with each other eventually, and he hoped they'd do so before either of them found Reed. The outlaw was wanted in three states. He wouldn't hesitate to kill if he felt trapped.

Sam knew there were others besides Reed out there looking to put a bullet in him, but Reed irritated him more than most. Some men became outlaws out of anger, or looking for a fast way to make money during hard times. But Reed was just mean to the core. Everyone he touched suffered.

When Sam spread his bedroll by the fire, he wasn't surprised Sarah put hers a few inches away. The need to make love to her had long ago become an ache deep inside him, sweet and torturing at the same time. Wanting her made him know he was still alive, still a man. In the past few years he'd closed down until he sometimes thought of himself as no more human than the Colt he wore. Everyone, but Sarah, looked at him the same way, but to her, he was a man . . . her man.

He wanted to ask her again if she'd decided that now might be a good time to start a real marriage. Their days together could be running out. He thought of promising her it would be nothing like what she had before. But Sam had finally found one skill he wasn't sure of. What if she felt nothing when they made love? What if he were as poor a lover as she was a shot? He tried to comfort himself by thinking the few women he'd been with had not complained. But that logic offered little peace when he knew they were being paid by the hour.

He smiled. Sarah seemed to enjoy his touch at dawn, and he'd never forget the way she kissed him before they left the hotel room. Still the question nagged at him. Maybe the trick was making her want him. He tried to relax on the bedroll. It wouldn't be an easy job when all he could think about was wanting her. He wished he had the right words to say, but he had always thought of words as a waste of time between a man and a woman.

As she did every night, Sarah untied her long braid and combed her hair out. Then she unlaced her moccasins and set them beside his boots. She slipped beneath the covers only inches from him.

He waited, thinking he should have told her she was pretty before it got too dark to see. He thought about complimenting her on something, but all he could think of was her shooting. If he said anything good about that, she'd know he was a liar.

"Sam," she broke the silence. "You think you could kiss me good night, if it's not too much trouble?"

He rolled to his side and spread his hand out on her middle. Gently he touched her, fighting a desire to grab her and bury her beneath him. He concentrated on the rivets on her pants that were bumping against his fingers. The denim trousers Levi Strauss had made for men were rough to his touch, but Sam knew the softness that lay just beneath. She'd pulled the cinch straps tight in the back, but they were still too big in the waist for her.

Sam leaned close and smelled her hair. "Someday, when the time is right, how would you feel if you had a child inside of you? My child."

She didn't answer. The intake of her breath allowed him to easily tug her shirt free from the waistband. He slipped his cool fingers beneath her shirt.

He lost himself in the way her body moved as she breathed. "I wouldn't mind having another child," she finally whispered. "Someday."

He leaned and kissed her mouth so lightly, he heard her sigh.

"Do you mind, Sarah, if I touch you while I kiss you good night?" Her body was already telling him the answer he wanted to hear.

"You won't go beyond a touch, Sam? You swear?"

"I swear." He lowered his mouth to cover hers as his fingers tugged the first rivet free on her trousers.

For a while he kissed her as though he planned to do so all evening. Each time they both learned more about pleasing the other. He tasted the inside of her mouth and enjoyed the way she shuddered with pleasure. One at a time he freed the buttons of her shirt until it parted to her waist, but he didn't push the material to reveal her flesh.

His hand slid down to find hers and he brought her fingers to his shirt, letting her do the same to him as he'd done to her. She was nervous, fumbling with the buttons, but he didn't care. When she finished, she slid her hands over his chest.

"I like the feel of you without bandages covering you," she whispered.

"I like the feel of you with nothing but my hand covering you," he answered and felt her laughter against his throat.

Suddenly he sat up and pulled her with him. He crossed his legs and lifted her into his lap, her legs spread on either side of his waist. His hands gripped her thighs and shifted her until she was as close to him as their clothes would allow.

"Sam!" She tried to pull away.

"It's all right," he whispered. "I'm not going to hurt you or break my word."

Her head gave a nervous nod. She trusted him enough to continue into the unknown.

One hand held her tightly in place as the other cupped the back of her head and drew her mouth to his. He kissed her fully, holding nothing back, releasing her only long enough to shove the cotton of their shirts aside. Her soft breasts brushed his chest, taking his breath away with pleasure.

At first she jerked, not knowing what was happening to her senses, then suddenly she met his passion with her own. The knowledge shook Sam. He wrapped his arms around her and pulled her against him. Her arms circled his neck and held tightly as she trembled.

He gently kissed her throat, brushing away her hair as he moved down. She melted to his touch, leaning back until the firelight danced off her bare flesh. He wanted to see her, but the need to feel her heart against his with nothing in-between was too great. He pulled her back against him.

Her arms rested lightly on his shoulders as she let him move her as he pleased. Slowly she relaxed, trusting him as she drifted with the feelings, newborn and raw with need.

When he placed her back on the bedroll, she stretched and smiled as his hand moved from her throat to her trousers. Watching her, he unfastened another hold on the pants, then another.

Her hand covered his. "No, Sam," she whispered. "Leave them on."

"All right, love," he answered against her ear. "As long as I can touch you."

He moved down to boldly claim one of her breasts with his mouth, and she began to sway in a dance as old as time. Her hand rode atop his fingers as he slid beneath her waistband to the warmth below.

She cried out as he touched her lightly at first, then bolder.

He kissed her mouth tenderly. "Tell me to stop, Sarah. Push me away."

His hand touched the very soul of her.

"No," she answered, out of breath.

He kissed her then, deeply. Moving his tongue in gentle strokes as he moved his fingers.

She broke the kiss, needing to breathe, wanting to tell him how he made her feel, but all that would come were sighs of pleasure and sounds of pure joy.

His mouth crossed back to her breast, and unbelievably the passion doubled.

Suddenly lightning struck her very center, and she felt her body tighten.

Sam pulled her against his side and held her then as she drifted slowly back to earth. He didn't touch her, or even kiss her. He just held her, letting her body tremble against his, he took the shock of her passion the same way he took her reaction when she'd fired the gun.

When Sarah could finally talk, she realized he'd pulled her clothes back together and was very still beside her. One hand rested on her, the other circled into her hair.

"I never knew anything like that," she whispered. "Sam you'll never believe what happened to me."

He didn't answer and she realized she'd been so wrapped up in the feelings washing over her that she hadn't given a thought to him.

"Oh, Sam." She stretched and kissed his jaw. "Did you know that would happen?"

He pushed a strand of hair from her cheek. "I thought it might."

"Would you do that again sometime, please?"

She felt laughter rumble in his chest. "I'll think about it."

She placed her hand over his heart and rested her head on his shoulder. "Good night, Sam." His name was almost lost in her yawn.

"Good night, Sarah."

He listened to the soft sound of her sleeping as he stared up into the night. He'd made her happy. If he could do it with a touch, he could do it when they made love. Slowly he was getting to know her, getting to understand what she wanted and how she liked to be touched. The only problem was if he had to court his wife much longer he would go insane with need for her.

Sam didn't bother to close his eyes. Since he married, he'd given up sleep.

TWENTY-FOUR

Sᴀʀᴀʜ ᴀᴡᴏᴋᴇ ᴡɪᴛʜ ᴛʜᴇ ꜱᴜɴ ꜰʟɪᴄᴋᴇʀɪɴɢ ᴛʜʀᴏᴜɢʜ the trees. The fire was low, but still hot, and Sam's bedroll lay over her, keeping her snug in the cold morning air. She stretched and rubbed her eyes.

Sam was gone.

For a moment she wanted to cuddle down into the covers and remember how he'd kissed her, how he'd touched her, but the knowledge that he'd left her sometime in the night frightened her.

"Sam," she said, praying that he'd answer. "Sam!"

She pulled the blankets around her and sat up. "Sam!"

Something moved in the trees.

"Sam. Where are you?" She closed her eyes. "Sam!" she cried. "Don't leave me!"

The noise in the trees increased, and she opened her eyes to see Sam running toward her. He knelt down and pulled her, covers and all, into his arms. "Sarah! What is it?"

She buried her face against his chest and tried to calm her heart. "Oh, Sam. I thought you left me."

He gripped her shoulders and pushed her a few inches away. "When are you going to stop thinking every time I'm out of your sight that I'm abandoning you? I was just watering the horses."

She felt like a fool. She wouldn't blame him for leaving her; she was sure she was about as near to crazy as she could get. "I'm sorry."

He pulled her back into his arms and chuckled. "First, you don't like me, decide I'm no good, and now you don't want me out of your sight. You're one confusing female."

He brushed her tears away with his thumb and kissed her soundly on the mouth. "Your lips are puffy this morning. If I was a bettin' man, I'd say you were kissed long and well last night."

"I was." She smiled. "Remember when I asked you why folks kiss on the mouth?"

"Yes."

"Well, forget I ever asked. I know the answer."

Sam grinned. "Don't look at me that way, or we won't make any miles this day. We need to ride fast to make up for the time we lost yesterday. I want you to tell me when you get tired."

She nodded and reluctantly left his arms.

Half an hour later they were crossing the open country between Dallas and Fort Worth at breakneck speed. Sarah loved it. She couldn't explain it, but each day she was with Sam she felt stronger. Somehow, maybe because he never complained about her being fragile, she no longer saw herself as such.

At noon they stopped by a stream and finished off the rest of Ruthie's supply pack.

"That's it," Sam said, folding the flour sack and sticking it in his saddlebag.

"I'll shoot us a rabbit for supper," she promised.

He laughed. "We'll starve."

By late afternoon Sarah was too tired to talk. Sam found a quiet spot and made camp. The morning had been warm and sunny, but the day ended cloudy with the promise of rain. Though she looked tired, she helped him with the horses, enjoying taking care of her own mount.

When Sam unloaded the saddles and supplies beneath an overhang, Sarah sat down to rest for a few minutes before building a fire. She leaned her head against the saddle, and the next thing she knew, a crackling fire startled her awake.

Sarah sat up, realizing she must have been asleep for some time. Sam had covered her with a blanket. Stretching, she saw him standing on the other side of the campfire watching the night.

"How long have I been asleep?"

He turned. "Long enough for me to build the fire and catch supper."

"Rabbit?"

"No, I'm saving them for you to shoot. I caught a few fish and opened a can of beans. Your plate is there close to the fire, if you're hungry, but I'm afraid I'm not much of a cook."

"Thanks." Sarah felt guilty for not doing her share, but the food tasted delicious anyway. "You're a great cook," she said between bites.

"When we get to my place, I'm kind of hoping you'll take over the job. Except for the few things Ruthie bakes or makes me, everything I've worn or tasted in years has been store-bought. Can you make pie?"

"Yes." She laughed. "I promise."

"I'm looking forward to that."

She paused. "Sam, do you truly have a place, or is it just a dream?"

"It's a place. I bought it for almost nothing a few years after the war, but every time I had a little money extra, I'd fix it up."

"Tell me about it."

He walked around the fire and sat on his saddle. "The house is not too big, but it's got a nice kitchen and a loft that would sleep several kids. It's got a new barn and a corral. The well is good, too, and I can walk to the fishing hole. There's a little town nearby. It's not much right now, but folks around are talking about getting a school started."

Sam watched her closely. In all their days together neither of them had spent much time bringing up the future. "I thought I could set you up there. You'd be safe, no one around there knows me. The times I've done work there, I've always told anyone who stopped by that I was just a hired hand. I thought about making sure you were well stocked for the winter this year, and next spring you can plant a good garden."

Sarah watched him. "If I'm there, where would you be?"

"I'd still do my job, but I'd have a place to come to when I'm tired and need rest. You'd have your house, and I'd have a safe place to hide out."

"You wouldn't live with me?"

"I thought that was what you wanted, Sarah, a home to call your own. You'd never have to worry about money, I have an account that will stand in the black for years."

Sarah stared at this strange man. He was offering her everything she'd ever thought she'd wanted. A home. A place to belong. Why did it feel so empty?

"Why are you doing this, Sam?"

He rubbed his hands together. "When I saw you back in Cedar Point being raffled off, I thought maybe there was a woman who would consider being married to me. I'm not the best catch in Texas. Maybe she'd give me a place where I could have some peace. It seems like a fair bargain; I'd take care of you."

"But you'd leave."

"Not for always. I'd come back now and then, maybe for a night or two. Maybe longer if you needed me."

Sarah sat her plate down and curled into the blanket. "We'd be like your friend Frank and his wife, Molly. We'd be married, but not married."

Sam frowned. She made his plan sound like some half-baked idea. He'd given it a lot of thought. He made his living as a bounty hunter. He couldn't just settle down and farm or ranch. He thought she would think living in a nice house would be far better than being in jail, but she looked at him as if he were offering her second prize.

He waited another hour before he joined her. The night air was so thick it stuck to his face. He finally lay down beside her and tried to offer his arm as a pillow, but she'd fallen asleep rolled into a ball beside her saddle. She hadn't even asked him to kiss her good night.

The next morning she was up and had coffee on by the time he stretched, working the soreness of sleeping on the ground out of his muscles. He tried a few times to talk, but for once she didn't have much to say. She didn't seem mad at him. When Sarah was angry, he could usually tell as soon as he got within shouting distance. Maybe she was just tired, he decided. The road was no place for her.

They pulled on dusters he'd added at the last minute to their supplies and moved out into the rainy morning. With her big hat and duster collar pulled high, he could barely see her face. As the road turned to mud, she seemed content to follow and made no effort to ride at his side.

By mid-afternoon his mood was as bad as the weather. He pushed hard, knowing of an old stagecoach station that took in travelers for the night. He hadn't used it in years, preferring to be alone even if the weather was poor. Sleeping in the rain always looked better than listening to others snore. The old station manager used to rent the rooms four to a bed. If you got in early, you went to sleep thinking you were the only one in the room, and by morning three others were sleeping next to you.

Sam had no idea what the arrangements were for women to stay. He guessed they also shared a room. Maybe if it wasn't too crowded, Sam could talk the man into letting him sleep with his wife.

She nodded when he pointed to the outline of the station and followed him in.

As they neared, something didn't feel right to Sam. The drizzle hampered his view, but he saw no activity. By the time they were to the far end of the corral, Sam realized the place was deserted. He pulled his mount back to Sarah. "At least we'll be out of the rain."

She agreed and he rode in first.

After looking around at the shell of a station, they decided the barn would be both cleaner and provide better shelter. Though the station house roof had burned, then caved in, the barn was in fair order. Hay had been stored in the back, probably by some farmer in the area.

While Sam took care of the horses, Sarah built a fire on the dirt floor where the roof was highest. It offered both warmth and light. She rummaged through the supplies, but found only beans, jerky, and peaches.

"Is this all you ever eat on the road?" she asked, holding up the cans.

"Pretty much." Sam saw little point to the question, but at least they were talking.

"Let me guess, when I make your favorite pie, it will be peach."

Sam smiled. "Apple. And while I think about it, promise never to serve me beans or jerky."

They ate close to the fire, then Sam stood guard for a while, watching the rain. Out of the corner of his eye he watched her pull hay from the back and build a bed near the fire. The old barn was just drafty enough to allow the smoke from the fire to drift up, yet the heat warmed the corner.

It had been two days since he'd touched her, and the need to hold Sarah built in him. He watched as she undressed in the shadows and slowly washed from a bucket of rainwater. She couldn't be dirty; they were both soaked to the bone despite their dusters. After pulling a nightgown from her bag, she slipped it on, then hung her wet clothes to dry.

When she slipped beneath her blanket, Sam decided he could wait no longer. He crossed to her. He pulled off his duster and Colts and put them within easy reach.

"Sarah," he said, leaning down on one knee to touch her shoulder.

She looked up at him. "Good night, Sam." She closed her eyes once more.

"No, wait a minute. I'm not ready to say good night." He wiggled her shoulder again, wishing she'd ask him to kiss her and touch her. When she didn't, he added, "I need to talk to you about something."

Sarah propped her head on her arm. "All right, Sam. What is it you want to talk about?"

He had to start somewhere. "Do you like the way I kiss you?"

She smiled. "You know I do, Sam. But I understand that married people can't go around kissing all the time, so I try not to ask too often."

"You don't have to ask me to kiss you, Sarah. Just nuzzle up to me and I'll get the hint." He thought of mentioning how her gray mare had been acting around his horse, but he didn't know if she would appreciate being compared to a horse. Besides, that wasn't the direction he wanted this conversation to go.

Sarah's arm folded into a pillow. "I'll remember." She snuggled back down in her covers.

He poked her shoulder again. "I wasn't finished."

With effort she propped her head up once more. "I'm sorry. I guess I was just thinking of sleep. It seemed like we rode for two days in the rain before stopping."

Sam reconsidered his planned conversation. She was tired. But he didn't know how many days they would have left together. "Do you like the way I touch you?"

"Yes, Sam," she answered, looking more awake. "I never dreamed a man would ever touch me and make me feel the way you do."

"And do you find me tolerable to be around? Tolerable to look at?"

"Yes, Sam." She raised one eyebrow, suddenly interested in the conversation. "I find you more than tolerable."

He smiled. "Well, I've been thinking that it's about time for you to change your mind about our marriage being in name only. After all, we both know it's a forever marriage, so you're just putting off the inevitable." He tried to read her face, but there were too many shadows. "You even said you wouldn't mind having my child, and I don't see how that's going to happen unless we get a little friendlier."

"I'll think about it." Sarah sat up and pulled her knees

to her chin. "You said you'd wait until I was ready."

"I did." Sam nodded. "But I'm thinking you're about ready."

"No, Sam." She lifted her chin. "I'm the one who says it's the right time."

"Well, I'm saying tonight is the right time." His words came out harsher than he'd meant them to be. He'd thought if he brought the subject up, she'd go along. But she didn't seem to want to talk about it, much less do anything. "Tonight seems like a good time to me."

She stood, suddenly the ball of fire he'd seen before. "Sam Gatlin, you are not going to tell me when the right time is."

"Well, maybe I should!" He climbed off the bedroll and paced a few steps before returning to meet her stare. "I'm your husband and I think I know."

"You're not forcing me into anything!"

"Hell, woman, it's been you forcing me into stuff since the night we married. I've given in until I'm about up to here with giving in." This wasn't at all the way he planned it. He pointed toward the bedrolls. "Like I said the first night, get in that bed and get ready. It's about time I won an argument in this marriage."

She placed her fists on her hips, preparing for a fight. For a long time the only sound in the barn was the rain on the roof.

"No," she said in little more than a whisper.

"You know what to expect, so this discussion is pointless. I say it's time we started acting like we were married."

He'd read once in a book that women like their men to be forceful, strong, but Sarah never read the same book. She glared at him as if he hadn't already been the most patient man on this earth. He wasn't asking her to do something she wouldn't enjoy. He'd see to that. But after this night there would be no question of Sheriff Riley calling the whole thing off between them. After this night she'd be his wife in more than name.

She moved away from the bedrolls. "You're not taking me by force."

"Of course not!" Sam resented her even thinking such a thing. "And I don't want you lying there all froze up. What I'm doing is changing your mind. I'm not going to bed you, Sarah; I'm going to make love to you the way a man makes love to his wife."

"You're breaking your word to me."

"I am not. I'm just helping you decide to make up your mind. Now, get in bed."

In an instant, faster than any gunfighter he'd ever seen, Sarah pulled one of his Colts from the holster hanging by his coat and fired.

TWENTY-FIVE

"SARAH!" SAM YELLED AS THE FIRST BULLET HIT THE
dirt to his left. "Put down that gun!"

The second shot was a foot to his right.

"Stop ordering me around!" She lifted the Colt with
both hands. "I'm not the same frightened girl you married.
I'm not going to be bullied into anything, not even by a
man I love."

The third shot rattled somewhere against the barn wall
behind Sam, but he swore it brushed his ear on the journey.

"Well, if you love me so much, why are you trying to
kill me?" He took a step toward her.

She waved the barrel of the gun. "I can love the mem
ory of you just as easily."

A low thundering sound rattled through the barn, shaking the flimsy walls.

The storm had suddenly decided to come inside.

Sam glanced at the door as a horse broke through the

curtain of rain and stomped across the wide barn floor.

The rider jerked on the reins, and the horse danced in a circle, spraying water in every direction. Before the horse had settled down, a rider in black jumped from the saddle and pulled his guns.

"Jacob?" Sarah said in a frightened whisper.

"I'm here, Sarah!" he yelled. "He's not going to hurt you. I could hear you yelling even through the rain."

"Dalton!" Sam raised his hands slowly. "Stay out of this."

Jacob spit the words as he moved closer. "I told you once, Sam, I wouldn't stand for you hurting her, even if she is your wife."

"Dalton, I always knew you had mud for brains!" Sam shouted. "I'm not hurting her. She's shooting at *me*!"

The young Ranger looked confused as he glanced from Sarah to Sam. When he stared at Sam, his voice lowered only slightly. "What did you do to make her so mad?"

Suddenly it was all Sam's fault. His wife planned to shoot him in cold blood, and it was all his doing.

"What makes you think I did anything?" Sam turned his anger to Jacob. "Besides, it's none of your damn business."

"So you're just going to stand there and let her kill you?" Jacob holstered his weapon and folded his arms. "And you have the nerve to say *I* have mud for brains."

"She's not going to kill me. I'm in no danger. I'm standing right in front of her."

Jacob shook his head and turned to Sarah. "Now, Sarah, you can't go killing him, no matter how worthless a husband he is."

Sarah's Colt shifted to Jacob, and unlike Sam, he had trouble standing his ground. "Be careful about the way you talk about my husband, Ranger. I may have to shoot him, but that doesn't mean I don't love him."

Sam laughed. The Ranger looked nervous. He was starting to get a grip on the problem he'd stepped into.

"Now, Sarah, love . . ." Sam tried again.

"Don't you 'Sarah, love' me, Sam Gatlin. Are you standing by your word or not?"

"Of course I'm standing by it. I never said I wasn't."

"Drop the gun, Sarah. Put it down slow," the Ranger encouraged, but no one was listening.

"And you can stop bossing me around. I swear, Sam, you act like you've never been around a woman long enough to have a conversation."

"That's probably right," Jacob said calmly, taking a step toward Sarah. "Go ahead and shoot him, Sarah. I'm sure whatever he did, he deserves to die."

"Shut up, Dalton!" Sam snapped. "What kind of help is that?"

"Well, I don't know," Jacob defended himself. "I never run across a bounty hunter and a confessed murderer's nest before. For all I know you two do this every night as some kind of mating call. Half the people in this state seemed to be trying to kill you, and you're shooting at each other."

He took another step toward Sarah.

"Stay back, Jacob," Sarah ordered. "I don't want to have to bury you, too."

"She's not going to kill you," Sam said. "She can't hit the broad side of this barn. She's already fired three shots and I'm still standing."

Sarah turned her attention back to Sam, ignoring Jacob as he took another step. "Stop running me down, Sam." She raised the Colt and fired. A rope hanging a few feet above his head danced with the shot.

Before Sam could react, she squeezed off two more shots, keeping the rope dancing.

Both men froze as they watched the rope settle back into place.

"If I'd wanted you dead, I would only have needed one bullet." Sarah slipped the Colt back in its holster.

"But the other day in the woods?" Sam moved toward her. "Why'd you act like you couldn't shoot?"

"I liked the lesson." She grinned as he lifted her off her feet and kissed her.

"I liked it better when she was shooting at you." Jacob pulled off his hat. "It makes more sense than the lady liking you."

Sam broke the kiss, but didn't loosen his hold on Sarah. "Next time my wife and I have an argument, do me a favor and stay out of it."

"No problem. How about you send me a telegraph, and I'll make sure I'm not even in the same county."

Sarah pushed on Sam's chest, and he reluctantly set her down. "Thanks for coming to my aid, Jacob. It was very kind of you, but if I hadn't learned to shoot as a child, the old woman I lived with and I would have starved."

"You're not going to hug the man again, are you, Sarah?" Sam asked. "Because if you are, I swear, I'll have to hit him a few times."

She offered her hand to Jacob. "Thank you," she said. "Have you had supper? I could make some coffee to warm you up."

"We'll need it." Jacob's stare met Sam's. "I've got news."

For the next hour Jacob told them of the trouble Reed and his gang had been causing in Fort Worth. It seemed a sheriff tried to kick Reed out of town, and the outlaw planned to stir up as much trouble as possible. Three men were dead already in gunfights, and the sheriff claimed a woman who was cut up in one of the bars identified Reed.

"I've circled around, waiting for you." Jacob finished off his coffee. "We've got to catch Reed when he's not expecting anything, or more folks will die."

Sam agreed.

Jacob nodded toward Sarah, who had curled beneath a blanket and fallen asleep several minutes before. "I thought you were going to leave her somewhere safe."

"I tried. I can't win an argument with that woman. I swear, she doesn't look it, but she's tougher than either of us." Sam smiled. "And probably a better shot."

"We'll keep her between us, if trouble comes," Jacob said. "She'll be safe there."

Sam agreed. "You're welcome to share our fire."

"No, thanks. I'll bunk in the loft. It's probably safer up there in case she wakes and the two of you decide to continue the discussion I walked in on."

TWENTY-SIX

SARAH DRIFTED IN AND OUT OF SLEEP AS SAM PULLED off his boots and slipped in next to her. As he always did, he tucked the covers over her before leaning back.

"Sam?" she whispered, rolling over.

"Yes," he answered.

"Will you hold me, tonight, or are you too mad at me?"

He circled his arm around her and pulled her against his chest. "I'm still mad, but I'll hold you." His warmth moved in around her as he added, "You're driving me crazy, you know."

"I know. I feel bad about that, I truly do." She could hear Jacob stomping around above them. She snuggled closer to Sam. She was glad the Ranger was up there, but she needed to be with Sam.

"Why didn't you tell the Ranger the reason you were shooting at me?" Sam whispered against her ear.

She crawled atop him and put her mouth close to his

ear to answer. "I couldn't. Then he'd know that I was breaking one of the rules."

Sam held her head in his hand. "Sarah, there are no rules between a man and a woman. Even if there were, I wouldn't know them." He rubbed his cheek against hers. "All I know is I want you. I want you so bad it may take a lifetime to get my fill. No rules matter except the ones we make."

He kissed her then, soft and sweet, like their first kiss should have been. Both of them had learned a great deal of the art. She marveled at how this one man could make her melt inside. She drank in sweet fire that only burned when it reached her belly, then the heat spread all the way to her toes.

While the kiss continued, he moved his hand down her back and gripped her hip.

"Sam, we can't do this. Jacob might hear."

Sam rolled her to her back and whispered, "I won't make a sound, but if you've no objection, I plan to touch my wife tonight. You've been asking to be held all day."

"No, I haven't." She buried a giggle against his chest.

"Yes, you have. In the way you move. In the way you look at me. Even when you were shooting at me, you were begging me to hold you tight."

She relaxed as his hands crossed over her gown. He didn't unbutton the tiny buttons that ran to her waist or try to pull up the hem, he just explored her body with the thin layer of cotton between them.

"When you come to me as a wife, Sarah, come to me without anything covering you, not even this thin gown. Come to me in the light so I can see you and touch you without having to take anything off of you. Promise me."

His hand closed around her breast as his words drifted across her cheek.

"I promise," she whispered.

His hand continued to roam, warming her beneath the material. He kissed her until all thought left her mind and she drifted with him in pleasure. He broke the kiss finally and moved his mouth once more against her ear. His breath was ragged as he whispered, "The next time you say you love me, it better not be because of some rule. Love me, or hate me, but do what you feel and nothing more. I have to know how you feel inside and not just what you think you are supposed to say."

"All right, Sam," she answered.

He turned her so that her backside fit against him and added, "We'd better get some sleep. If Jacob is right, we should hit trouble by mid-morning. No matter what happens, stay close to me and do what I tell you. Both our lives could depend on it."

"I'll remember." She moved closer. "Good night."

"Mind if I touch you while we sleep?" His hand already held her breast. "I seem to be developing a habit. I know no peace without the feel of you next to me."

"No," she answered. "I don't mind."

She listened as his breathing grew steady, but his hand still held her firmly in his grasp. He wasn't the only one developing a habit. She felt complete next to him.

Hours later, when the fire had burned low and the storm had settled to a shower, she awoke to his touch. He'd unbuttoned her gown enough to move his hand inside and was gently crossing his thumb back and forth across her nipple. The pleasure rocked her as if she were still dreaming.

When she sighed, he looked up, his dark eyes fiery with

passion. Neither said a word; they'd both said all there was to be said.

He closed her gown and rolled to his back. For a long time they just lay side by side, not touching, but listening to the other breathe. She wanted to tell him how easily she responded to him. How much she wanted him. How she'd been wrong to make him promise. He wanted her, she wanted him, they were married.

Most of all, she wanted to tell him what it meant to her that he waited. She was putting him through hell. But he waited. Maybe she was putting them both through hell, and she couldn't find the words to let him know that by this one act, he honored her. By waiting, he gave her the respect she'd longed for all her life. She was no longer someone to be passed from place to place, someone without value. Sam had made her feel cherished. He'd made her feel worth waiting for.

"Sam," she whispered, knowing he wasn't asleep.

"Try to get some sleep, Sarah. It's almost dawn, and this promises to be one hell of a day. I didn't mean to wake you. I just wanted to touch you one more time."

"Sam, I want to say one thing before we start this day."

"All right."

She found his hand resting between them and held it tightly as she whispered, "I love you."

He gripped her hand in his for a moment, then stood and moved to the barn opening.

She followed.

He wrapped his arms around her and held her as they watched the sun come up. He leaned his head so that he could breathe in the smell of her hair and added, "I love you, too."

TWENTY-SEVEN

SARAH KNELT BEHIND A PILE OF ROCKS AND WATCHED Sam and Jacob moving closer to Reed's camp. It had taken them until almost sundown to find the outlaws, but now that they were here, all the exhaustion of the ride vanished as fear ran through her veins.

The feeling that finally Sam would be rid of this man who had haunted them settled over her. If Zeb Whitaker truly made it to jail and they killed or captured Reed tonight, she and Sam might both know a little peace.

She lifted the rifle Sam had insisted she keep and stared down the barrel. Two men sat by the fire; one other stood several feet away, staring toward the west. The night was still after the storm the day before, and their voices drifted to her. She couldn't make out words, but she knew they were arguing.

Sam told her he didn't think Reed was among them. He'd said the man was thin to the point of bone and liked to wear a black leather coat with fringe on the sleeves.

Though they'd been told Reed and his men were camped along this bend in the Trinity River, the informers could be wrong. Sam and Jacob had to make sure before they rode into a camp firing.

No man in the camp fit the description of Reed. Sarah leaned back and tried to relax. Jacob planned to ride into the camp and ask a few questions with Sam hanging behind on guard. She'd noticed the Ranger slipped his badge into his pocket before they'd left her at the rocks. Even if the men by the river were Reed's men, there was no point in having a shoot-out with them and take the chance of scaring Reed further into hiding.

She heard her horse make a sound and glanced up to see if anyone in the camp had heard it, too. She doubted it, but Sam told her to stay down and out of sight. He also told her if shooting started, to aim and fire at anything that didn't look like him or the Ranger.

She studied the men at the camp, trying to guess if she were close enough to hit any one of them. Sam's attempt to keep her safe might not be the best thing if she could be of no help when he ran into trouble.

Something rattled in the brush behind her, and Sarah realized she was no safer here than she would be closer to the action.

Lifting her rifle, she silently moved through the shadows along the tree line, cutting the distance between her hideout and the camp in half. Her moccasins didn't make a sound as she ran. Within minutes she reached a place so thick with branches the trees seemed to be growing on top of one another. Just for safety, she pushed her shoulders against a twisted tree trunk. No one would see her here, but she had a clear view of the camp, or a clear shot if need be.

Again she heard something moving behind her. This

time the shuffling sounded more like boots trying to walk softly over the ground littered with leaves. Her first thought was that it might be Sam, returning to check on her. But then she realized he'd been in front of her only minutes before. He wouldn't have had time to circle behind her. Also, he thought she was out of harm's way, so he would be more likely to stay with Jacob, who would be facing down three-to-one odds if Sam didn't back him up.

She pressed farther into the tree as a black shadow passed between her and the edge of the tree line. He was almost close enough to touch. A thin man. She could hear the soft swish of his leather coat and see the fringe dance between her and the camp's fire.

Holding her breath, she realized she was almost close enough to smell Reed. He didn't seem to be in any hurry. It was almost as if he strolled in the darkness, waiting for something.

She heard the click of his knife as he tapped the blade. For a moment she thought he might have seen her running and was playing with her now, knowing she hid somewhere near. But as he continued to wait, she realized all his attention was focused on the camp.

Reed was doing the same thing she was doing. He was waiting in the safety of the trees until trouble started.

Without letting Reed out of her sight, she watched Jacob ride toward the camp, his head low, his body loose as though he were almost asleep in the saddle.

"Hello the camp!" he finally yelled. "All right to ride in?"

The two men who'd been arguing by the fire stood. "Come on in, slow and easy, mister," one answered as all three men in camp readied their guns.

Jacob moved closer. "I saw your fire and thought you

might be the couple I'm looking for. A man and his wife on their way to Fort Worth."

The two men by the fire seemed to relax, but the third man on the edge of the light stood ready.

"We're just a few wranglers heading back home," the man who'd spoken before said.

Sarah knew little about wranglers, but these men were not dressed like men who herded cattle. They wore no chaps, and the wool of their trousers would never take the rough work around cattle.

If Jacob noticed he didn't comment as he climbed from his horse. It was considered good manners to offer any stranger who came in unarmed a cup of coffee, if not supper.

Not one of the three men offered.

Jacob checked his saddle. "Well, I'll be moving on."

All three men waited for him to leave. They weren't looking for trouble, but they weren't inviting any in. Silence stretched.

Finally the only man who'd spoken said, "I think I saw a couple camped a few miles back. You might want to check before you stop, stranger."

Jacob nodded and lifted his rifle from the saddle. "Raise those hands nice and easy, boys. I'm a Texas Ranger and I think it's about time you came with me."

The two men did as he asked, but the third went for his gun. A gun fired from the shadows and the lookout fell. Jacob kept his rifle steady on the two remaining outlaws.

Sarah searched the area where the shot must have come from, but she couldn't see Sam. When she looked back, the thin shadow of Reed had also vanished.

"I didn't come alone." Jacob motioned with his rifle for the two by the fire to keep their hands high.

Sarah heard movement in the trees several yards away. Suddenly Sam stepped out, his hands in the air. A moment later the thin man moved behind him, a gun shoved against Sam's back. "Drop that gun, Ranger, or your friend will not take another step."

Jacob swore and lowered his rifle.

In horror Sarah watched as Sam was herded into camp.

"We've been waiting all day for you two boys to show up." Reed laughed. "I knew if I stopped looking for you, you'd find me. And this spot had too many hiding places near to pass up."

"Come on in, boys!" he yelled.

Men, well armed, materialized from around the camp. If she would have tried to get another ten feet closer to the fire, she would have almost stepped over one. She counted six.

The two men who'd been arguing at the camp earlier quickly grabbed Jacob's weapons and tied his hands behind his back.

"You'll never get away with this." He shoved at the men who tried to hold him.

"Oh, but I will," Reed answered. "All we have to do is toss your body in the river. You'll float for miles, and no one will even be able to guess where you were shot. Since there's no scene of the crime, lawmen will all think some-one else will handle the details."

"That's not the way the Texas Rangers work. Someone will come after you."

"Me!" Reed yelled. "By the time they find your body, I'll have witnesses that put me nowhere near this river."

"You can't murder us and get away with it." A bit of nervousness flickered in Jacob's voice, but Sarah noticed Sam hadn't said a word.

She lifted her rifle. If any man tried to open fire, she'd

down one, maybe two, before they could hit Sam and Jacob.

"You, I *can* kill." Reed laughed. "One Ranger in the state, more or less, won't matter, but the great Sam Gatlin is another story. My name will be whispered with respect in every saloon in the state when folks know I downed the legend."

Sarah couldn't believe Sam wasn't making a sound. In fact, he seemed to be just listening, as if he had only passing interest in the conversation.

"Shot him in the back, you mean," Jacob hissed.

Reed eased Sam's guns from their holster. "I'm not going to shoot him in the back, I'm going to face him and kill him while he's armed." He motioned for two of his men to move closer. When they each held one of Sam's arms, Reed ordered, "String him between those two trees, boys. Pull his arms out tight."

The moment Reed pulled the gun from Sam's back, Sam shot into action. He grabbed the man on his left and sent him flying into the fire. The man on his right put up a fight, but he was no match for Sam. Within a few blows he lay flat out on the ground, moaning in pain.

Reed fired one shot between Sam's legs. Sam froze. Reed pointed his gun at the Ranger. "Go along nicely, Sam, or I'll kill your friend before you can make it two steps toward me."

Sam hesitated as if debating.

"Do what you must, Sam!" Jacob shouted. "I'm dead anyway. Take any chance you have."

One of the men holding Jacob slammed the butt of his gun against the Ranger's mouth.

Jacob jerked so violently the man stumbled and fell. He jumped up, embarrassed that a tied-up Ranger could get the better of him. Swearing, he hit Jacob again, hard enough this time to drop the Ranger to his knee.

Reed smiled, obviously enjoying watching the Ranger bleed. "Tell you what, Gatlin, I'll let the Ranger go after my men rough him up a bit, if you'll face me in a fair fight."

Sam stared at him. "A fair fight?"

"As fair as I'm ever going to offer you. I want to start with your hands away from your guns. You let my men tie one hand to each of those trees. When I yell, my man will cut the rope on your left hand. We draw."

"You know I'm right-handed," Sam commented.

"I know, that's why I'm giving you a gun in your right holster. You beat me, left hand having to pull your right gun, and I figure I'm too slow to live anyway. I'll leave orders for none of my men to interfere and to leave the Ranger breathing. Fair enough?"

"Fair enough." Sam stepped between the trees and lifted his arms shoulder high. Hesitantly outlaws stepped forward to tie his hands, pulling him between the two trees.

Sarah fought back tears as she stared at the man she loved and tried to decide how to help.

One of the men Sam had fought and burned in the campfire hurried forward once the bounty hunter was tied. He slammed his fist into Sam's face several times.

"That's enough, Roy," Reed ordered. "I want to get on with the gunfight."

Roy doubled back and slammed his fist into Sam's face one more time before backing away.

Sarah lifted the rifle, trying to decide which man to shoot first. She knew she only had one shot, maybe two before the outlaws filled both Sam and Jacob full of lead. Both men were bleeding, Jacob from the mouth and Sam from cuts over his left eye and along his cheek.

"Is there anything you want to say before I order the rope cut?" Reed shouted. "The second it falls we both have the same time to pull our guns. You'll just be reaching a little farther than me. And when I've killed you, I'll be the legend and you'll just be one dead bounty hunter."

Sam stared at Reed. "I've got a guardian angel you haven't counted on. She can make a rope dance with one bullet."

Reed laughed, commenting to his men that the legend must have already been hit one too many times in the head. He ordered them all to stand back as Roy held the knife above the rope that bound Sam's left hand.

Sarah raised her rifle. Reed moved his fingers an inch above his weapon and prepared to draw.

"Now!" he shouted.

Roy slit the rope the exact second Sarah fired into the rope that bound Sam's right hand. With lightning quickness Sam drew, downing Reed even before the outlaw's gun was clear of its holster.

He whirled around to the other men. "Touch your weapons, boys, and you're dead."

All of their bravery drained out of them as blood spread across Reed's chest.

Sam shoved Roy toward the others, pulling guns and tossing them away as he moved. "Untie the Ranger," he ordered.

Sarah stood prepared to fire if any man moved.

Jacob rubbed his wrist, then collected his guns. "Thanks." he glanced at Sam. "I owe you one." He moved to tie the remaining members of the gang while Sam stood guard.

Sam looked over his shoulder and saw Sarah step out of the shadows. "I thought I told you to stay put where you'd be safe." His voice was a growl, but a smile lifted the corner of his mouth.

"But, Sam—" Jacob yelled.

"Stay out of it, Ranger!" they both yelled back.

"If I'd have listened, you'd be dead right now," she whispered when she neared.

"If you'd listen, you'd be pregnant right now," he answered.

TWENTY-EIGHT

THE DEPUTIES FROM FORT WORTH JACOB HAD SWORN would meet them at Reed's camp showed up about the time all the outlaws were tied. They agreed to take the men into Fort Worth while Sarah pestered both Jacob and Sam until they allowed her to treat their wounds.

"For such strong, big men, you both sure whine when it's time to patch you up," she complained until they both let her work.

Sam didn't miss the way the Ranger looked at Sarah while she leaned close to him and cleaned the cuts on his face. He couldn't blame the man for staring at her, hell, he'd been around her for two weeks, and her beauty still crept up on him and took his breath away sometimes.

When Sarah went down to the river to wash up, Jacob looked at him. "You don't deserve her, you know."

"We've had this conversation before."

"I know, but I might just tell you every time I see you so you don't forget." Jacob flinched as he tried to smile.

His lip had finally stopped bleeding, but it was swollen almost double in size.

"I'm not likely to forget." Sam kept Sarah in his sight even as he talked. "When I married her, it was more to get her out of that jail than anything else, but now . . ."

"You don't know how you'd live without her," Jacob finished the sentence.

"Something like that," Sam answered. "But I can't stay. Even if I tried to settle down with her, there would always be some Reed looking for me. I got a place not too far from here that I can set her up in. She'll have all she needs, and I'll check in on her from time to time."

"She'll hate it," Jacob offered.

"Why would she hate it? She hasn't seen it yet. In fact, she doesn't believe it's real. She thinks it's like a fairy tale I tell her about now and then."

"She'll hate it if you're not there."

Sam frowned. "So you think I should let her go and she'll find some nice 'stay around' farmer to marry next. I don't know if I could do that."

"It's too late anyway." Jacob stood and stretched. "She's already made up her mind that you're her man. Hell if I know why. You're not even nice to her half the time, and the way you snap at her, she should have shot you and not the rope."

"Thanks a lot. If she'd have missed that rope we'd both be dead."

"I know," the Ranger mumbled. "All I could think about when I was tied up was that you'd better survive for Sarah's sake."

"What are you hinting at?" Sam studied the younger man closely. "You think I should get out of the business?"

"You can't," Jacob answered. "Legends may die, but they don't just walk away. Folks don't let them."

Sarah returned and the conversation died. Sam leaned back against his bedroll and tried to find an answer, but there wasn't any. They were all too tired to eat. Jacob bedded down across the fire from Sam and Sarah. He turned his back to the fire and was snoring within minutes.

Sarah giggled softly at Sam's side. "The Ranger may have trouble finding a wife if she knows he snores."

Sam pulled her covers over her shoulder. "Men like him are better off staying single."

She rolled to face him. "Men like him? You're a man like him."

"That's right," Sam answered.

She was quiet for a while, then whispered, "Sam, are you sorry you married me?"

He pulled her close. "No. How about you?"

"No, Sam. I'm lucky to have found you."

Sam thought about what the Ranger had said about how he yelled at Sarah and acted mean to her half the time. Looking back he could remember more words said in anger than he'd like to think about. But his yelling didn't seem to affect her much; she did whatever she wanted to.

"You know, Sarah, Sheriff Riley might let you out of the fine and then there wouldn't be any reason you had to be married to me."

She placed her hands on his sore, bruised faced. "I *am* married to you Sam. Now go to sleep. Tomorrow we will finally be at our house."

Our house, Sam thought. He'd begun to think of it as hers. It was all he had to offer her, a safe place, a place all her own. Maybe Jacob was wrong, maybe she would love the house and not mind so much that he wasn't around.

But dawn arrived with him dreading the day. He'd set

her up in the place and ride away. Because if he didn't she would never be safe.

Jacob said farewell to them where the road divided. He planned to ride into Denton and catch the train north. He promised to telegram Sam as soon as he knew Zeb Whitaker was safely locked away. Sam let Sarah believe she had nothing to worry about, but both men knew a rumor told in a bar was not to be believed completely.

When they left Jacob, Sam gave his horse full rein, suddenly in a hurry to show Sarah his place. She caught up to him, and they raced northwest toward open country.

As they climbed the last hill, Sam saw the chimney peeking up over the horizon, the roof of the barn reflected off the afternoon sun. Sam pointed a moment before he knew something was wrong. With a sudden kick of his horse, he bolted forward, dreading what he knew he would see even before he cleared the hill.

"What?" was all he heard Sarah say as he rode away from her.

He reached the top of the hill and pulled his mount. There before him was the valley he'd thought of as home for years. The barn, the corral, the trees down by the pond. But the house, all except for the chimney, had been replaced by a pile of burned rubble.

For a moment, Sam couldn't make his mind believe what he knew his eyes saw. The house hadn't been big, but it had been solid. It could have withstood any storm.

Sarah caught up with him, but he hardly noticed. She reached for his hand, but he pulled away and rode down the hill.

She found him again standing in the cold ashes of his home, a note in his hand.

"What happened?" She stood on the edge of the mess. She waited on what once had been a porch he'd built for watching sunsets. Sam looked up at her, thinking he could never remember watching one, only planning to someday. Now it was too late.

"A neighbor left me a note. He says the fire was set. The town folks overheard a group of wild young boys bragging about watching it burn." Sam glanced down at the paper he'd pulled off one of the few poles left standing. "He said the sheriff's not sure if it was directed at me, or if the boys just wanted to do some damage and knew this house sat empty." Sam handed her the letter.

"You're Mr. Garrett here, also?"

Sam took a deep breath, hating the smell that filled his lungs. "Garrett's my real name, Sarah. I just used Gatlin because I thought it sounded hard like the gun. I bought the place under my real name thinking no one would find me here."

"You don't know that they have."

"I don't know that they haven't." Sam kicked at what had once been a chair. "We should ride into town and check with a clerk named Willoby, who serves part-time as the town sheriff. Maybe he'll be able to tell us more."

"I'm staying here," she said, as if there would be no further discussion.

"You can't," he answered. "There's nothing here."

Sarah's light blue eyes stared up at him. "There's my home here. I'll be here when you get back."

Sam needed time to himself anyway, so he didn't argue. If she wanted to stay and cry over the loss of her home, she had a right, he guessed. He rode into town trying to make sense out of what had happened. Before he reached the cluster of buildings, he removed his gun belt, placed it over the saddle horn, and covered it with his duster.

To his surprise the sheriff seemed both interested and sorry for his loss, but could offer little in the way of information. He thought the boys were only passing through, coming home from a cattle drive. Sam had a gut feeling that whoever burned his place did so knowing whom they were making mad.

The owner of the mercantile seemed interested in Sam's problem. He even offered to cut the usual cost of lumber if he planned to rebuild. The town's saloon consisted of a small room in the back of the general store. When Sam passed through to look at the lumber on hand, several of the men joined in the discussion of what a crime the burning was in a place that had prided itself in having little trouble.

They asked about the cuts on Sam's face, and he easily explained that he'd fallen from his horse a few days back. The townfolk took that as a reason, never guessing that the legend Sam Gatlin would never fall from his mount.

When Sam mentioned he had to get back to his wife, all at once he was family. One old man even slapped him on the back and said it was about time he brought the little woman out. The store owner's wife insisted on wrapping up food for them and even said if they would like, they were welcome to spend the night in their kitchen. After all, she said, they were neighbors.

Sam left the place bewildered. He'd never been more than a shadow in this town. Buying what he needed from time to time when he fixed up things. He'd never taken the time to talk to any of them more than to say hello. But they all seemed to know him. A part of him wished he could step into this life and be one of them.

Only, how would they react when they found out who he really was? They'd pull their children away when he walked down the street. They'd tell stories about what he'd done, as if he were the devil walking on earth.

The night was cool, but Sam hardly noticed. His thoughts were full of Sarah and how he'd let her down. He'd promised her a home, a place where she'd be safe. Now he wasn't sure he would ever be able to give her either one of those things. He had the money to rebuild, but why? Someone would just burn it down again. Maybe a dream was meant to be just that, a dream.

He was surprised to see a light coming from his place as he turned the last bend in the road. Sarah had hung lanterns from the few poles left on the porch. There were also lanterns glowing from the barn loft.

He climbed down from his horse and stood in front of the house. Somehow, in the time he'd been gone, she'd swept the ashes away from the porch and along a path that led to the fireplace.

"Welcome home," she said as she stepped out of the darkness between the two buildings. She'd put on her dress and combed her hair out.

"Not much of a home," Sam answered as he handed her the bag of food. "But at least we've got something to eat."

To his surprise he didn't see the disappointment he'd expected in her eyes. She looked tired, and had a black smudge across her face, but she didn't look like a woman about to bury her dream.

They walked in silence to the barn. While he turned his horse into the corral with hers, she set the food he'd brought on a table she'd made out of extra boards she must have found in his supply room in the back of the barn.

He had to give her credit: she hadn't spent much time crying over her loss. She'd been busy since he'd been gone. One corner of the barn almost looked livable, with rough benches and their bedrolls spread on the hay.

Without thinking about it, he lifted his hand and rubbed the mark off her cheek. She curled into him, moving her face against his shirt, circling her arms about his waist.

When she lifted her face to him, he knew what she wanted. He'd told her she didn't have to ask, she just had to move close to him. With an ache deep in his soul, he leaned down and touched her lips with his. The kiss was tender, filled with all the longings of what might have been.

When she broke the kiss, she whispered, "Supper's ready."

He couldn't help but smile even though a part of him wanted to scream. She'd said the words as if she'd said them a thousand times.

They ate with him trying to figure out what to say to her.

"I'll have to thank the store owner's wife for sending this out. She's not much of a cook, but her kindness was great." Sarah didn't seem to notice he hadn't said a word. "I notice there are apple trees by the pond. I could make apple jelly next fall. It won't cost much, mostly just for the sugar and jars. Who knows, maybe I could work out a trade at the general store."

He moved to the loft window and watched moonlight flicker across his land.

"You said there were fish in the pond. If no one's been fishing there, we should be able to live off of them and the game around here."

"Stop it, Sarah," he finally said. "We both know I let you down. We both know we can't stay here."

"Of course we can, Sam." She dimmed the light. "We can live in the barn until we get the house rebuilt. I think I could even use the fireplace to cook one meal a day. The horses have plenty to eat."

He could hear her getting ready for bed as though they had a bedroom or a bed to sleep in. How many nights? he asked himself. How many nights had she slept on the ground since they'd been married, and how many times had he told her of a home he had waiting for her? A home that was no more than ashes. Maybe it had been just boys having fun, but Sam would always wonder if one of the outlaws he'd sent to jail or killed their kin wasn't trying to even the score.

"You'll see, it won't be that long until I can plant a garden." Sarah pulled him back from his thoughts. "I'm really quite good at it, Sam. In time I'll find some of the herbs Granny Vee used and transplant them from the wild to little window boxes so I can keep an eye on them and cut them at the right time."

He looked over his shoulder, knowing he would have to make her understand. There could be no future for them. She'd be smart to take Sheriff Riley's offer when he told her he'd call the whole marriage off since they knew she wasn't a killer.

The sight before him made him forget what he'd been about to say. Sarah stood in the moonlight totally nude.

He turned slowly and envied the moonlight as it shone over his shoulder and caressed her body. Her hair tumbled past her waist, looking almost silver in the light. He'd always thought of her as small, but now he realized she was perfect. Her breasts were high and rounded to perfection just as he knew they would be. Her waist was small, her hips rounded.

He stopped and looked away. "Sarah, what do you think you are doing?"

I'm going to bed," she answered. "Like you told me," she added.

Sam felt as if he would starve for the sight of her if he

didn't turn around. But this time the beauty before him was no less of a shock to his senses. "I never told you to take off your clothes."

She laughed and took a step toward him. "Yes, you did. You said when I'm ready to be your wife in more than name only I should come to you without any clothes on."

"But, Sarah, I promised you so much."

"I know. I'm ready now."

He smiled. "I mean I promised you a home and a place where you would be safe."

She was only inches away from him. He could smell the honeysuckle aroma in the air.

"Make love to me," she whispered as she closed the space between them.

Sam let his hands slide over her body as he leaned down and met her kiss. All sanity slipped away as his senses filled with Sarah. Her mouth was hungry, her body warm.

She pulled at his clothes, and he let her help him. He wanted to feel her skin against his as dearly as she seemed to need it. He unstrapped his gunbelt and let it hit the floor as he lifted her in his arms and walked toward the bedrolls.

He spread her out across the blankets and watched her stretch as she smiled up at him. For a moment he was afraid to touch her. How could such perfection be real?

Her small hands moved up and opened his shirt. When her fingers crossed over his heart, he was lost. Lowering slowly, he let his chest gently press against her. She moved in response, sending heat rushing through his veins.

Slowly, he reminded himself. Go slowly. But her body was warm with need as she begged for his touch.

He'd meant to make love to her with great care, but she opened her legs to him and he couldn't pull away. He moved inside her as his body pressed her into the soft bed of hay.

She kissed him, pulling him to her with her arms. Slender chains he couldn't have broken. Sam pushed deeper inside her, and without warning heaven exploded and all he could do was ride passion.

When he collapsed, he carefully twisted to his side so that she wouldn't have to take the weight of him.

He was out of breath, shaking, sweating all over, and she was calmly watching him.

Sam buried his head in her hair. Where had he gotten the idea that he could be a lover? He thought about saying he was sorry, he'd thought only of himself and not her, but he remembered how she'd told him her first husband had used her, but always said he was sorry afterward.

"Sam?"

"Yes, love?" he answered.

"Is that all?"

TWENTY-NINE

Sam pulled the covers over her and rose up on one elbow. She could see his dark eyes shining even in the low glow of the lantern.

"No, my love, that is not all."

His smile made her want to laugh.

"But I need you to cover up so that I can unwrap this great gift you've given me a little at a time."

She watched him closely. "I thought I already gave you the gift."

He silenced her with a warm kiss. She thought of pulling away and asking him to explain, for it seemed to her she'd already been bedded. His seed had been planted deep inside her, of that she was sure. But Sam seemed to think their loving was not finished, and his kiss felt so good, Sarah decided to save her questions for later.

As he had before, he kissed her until all thought left her mind and she began to float in a warm ocean of passion where every touch brought both pleasure and need.

He moved his big hands into her hair and moved her head first one way and then the other so that he could fully kiss her.

She leaned back and relaxed, letting him do with her what he pleased, for it all pleased her. Finally, when her lips were swollen from his kisses, he moved to her neck and began tasting her skin. She felt his warm breath along her damp flesh as he moved from her ear to her throat.

"Sarah," he whispered. "Are you my wife, my full and true wife?"

She sighed and leaned her head back so that he could journey down her throat.

"Say it, Sarah," he asked again. "Tell me how you feel."

"I'm your wife," she answered as he moved lower, pulling the blanket down to her breasts. "Oh, Sam I love you."

He closed his mouth over her breast then and sent her beyond word, deep into a passion only he knew how to take her to. His hands moved over her body, claiming every inch as his as the blanket slipped lower and lower an inch at a time.

Sarah began to rock with his touch, and he rewarded her with bolder movements. When he took the time away from her body to return to kiss her, she was hungry for his mouth on hers, but twisted with need until his hands caressed her, reassuring her that he'd return to taste her flesh once more.

His hand moved lower until he found the warmth between her legs. She pushed against him, suddenly needing more. He held her there, letting her beg for more while he took the time to kiss her deeply one more time. Then, with a swift movement, he spread her legs and shifted above her.

This time Sarah was ready for his mating. This time

her body also throbbed with need, and her skin grew damp with sweat. A raging fire built within her, for this time he was in no hurry.

They rode the passion together until Sarah's body shattered with pleasure. A moment later she felt him shake and knew he had crossed into paradise with her.

She wrapped her damp arms around him and held on as tight as she could, never wanting the moment to end. Never had she dreamed that a mating could be like this.

After a long while Sam tried to pull away, but she held tight.

"It's all right."

She felt his laughter against her chest.

"It's all right, Sarah," he whispered. "We can do it again. You can let go."

"When?" she asked as she loosened her grip around him. "When can we do it again?"

He collapsed beside her. "Soon. I have to have a little time."

"Is this one of the things I shouldn't ask of you often?"

Sam pulled her mouth to his and kissed her lightly. "No. You can ask it of me anytime you like. I'll just need to rest a while between times."

"How long?"

"You're a demanding woman, Mrs. Garrett."

She sat up and watched him, suddenly not the least shy. He closed his eyes for a few minutes, then opened one eye. "What are you doing?"

"Waiting," she answered.

He grabbed her and pulled her beneath the covers. "I've got a better idea. How about I hold you while we wait."

His hand slid down to her backside. "You are the most beautiful creature I've ever seen."

She relaxed, realizing how exhausted she was. The

warmth of his hand felt as if it belonged on her hip. She liked the feel of his body against hers. The thought crossed her mind that she might ask him why people wore so many clothes when it felt so good to be without them.

She drifted into sleep with his warm breath brushing her cheek.

Much later, in the time before dawn, she awoke to him touching her, to his hungry warm mouth on her breast.

She stretched and realized her body was already longing for him.

When he noticed she was awake, he moved to her ear. "Would you mind mating with me again, my love?"

Her arms went round his neck. "No, I wouldn't mind. Thank you for asking."

"You're welcome," he answered as he kissed her ear.

This time the journey was familiar. She knew what waited at the end of passion's ride, and she looked forward to it even while cherishing each step along the way. She moved to his every touch and welcomed the opportunity to feel of him as well. When her hands moved over him she felt powerful for his muscles tightened with her caress and he let out a low moan when she grew bold.

They took their time discovering each other, playing at lovemaking, swimming in passion. When finally they were both hurting with a need for the other, he rose above her once more and ended the delicious torture. They climbed together and fell into heaven wrapped in each other's arms.

When her breathing returned to normal, Sarah laid her hand over Sam's heart and whispered, "I'm home, Sam. Right here circled in your arms is where I belong."

THIRTY

Sarah awoke long after sunrise. The barn was bright with light. Sam stood by the loft window looking out on the day. When she stretched and yawned, he turned her direction.

"Morning," he said. She thought he looked younger, not as cold as he once had with a frown carved into his face.

"Good morning. I'm sorry I overslept."

"Don't worry about it." He smiled. "You didn't get much sleep."

Sarah pulled on her undergarments and looked around for her dress. "I'll get the coffee on and see what we have in the supply sack for breakfast." She hurried to where she'd left the saddlebags.

Sam stepped in her path. "First, good morning."

She looked at him, confused. "You already said that."

"Not the way I'd like to say it." He pulled her close

and kissed her mouth so lightly she could barely feel his lips.

"Is it time to do it again?" she asked with a smile, wondering what the rules were on this new lovemaking thing he'd taught her.

Sam laughed. "No, I think we'd better rest and eat something." He looked worried. "Are you all right? Did I hurt you?"

Now was her time to laugh. "No, Sam, but thank you for asking."

He lifted her into one of his huge bear hugs.

An hour later, after they'd taken a shivering bath down in the pond and drunk a pot of hot coffee while wrapped in blankets, they finally got dressed and stepped out of the barn.

"Sarah, I wish you could have seen the house."

"I will. Not today, or tomorrow, but soon. And this time it will be the house that *we* built."

"I don't know. Maybe you'd be safer somewhere else."

Before she could answer, they noticed the sheriff coming up the road. Behind him was a line of wagons all loaded down with lumber.

Sam didn't know what to think. The men pulled onto his land as if they'd been asked. He might have said something, but he didn't want to worry Sarah.

The store owner jumped off his wagon first. "Now, I know you didn't tell me to order lumber, so I just brought all I could round up in the back. We may not be able to build a whole house, but we can get the frame up today and from then on, I'm guessing I can get supplies in as fast as you can build the rest of the house."

Sam could say nothing.

"And don't worry about paying for everything. I'll carry you if you need me to."

Sarah moved out from under Sam's arm and greeted each man as he pulled into the yard. Sam could see they were all charmed by her, each taking off his hat and greeting her.

"Now, don't worry, ma'am, about feeding us," one said. "Our wives will be out all together in a wagon after while, and they'll each be carrying an armful of victuals."

The men rolled up their sleeves and began pulling the burned lumber down. Sam wasn't sure what to say, but he pitched in. Slowly, as they asked questions about where he wanted a window, or how did he want to hang the door, Sam began to learn the men's names. He talked with them as he'd seen folks talk to one another. He didn't wear his guns. They didn't know who he was. No legend stood before them, just a man who'd lost his home, and they were his neighbors planning to help him out.

By lunch a few of the men were kidding him about how he must be a newlywed because his wife couldn't pass within a mile of him without patting on him. Sam tried to grumble, but ended up smiling. In truth, he loved her attention. She was, however, no good for his image as a tough man. It was hard to convince anyone to fear him with a butterfly landing on him every few minutes.

In truth he found himself glancing in her direction every few minutes. Even working, he could still feel her body against his. He had to fight the urge to tell all these good people to go home so he could make love to his wife.

Sarah fit right in with the women. They all seemed to talk at once, asking her a hundred questions without allowing her time to answer one. They brought food by the basketful and spread it out on a table made from extra boards. When one found out that Sarah was newly married, they all decided to give her a cup towel shower.

When Sarah looked confused, they explained that each woman would bring a small gift for the kitchen wrapped in a cup towel. When the party was over, Sarah would not only have all kinds of things for her kitchen, she'd also have a drawer of cup towels each with the initials of one of her new friends.

When the men came over to eat, Sarah had to sit with the women, but she hurried over, helping with the table when she could. Each time she passed Sam, she brushed against him until finally she drove him so crazy that he pulled her into his lap and kissed her soundly. The men hooted and the women blushed, but everyone seemed willing to excuse the newlyweds.

"Ain't no sin in loving your wife," the store owner said as he put his arm around his chubby little wife. "I've been doing it for twenty years."

The men returned to work, but not before Sarah saw the promise in Sam's eyes. By sundown the tired neighbors were all loaded in their wagons and ready to head home.

Sam stood with the sheriff and Luke, the store owner. "Thanks," he said, extending his hand to each.

"You're welcome," Luke answered. "You'd do the same for me."

"That I would," Sam answered and realized he meant it.

Luke climbed into his wagon and moved down the road. Sam glanced over at the house, where Sarah was arranging imaginary furniture in a house without walls.

"Long day, Sam," Willoby, who served as sheriff, said, as if they'd been friends for a long time. "I best be moving on."

Sam had to be honest with the man before him. "I need to tell you something about me. As the sheriff, you'll probably find out soon enough."

The older man shook his head. "I know all I need to know about you."

"But—" Sam tried again. It would only be a matter of time before someone recognized him, and then folks would talk.

"Tell you what, Sam, you get this house built for your little lady, and then we'll talk. Winter's coming on and I wouldn't want her out here without a home."

Sam felt as if someone were offering him a suspended sentence. He knew it wouldn't last but for a matter of days, but he'd take it. This might be the only time he had to feel like a regular man.

For the next couple of weeks Sam worked on the house until his hands bled with blisters, but he didn't care. He liked working all day and loving Sarah all night. They'd go round and round over some detail about the house, for she had her mind set on how she wanted every detail to be, but at night under the covers there were no arguments.

The kitchen was finished first, and she set about proving she could cook. Every time she went to town, something seemed to follow her home. First a cow, then two goats, then a dozen chickens, and finally a puppy. The place was suddenly overrun. The cow kicked Sam every time he got within three feet of her; the chickens kept trying to roost in whatever part of the house he was working on.

Sarah only laughed until one of the goats ate one of her new cup towels. Sam thought they might have goat stew for dinner when she found out.

The first night they slept in their own bed, they didn't make love. They just held each other all night long.

Three weeks to the day she'd become his real wife, Sam looked up from his work on the roof to see Sheriff Willoby and two other men riding toward his new home. He watched as Sheriff Riley and Jacob Dalton came into view. He felt as if his heart fell out of his chest.

His life with Sarah was about to end.

THIRTY-ONE

SARAH WATCHED THE FOUR MEN WALK TOWARD THE
barn. She had no idea why they'd come, but from the
look on Sam's face, it couldn't be good news. Sam had
told her to stay in the house as he stared at her with a
longing in his dark eyes. She'd seen the look before in
the silence of the night when he thought she was asleep.
A gaze that memorized her as though he knew he'd never
see her again.

She waited as he'd told her, until they closed the barn
door. Then she hurried through the kitchen and ran to the
corral opening near the back of the barn. She slipped into
the shadows between the stalls and tried to figure out what
they were talking about.

"We all know why we're here," Willoby started. "I
knew Sam Garrett and Sam Gatlin were the same man
when he bought the land. I'd seen him before down in
Waco when I was keeping books for an undertaker. He
had no reason to even notice me as he brought two out-

laws and a body into town." The part-time sheriff looked at Sam. "I didn't believe all those stories I heard about you then, and I don't believe them now. You had the decency to offer to pay me for burying the man strapped over his horse, and not many would do that."

Sheriff Riley sat down on a stool, then stood slowly, looking older than he had when he married Sarah to Sam months ago. "We're all here because we know Sam ain't a bad man. But he's never going to know any peace if we don't do something."

Jacob agreed. "He's a legend. It's getting so bad his legend grows when we know he's down here doing nothing. I can think of three tales that have started about him since he's been building his house."

"There are probably boys practicing their shooting now hoping to get a chance to gun him down in a fight." Riley pulled out his papers and pouch and started rolling a cigarette. "It's just a matter of time before one finds him."

Sam had had enough. "I don't care what you three think of me. I'm not a wanted man. I can live anywhere I want to live. So if you think you'll gang up on me and get me to run, you'd better think again. My wife wants to live in this place, on this land, and as long as there is breath in me, that's exactly the way it's going to be."

"Now, hold on Sam." Jacob squared his shoulders. "There's no point to you going off half-cocked. We're just here to help you. A bounty hunter doesn't just hang up his guns and decide to be a farmer."

"Help me? You'd all three help me by forgetting you ever knew me."

"Now, wait a minute." Sheriff Riley pointed his tobacco-stained finger at Sam. "Sam's got a great idea."

The other two look confused. Sam didn't look as if he cared if he heard the sheriff's point.

"Sam said as long as there's breath in him."

Jacob raised an eyebrow. "What are you suggesting, Riley? That Sam dies?"

"Of course not." Riley looked offended. "I think it would be much better if someone killed him. If he's dead, there ain't no one going to be looking for him, and we all know that once the man dies, the legend fades."

Sarah gasped for air, and all the men, except Sam, turned toward her.

After a silence Sam said calmly, "Come on out, Sarah, love. I had a feeling you wouldn't stay in the house."

She stormed to the center of the barn. "Why should I stay in the house when you men are out here thinking of killing my husband?"

"It's the only way, darlin'." Sheriff Riley sounded as if he were talking to one of his daughters. "Don't you see, if Sam is dead, no one will be looking for him. No half-grown kid wanting to make a name for himself. No outlaw getting out of jail, planning to even the score for Sam bringing him in. No relative who blames Sam for his brother or father or son dying."

Sam grabbed her hand and pulled her closer to him. "It's the only way. I got to die."

"And you've got to stay dead. No coming back in a few years to pick up extra money by bringing in a few outlaws." Riley shrugged. "The only problem is which one of us is going to kill him."

Jacob stepped up. "I could do it. Claim he got caught in the crossfire with an outlaw." Jacob grinned. "I could shoot him in the head, where there's likely to be little damage."

Sam glared at the young Ranger.

"No," Riley said. "You're too good a shot to let that happen."   •

"I could do it," Willoby spoke up. "I could say I thought he was breaking into a store, and I shot before I saw who it was. I'm not that great a sheriff. An accident wouldn't be that unusual."

Riley shook his head. "No one would believe you were that good, or that lucky. Men like Sam Gatlin don't get shot by accident. Haven't you heard the tales? He can move like darkness over the land without making a sound."

Sam rolled his eyes.

Sarah finally figured out what they were talking about. "I could shoot him. I'm a good enough shot, I could hit him in the shoulder and then patch him up."

"Too risky." Riley began to pace. "No one would believe you'd shoot him. You're always patting on him like you can't stay away from the man." The old sheriff shook his head. "Hell if any of us can figure out why."

All at once everyone in the barn was arguing over who would get to shoot Sam.

Finally Sam yelled for them all to stop. "Enough!" He added when they settled down, "How about I shoot myself. If you all keep this up, I might do it just to get some peace."

Riley looked as if he was considering the possibility, but said, "That wouldn't work."

Before anyone could start arguing again, a low southern voice sounded from the shadows. "I'll shoot you, Sam. It's the least I can do."

No one moved but Sam. He walked to the edge of the lantern's light. "Forget it. It would put you at too great a risk. You've got the kids to think about."

"Who is that?" Riley whispered as Jacob rested his hand on his gun.

"I wouldn't have my kids if it hadn't been for you. I

said I'd pay you back one day. Be in Fort Worth in the streets where lots of folks will see you die on New Year's Eve. At midnight, when the shooting starts celebrating the new year, you'll fall."

"It might work," Riley said. "You'd die in front of half the town. No one would know who made the shot, but any fool who wants to can claim it was him."

Jacob pulled his Colt. "Step out from the shadows, stranger."

All was still. No one moved or heard anything but the wind from the open window in the loft.

Sarah thought she heard the sound of a horse riding fast in the general direction of a place known as Satan's Canyon.

THIRTY-TWO

Sarah paced the wood planks in front of the general store waiting for the mail delivery to come in on the noon stage. For the hundredth time she wished she'd gone with Sam. He needed her.

"They may be late today, ma'am, what with yesterday being the first and all. It usually takes the drivers a few days to sober up enough to make their runs."

Sarah tried her best to act calm. "I know, I'm just expecting a letter from my husband." Sam had been gone over a month. Riley convinced him he needed to be everywhere in the state, except around home. That way folks could say they saw him in Waco or Abilene just before he got shot.

"There's the stage now!" someone yelled.

Sarah didn't move. She'd been trying to keep from throwing up her breakfast all morning. This plot of Riley's must be upsetting her more than she'd guessed. She almost laughed. Who wouldn't be upset to know that two nights ago her husband had been shot on a street? A hundred things could have gone wrong. What if Frank's aim was off? What if Sam moved at the last second and the bullet hit his heart? What if someone realized he wasn't dead?

"Mrs. Garrett," the store owner said. "I'm sorry, there was no letter from your husband, but here's the paper from Fort Worth you asked for."

"Thanks." Sarah forced herself not to look at the paper. "Maybe there will be one tomorrow." She needed to talk to someone if only for a moment. "We've never been separated before."

"Don't you worry none, that man of yours will get his buying done up in Kansas City and be home before you know it."

Sarah nodded, wishing it were true that Sam had gone to Kansas City to buy horses. No one in town knew where he really was. No one but the sheriff would ever know. If Sam lived through his killing, he would be Sam Garrett from now on. They'd work the farm and raise horses and grow old together.

She drove halfway home before she could wait no longer. Sarah stopped the wagon and opened the paper. There, in the corner of the front page, were the words she hated to read. "Sam Gatlin murdered at midnight."

She tried to blink away the tears long enough to read the details. No one knew who fired the shot. A Texas Ranger confirmed his identity and his death. A sister of the church knelt beside him and prayed while everyone else passed by, staring at the man who had been a legend.

Sarah couldn't read more. She moved on toward home, glad that Ruthie had been with him, but heartbroken that Sam wouldn't allow her to go to Fort Worth. This time, he'd said, he didn't need an angel to save him.

As Sarah rounded the last bend, she saw a wagon pulled up to her house.

Jacob Dalton stepped off the porch and waited for her. He was alone.

Sarah hurried, jumping from the wagon even before her horse stopped. "Jacob! How did it go?"

He caught her and held her close as he whispered, "I'm sorry, Sarah."

She felt her heart stop.

"I did the best I could to keep him sober, but the damn fool thinks he needs to drink when he's been shot."

Sarah jerked away. "He's alive?"

Jacob lifted the tarp off the wagon's bed. "And meaner than hell. He's threatened to kill me several times since I picked him up at the cemetery. Claims we left him in the coffin too long."

Sarah stared at her husband, dirty, covered in blood, and smelling like a saloon.

"I tried to get him to let me clean the wound and bandage it for him, but he said he wanted you to do that. Wouldn't let anyone touch him. So I bought enough whiskey to last, and we headed here."

The smell of blood and dirt and whiskey made her stomach turn over, but she knew what she had to do.

"Help me get him up and in the house."

Jacob pulled on Sam's arm. "Whoever did the shooting caught him on the left arm. All Sam had to do was lay his wound over his chest, and everyone thought he'd been shot in the heart." Jacob took the weight of Sam's arm across his shoulder. "I tried to tell where the shot came from, but it was like a ghost made the shot and disappeared. I'd like to have known the man Sam Gatlin trusted with his life."

Sam swore, then looked up. Pain-filled eyes met hers. "Morning, ma'am. Name's Sam Garrett."

She smiled. "I know who you are, you id . . . who did *you say you were?*"

He took her hand. "Sam Garrett."

Suddenly the blood and dirt didn't matter; she hugged him wildly.

He moaned in pain. "Could you wait a few days before you kill me again, Sarah, my love?"

An hour later Sarah had bandaged Sam's wound and scrubbed him clean. He offered Jacob his hand. "Thanks, friend."

Jacob nodded toward Sarah. "You don't deserve her," he said.

"I know, but I plan on being right here by her side until they bury me instead of rocks in my coffin."

"Did you tell her she can get out of the marriage if she wants to?"

"How about you tell her." Sam grinned. "I'd like someone to see her temper if she even thought you might take her away from me."

Jacob shook his head. "Unlike you, Sam, I'm in no hurry to die."

Standing, Jacob reached for his hat. "Rest in Peace, Sam."

TURN THE PAGE FOR A PREVIEW OF

JODI THOMAS'S

NEXT HISTORICAL ROMANCE TELLING
LACY'S STORY.

COMING SOON FROM JOVE BOOKS

Cottonwood, Texas
1883

CAPTAIN WALKER LARSON GRITTED HIS TEETH AS SER-
geant Harris ushered in another of the prostitutes who
came to complain about the evacuation order. As usual,
the tall, lanky sergeant grinned at the woman as if he were
guiding her into the front pew on Sunday morning.

They had a matter of hours to clear the little town before an all-out range war started and the sergeant acted
like the army was there to serve tea. Cowhands from the
warring ranches were already swallowing courage at saloons. By nightfall they would be itching to fight and
nothing Walker and his handful of men could do would
stop them.

Walker frowned at the paperwork stacked on his desk.
Since he moved into the abandoned sheriff's quarters,
he'd had nothing but trouble walk through the door. Why
couldn't these women understand that all hell was about

to break loose? They'd be better off to collect their belongings and go like most of the civilians. Trouble twisted in the streets, a building tornado, but these 'ladies of the night' didn't seem to hear the wind.

"Captain, this one insists on seeing you right away." Harris removed his hat and pointed her toward the only chair in the room other than the one Walker sat in behind his desk. "Says it's real important."

Walker cleared his throat as he prepared to say what he'd said to everyone of the doves who'd come to complain. The army had a responsibility to protect them, whether they wanted help or not. With a range war threatening, what little peace this town knew was gone. Every man seemed to have chosen a side and it was only a matter of time before someone started the fight. No one would be safe and the saloons, where these women roamed, were waiting powder casks.

This one was a beauty, though. Rich, walnut-colored hair he wouldn't mind folding inside his grip. And young. Far too young, Walker decided, to be in such a business. But he guessed the ones who managed to hang on to their youthful looks could demand higher prices.

She appeared wearier than the rest, as if she'd traveled a long distance. Her dusty red coat was well made but did little to hide her wares beneath. He didn't miss the fullness of her breasts, or the way her jacket pulled in sharply along the waist.

He forgot his standard speech as he raised his gaze and stared into eyes the warm brown of polished leather. She was the first woman in a long time who tempted him to visit the back streets.

"There are no exceptions, Miss. We have to evacuate you with the rest of the ladies." He felt sorry for her. She looked frightened and a little lost, as if her world were about to end. She was a master at playing the innocent, for she almost made him believe it.

"I'm not with the others," she said in little more than a whisper. "I came to see you."

He waited, wondering what she'd offer to be allowed to stay behind. Whatever it was, no matter how tempting, wouldn't be enough for him to bend the rules. He hadn't made it to captain at twenty-five by bending.

She looked up at him with those beautiful eyes again. "The sergeant said your name was Larson . . . Frank Larson, sir."

"That's right." He nodded, finding himself wishing she had come to see him about something else. Frank was his first name, but no one but his father had ever called him that. His mother had liked her family name, Walker, best. "I'm Captain Larson," he stated, reminding her this was not a social call.

He couldn't tell if she were relieved by the information, or more frightened for some reason. He half expected her to bolt and run by the way she clung to the strings of her tattered handbag.

"And you are?" He really didn't have time to mess with learning her name, but he asked just the same.

"Mrs. Larson," she answered lifting her chin slightly. "Mrs. Frank Larson."

Walker smiled and stood. He had no idea what kind of game she was playing, but Larson was a common name. She might be married to a man who had the same name as him. That wouldn't change a thing. His job was to try and save lives. The only way he could do that was to get her and all other women and children out of town. Except for a few widows and these prostitutes, most of the women had menfolk to look after them.

"Nice to meet you, Mrs. Larson. Where might your

husband be?" He tried to keep his words formal as he moved around the corner of the desk. Perhaps he'd been wrong about her occupation. Maybe she was a shop-keeper's wife or a rancher's daughter who'd been sepa-rated from her family.

Her eyebrows shot up in shock. "Why, right before me, sir."

The words hit Walker like a powerful blow to his gut. He didn't move. The tiny possibility that she spoke the truth seeped through a crack in the wall he'd spent years building around himself.

She twisted the cord of her bag about her fingers that appeared to be stained with ink.

He'd seen those kinds of stains on his father's hands many times . . . printer's ink. The clock on his cluttered desk ticked away seconds as though they both had all the time in the world.

"You must be mistaken," he said at last. "There is no one in the room, Ma'am."

Her unsettling gaze watched him closely. "You are in the room, sir. I'm Lacy Larson, your wife."

Sergeant Harris opened the door suddenly, following his words into the room. "Last stage will be leaving in ten minutes, Captain." Harris had acted as doorman for the captain for four years. He jerked back a step, well aware that he'd interrupted something even though Wal-ker hadn't said a word. "Begging your pardon, sir."

"Hold the stage," Walker said without taking his gaze off of Lacy. "I need a few minutes with this lady."

"I don't know if I can," the sergeant mumbled. "That driver is in a powerful hurry and don't look like he cares much what the army has to say."

Walker's cold stare shifted to Harris. "Hold it at gunpoint if you have to, but that stage doesn't leave until this woman is on it!"

Harris nodded and backed out of the room, closing the door behind him.

Walker turned his full attention to Lacy Larson. "You are the woman my father bailed out of jail and married me to by proxy three years ago." He found it hard to believe. She must have been little more than a child at the time.

His words hadn't been a question, but she nodded in answer anyway.

"How old are you?"

"Eighteen," she answered. "How old are you."

"Twenty-five," Walker snapped.

She watched him closely. "You seem older," she said more to herself than him. "Your father always called you his boy."

Walker walked in front of his desk choosing his words carefully. He didn't want to frighten the lady further, but she had become far more than his responsibility as an officer of the government.

She stared at the strings of her purse.

Walker shoved paperwork aside and leaned on his desk. He crossed his long legs as he folded his arms. He stood so close to her he could touch her if he shifted. He considered himself an honest, straightforward man, but for once, he tried to think of how to be kind. She looked so frightened. He blamed his father for this mess more than her. She'd been in jail. She'd done what she thought she must to survive. But his father had paid her bail and started this whole muddle. The old man should have stayed out of his life, as well as hers. What kind of father buys his son a wife?

"I fought," Walker began, "to get the marriage annulled

when I found out what my father had done. I'm a soldier, Ma'am, I have no need or desire for a wife. You'd be better off married to someone else."

Light from the window flickered off his polished boots. She lowered her head and seemed to be focusing on the bouncing rays. He hoped he hadn't hurt her feelings by being so direct. Surely, she couldn't think he was turning her down. After all, until a few minutes ago he'd never seen her before. She'd probably make some farmer up near Cedar Point a great wife. She was certainly a beauty, even if she did have a questionable past.

"So we have not been legally married these past three years?"

She raised her chocolate-colored eyes to him.

Walker almost groaned aloud. He'd guess she could get about anything in this world she wanted with those eyes, but from some other man. Not him.

"Oh, we're married all right. Thanks to the power-of-attorney letter I left my father, the marriage is as solid as if I'd signed the paper with my own hand."

"You don't want to be married to me?" She looked like it had never crossed her mind that he wouldn't want her.

Walker flinched, hating that he was hurting her. He silently swore at his father who was a kind man, but always thought he knew what was best. "It's not that I don't want *you*, it's that I don't want a wife. Any wife."

He walked to the long, thin window that faced the dusty main street of this little town whose name he had trouble remembering. Since he'd left home, his life had been a string of battles. Walker didn't want to even think about what his life might have been like if he hadn't run away from home at seventeen and kept running. He never told his father why he'd left, and he didn't plan to tell this woman who thought she was his wife.

"How is the old man?" Walker asked, realizing he hadn't heard from his father in months.

Lacy stood and walked to the window. She didn't come to his shoulder, but he sensed her nearness even before he turned around.

"Your father died three months ago." Lacy touched his arm offering comfort he did not know how to accept.

"He'd been ill for almost a year, but he wouldn't let me write you and tell you." She took a deep breath. "I did the best I could, moving him in with me above the print shop as he grew weaker, partly to save money, but mostly so I could check on him more often. Though he was in pain, he seemed happier there than alone at the boarding house."

Walker clenched his teeth and stared out the window seeing nothing but memories.

Lacy continued, "I buried him next to your mother. I think everyone for twenty miles around came to the funeral. I'm sorry to have to tell you like this. I wrote you three letters, but when I didn't hear back, I knew they hadn't caught up with you."

"There's no easy way. Straight-out is fine. I knew he was failing, more crippled up every year." He faced her and was surprised to see unshed tears floating in her beautiful eyes. He covered her hand with his own, wishing he could grieve for his father as she obviously did. "Thank you for coming to tell me, but you really most go." They'd already wasted precious minutes.

"I didn't come just to tell you he died," she whispered, her bravery building with each word. "I came because I want to be your real wife."

Walker felt her fingers tremble beneath his. "Go back to Cedar Point. Sell the print shop, keep the money. I want no part of it." He didn't have time to explain. She needed to be on the stage. Even if she shared his name, she was no more to him than a stranger, a civilian. "Move away and change your name, or tell everyone I died. Get on with your life, Lacy. I've never been a part of it, I never will."

She shook her head. "No," she answered as though they talked of something debatable. "I'm not leaving until I'm your wife. Your real wife."

Harris tapped on the door before opening it, something Walker never remembered the sergeant doing. "The stage driver says he'll give us fifteen more . . ." Harris froze as he took in the scene. The sergeant's gaze stared at the point on Walker's sleeve where Lacy's hand rested.

Walker didn't introduce Lacy. After all, Harris would never see her again. In truth, all he needed was a few more minutes with this woman to convince her to move on with her life and forget about this make-believe marriage she thought they had.

"Fifteen minutes will be fine." When Harris didn't move, Walker added, "That is all, Sergeant."

Harris saluted and backed out of the room.

Walker listened for the latch to snap before he gave Lacy his full attention. "What are you talking about? You are my legal wife. The only one I'll probably ever have. But, I'm setting you free from whatever bargain you made with my father."

Her hand slipped from his arm.

"I wish we had time to talk, Lacy. I thank you for all you did for him, but you really must be on that stage. Your safety is my responsibility."

Lacy moved her head slowly back and forth.

"This is not a game or a clash of wills." Walker fought down anger. "You will be on that stage."

"Not until I'm your wife, full and proper."

Walker's limited patience snapped. "What are you suggesting, Mrs. Larson, that I bed you here and now before the stage leaves?"

To his surprise she nodded. "I'm not budging until I'm your wife. I'll not go back and wait to be a widow unless I've been a wife even if only for fifteen minutes."

It crossed his mind that he might be dealing with madness. No sane woman would want to stay in a town where trouble boiled. He frowned. No sane woman would want to bed a man she barely knew.

He decided frightening her might be his only weapon. "Well, if that is the way it has to be Mrs. Larson, my quarters are beyond that door." He motioned with his head toward the door behind his desk. "If those are your terms, we won't be disturbed in there."

To his shock, she moved to the door.

He followed, determined to call her bluff.

She walked to the center of the small, sparsely furnished bedroom and turned up the lantern's wick, casting shadows into corners. She didn't turn around as he threw the latch, insuring their privacy.

"Go ahead and take off your clothes." He fought down a smile, knowing she'd turn and run any moment. He'd seen the fear in her eyes when she'd first entered his office. She wouldn't be able to play this game for long. "You can lay them over the chair. I'm sorry about the small bed. I'm not in the habit of entertaining company in my quarters."

Without turning around, she removed her traveling jacket and placed it over the chair. A moment later, her skirts and petticoats pooled around her ankles.

Walker swallowed, wondering how far she planned to carry this challenge. Or, how far he did.

She stepped from her shoes and turned to face him,

unbuttoning her blouse as rapidly as her shaking hands could move.

He wondered how many times she'd played this game before. After all, she might look young and pure, but Walker remembered where she came from. Pure proper ladies don't buy their way out of jail. He hadn't even bothered to ask his father what she'd been accused of, or to what she'd confessed.

"Keep going," he ordered, determined to wait her out.

When her blouse parted it took every ounce of his control not to move. Her thin camisole did little to hide the body beneath. He saw the rise and fall of her breath in the exposed flesh of her breasts. Her skin was cream, from her cheek to where she tugged at the ribbons of her undergarment.

The lace and silk fell away and she stood before him a hundred times more beautiful than any picture of a woman he'd seen over any bar. To his amazement, she stretched and pulled the combs from her hair and let the brown locks tumble. Then, as though she'd done so a hundred times, she crawled between the sheets of his bed.

Walker searched for something to say in a brain filled to the rim with the vision before him. "I thought you'd run by now."

She looked at him with frightened, determined eyes. "I'm not leaving until I'm your real wife. I promise I'll not bother you again, but I'll not step foot on that stage until this marriage, no matter how it started, is consummated."

A hundred reasons should have come to mind about why he should not do this, but not one seemed to matter. Into his world filled with war and death and pain, something perfect had fallen. Even if she were a mirage, he had to hold her this once.

Walker crossed the room unbuttoning his uniform. He stood above her and ran his hand down the length of her body, marveling at the softness. He wanted to tell her how perfect she was, or how there had been no women in his life for years, but there was no time now. The stage would be leaving in a few minutes.

His jacket fell atop her coat as he leaned down, letting his chest press against her. The pure pleasure of her beneath him shot through him unlike anything he'd ever dreamed of experiencing. He thought of himself as a man of action whose emotions were buried years ago. Only this woman, who called herself his wife, brought them all back, an avalanche of sensation.

She didn't move. She only waited.

When he tried to kiss her, she turned her head away and he realized what he'd been about to do was not a necessary part to this mating she wanted. Anger and relief blended for he knew he'd never wanted to waste time kissing on the few brief encounters he'd had with women of the night. For some reason, she felt the same.

"Are you sure?" He had to know that this was what she wanted. "You'll leave as soon as I do this?"

She nodded.

He unbuttoned his trousers, reminding himself she was his wife. Though he'd never asked for the part, it was his duty to see her safe. He gripped her thigh and pulled her legs apart. Maybe this was his duty too. She'd asked for no love. No forever. No pretense. Only this.

Walker pushed into her hard and swift, angry that he'd allowed her to call his bluff, that he hadn't been able to stop after he saw her waiting. He had no idea what game she played, but he'd do his part and be done with her.

With his second thrust, all thought vanished as her body took him in, wrapping around him. A passion strong and wild jolted through him. His senses shot in rapid fire. The fragrance of her washed over him, the feel of her, the soft sound her breathing made, the perfection of her nearness, the taste of her skin as he opened his mouth against her throat.

He wasn't prepared when his very soul shattered. He pushed into her and let out a long breath that he felt he'd held in for years. They became one, two strangers married now on paper and by action.

When he was able to form a thought, he rose a few inches off her and looked down at this woman who insisted she was his wife. Her warm brown eyes were tightly closed, her teeth biting into her fist, holding back any sound as tears streamed from the corner of her eyes into her hair.

It took a few moments to realize that the unexpected ocean of pleasure that had washed over him like a tidal wave had held only pain for her.

Harris pounded on the door. "Two minutes!" he yelled. "The driver threatened to shoot me if I asked him to wait any longer."

"She'll be there!" Walker shouted back as he climbed from his bed and buttoned his trousers realizing he hadn't bothered to remove even his boots.

"I've done what you asked," he said, irritated that she seemed to be suffering through some great tragedy when she'd been the one who insisted on the mating. He glanced at her body one last time as she pushed back tears. The buckle from his uniform belt had scratched across her abdomen, marring perfection. "Now, you have to go, Lacy. We've no more time."

Walker grabbed his jacket and turned his back, hating himself more than he had since the night he'd left Cedar Point. He thought of saying something kind to her, but there were no words. What they'd done was as far from making love as heaven from hell. He wasn't fool enough to tell himself that it was all her doing. She might be his wife. She might have insisted. She might have had a body made for love. But he'd been the one who accepted her challenge when he should have turned away.

He waited, his back to her, telling himself he would allow her a margin of privacy while she dressed. Telling himself he wasn't afraid to face her.

Walker straightened his jacket and checked to make sure all was in place in the mirror over his wash stand. The reflection was the same as always. A young professional soldier on his way up in rank, but somehow, inside, something had changed. He didn't turn around until he heard her walk to the door. He wanted to speak, but could think of nothing to say. She'd gotten what she wanted, he had taken her.

He heard the latch move and the door opened, then close behind her.

Without a word, she was gone, leaving him fuming at how he'd been manipulated by a woman not out of her teens. Maybe she'd manipulated his father also, or the old sheriff in Cedar Point.

He was back in full control, not only of his men, but of himself. He didn't need anyone. He didn't want anyone in his life. No matter what her game was, he would not play it again.

All emotion drained from his mind as he glanced around his quarters, making sure she hadn't left something that might give her reason to return. A single hairpin rested on the table, forgotten in her haste. He slipped it into his pocket and looked toward the bed.

The lantern's light caught the few drops of blood staining the white sheets where she'd lain.

The sight knocked him to his knees.

Cedar Point
November 1885

Lacy folded a few dollar bills into the last pay envelope and stuffed it in the bottom drawer of her desk. She leaned back, breathing in the familiar smells of the print shop. Ink, sawdust, paper, poverty. Home.

In the two years since she had taken over the shop, she managed to make the payroll every month but one. Once she'd taken all the money from the cashbox and traveled halfway across Texas to meet her husband. She shrugged. Once she'd been eighteen and a fool.

As the wind howled outside, Lacy closed her eyes, remembering how excited she'd been when she learned that Frank Walker Larson was stationed little more than a day's ride by train and then stage from her. Finally, her husband would be more than just a name on the marriage license.

She'd dreamed of how it would be when they met. He would be young and handsome in his uniform. She'd run into his arms and he'd tell her everything was going to be all right. After the year of taking care of his father and keeping the shop running, Lacy would cuddle into his embrace and forget all her worries.

She opened her eyes to the shadowy world of her small print shop. The real world. Her husband had been handsome, she admitted. So tall and important he took her breath away. But he hadn't welcomed her. His arms had folded around her in duty, nothing more. The Frank Larson she ran to was only a cold captain who preferred to be called Walker.

Lacy pushed away a tear as she remembered riding back on the dusty stagecoach that day. Now twenty, she was old enough to realize what a fool she had made of herself with Larson. The ride home had only prolonged her agony. Her body hurt from being used, but the dreams he killed scarred. The coach had been crowded with women wearing too much perfume and men smoking cheap cigars. When Lacy threw up in her handkerchief, the passengers decided that she would benefit from more air.

At the first stop, she was encouraged to take the seat on top of the stage. She'd pulled on her bonnet and gladly crawled into the chair tied among the luggage. As she watched the sunset that day, Lacy took the letters from her bag that Walker had written to his father years ago. She fell in love with her husband through reading his letters of adventure, memorizing every line as if it were written to her.

One by one, she watched them blow out of her hands, drifting in the wind behind the stage like dead leaves. That day she put away childhood. That day she'd given up on dreams.

Lacy stood in the dimly lit shop and pulled her shawl around her as if the wool could hug her frame. She stretched tired muscles. It was late and tomorrow would be a busy day. Every Saturday after all the papers were sold and the flyers nailed, Lacy rode out to her friends' farm. There, she could relax for a few hours. She'd play with Bailee and Carter's children and remember how years ago, when Sarah, Bailee and she had been kicked off of a wagon train, they'd talked about what life would be like in Texas. Bailee had sworn she'd never marry and Sarah had thought she wouldn't live to see another winter. But Lacy, then fifteen, had boasted that she would marry and have so many children she would have to start numbering them because she'd run out of names.

"Five years ago," Lacy whispered to herself as she

climbed the stairs. Five years since they came to Texas half-starved, out of money, and out of luck. Bailee found her man and had three sons with another baby on the way. Sarah wrote often about her twins.

"And then there is me." Lacy walked into her small apartment above the shop. "I had a husband for fifteen minutes, once."

Her rooms welcomed her with colorful quilts she'd made and tattered books she'd collected. When she first moved in and began to learn the newspaper business, she could barely read, but Lacy studied hard. Her father-in-law never tired of helping her learn those first few years. He'd treated her like a treasure even though she'd been little more than a rag-a-muffin when he'd paid her bail and married her to his son by proxy. From the first he talked of what a grand jewel she'd be to his son when the boy finally came home from serving in the army.

On evenings like this, she missed the old man dearly. She longed for the way he always talked about Walker as if his son were still a boy, and the way he could quote every article he'd ever written as though it were only yesterday and not material from twenty years in the business.

Before Lacy could heat water for tea, someone tapped on the back door.

She lifted the old Navy Colt from the pie safe drawer and went to answer. No one ever climbed the stairs to her back door except Bailee and she wouldn't be calling so late.

The minute she saw Sheriff Riley's stooped outline through the glass, she relaxed and set the gun aside.

"Evening." She opened the door to a cold blast of air that almost took her breath away. "Want to come in for a cup of coffee, Sheriff? It's cold enough to snow." The little porch area at the top of a narrow flight of stairs held no protection from the night and lately, the sheriff was thin as bone.

Riley shook his head. "Now you know I can't do that. What would folks say, a lady like yourself having a male guest after dark?"

She grinned, knowing no one would think a thing about the old man coming in from the winter night to sit a spell, but she wouldn't spoil his fun. "You know you're the only gentleman I ask inside. I'd shoot any other man who came knocking after dark."

Riley nodded. "I'd hope so. You being a respectable lady and all. I wouldn't even bother with a trial if I found a body on this porch." Though he'd listened to their confessions of killing a robber on the road to Cedar Point five years ago, the sheriff had always treated Lacy, Sarah, and Bailee more like daughters than outlaws.

The sheriff, like everyone else in town, regarded her as if her husband had simply left for the day and would be back anytime. Here, she was Mrs. Larson and there was a solidness about it even if there was no substance to the man she married.

Riley shifted into his coat like an aging turtle. "I just came to tell you that I got a telegram a few minutes ago saying Zeb Whitaker will be getting out of jail next week. I promised you I'd let you know the minute I heard."

Lacy fought to keep from reaching for the Colt. Big Zeb Whitaker was an old nightmare she laid aside years ago when he'd finally gone to prison. She could still feel his hands on her when he'd grabbed her and ripped the front of her dress open to see if she were woman enough to kidnap. She thought she killed him once. She would kill him for real if she had to. He was the first man Bailee, Sarah, and she met when they came to Texas and if Zeb had his way he would have taken their wagon and left them for dead.

"Lacy?" Riley said as though he didn't think she listened.

"Yes." She balled her fist to keep her hands from trembling.

"Rumor is he still thinks one of you three women has his stash of gold. I wouldn't be surprised if he showed up around here. I'm not too worried about Bailee way out on the farm with Carter watching after her, and Sarah tucked away where Zeb will never find her." Riley's face wrinkled. "But you . . . with your man gone and all."

He didn't need to say more. She knew she was alone. Her man wasn't gone, Walker had never been here. Except for the one brief meeting he was no more than a name on a piece of paper.

"I think you should leave town, Lacy." When Riley met her stare, he added quickly. "Just for a few weeks. Go see Sarah. Or maybe you have family back East you could visit."

Lacy wanted to scream, 'with what!' There were times over the past few years when she didn't have enough money left to buy food. Once she survived on a basket of apples Bailee brought in from their farm. The two friends never discussed how Lacy was doing, but Bailee always brought apples and eggs and more from the farm, claiming she wanted to trade them for a newspaper. More often then not, Lacy swapped a ten cent paper for a week's worth of food.

Lacy didn't want the sheriff, or anyone else in town, to know how little she had. They all seemed to think her invisible husband sent her money regularly. "I'll be fine here, Sheriff, don't worry about me."

Riley shook his head. "I don't know, Lacy. I'm not as

spry as I used to be. I'm not sure I can face a man like Zeb Whitaker."

"He's aged too, you know. He's probably barely getting around. Who knows, he might come back to say he's sorry for causing us so much trouble five years ago."

"Mean don't age well." The sheriff frowned. "I'd feel a lot better if your man were here."

"Walker's down on the border fighting cattle rustlers," Lacy lied. She'd been using that excuse for months now; it was time she made up another reason. "I'll be all right. I have the gun you gave me."

Mumbling to himself, Riley turned and headed down the steep stairs. Lacy knew he wasn't happy about her staying, but this was her home, her only home, and she needed to run the shop. None of the three men who worked for her could take over her job.

Duncan was almost deaf. Folks coming in to place an ad had to stand next to his good ear and yell their order. Eli's bones bothered him so much in winter that he stayed on his feet most of the day. If he sat for more than a few minutes he seemed to rust. And, of course, Jay Boy was just a kid Lacy paid a man's wages because he supported his mother and little sister. He might be learning the business between errands, but he couldn't take over.

Lacy closed the back door and locked it. She had to stay. If Whitaker came, she'd fight. Maybe even die, but she wouldn't run.

For the next few days Lacy carefully locked every door and made sure the old Colt was not far from her hand. She caught herself jumping at the jingle of the front bell and waking each night when the wind rapped at her upstairs windows. As the days passed, she calmed, telling herself she was in the middle of town and had nothing to fear from an old buffalo hunter like Zeb Whitaker.

If he did come to town, he would need but one look at her shop to see that she couldn't have stolen the gold he said he had when he tried to take their wagon. Lacy remembered seeing coins spilling out of his saddlebags after she'd clubbed him, but she hadn't taken a single one.

One week went by, then another. Winter settled in, turning the usual mud holes in the streets to ice and frosting the air. Lacy worked in the shop by day and quilted by candlelight late into the night. She hated winter, for she never felt warm. Even standing in front of her small fire, only one side warmed, the other chilled.

Around midnight, she gave up trying to work. While she dressed for bed, thin bricks heated by the fire. In her gown, Lacy carefully wrapped each brick and stuffed it beneath the covers near the bottom of her bed. Then she jumped in bed, laughing at her own attempts to keep warm.

The wind rattled the windows along the back of the apartment even more than usual with a promise of snow.

Lacy poked her head out from beneath the quilts. She listened. The alley behind her shop sometimes sounded like a wind tunnel, dragging a howling winter into the shadows. The wooden frame of the shop below groaned. Somewhere boards popped as they shifted.

She slipped back under the blankets, hoping her breath would warm the space between the sheets.

Just as her icy toes thawed, thanks to the hot bricks, the back door rattled. The sound was muffled by a towel she'd placed to keep out the draft, but she thought she heard the creak of the door handle.

Lacy hesitated, weighing fear against being cold. The Colt rested on the dresser not three feet away, but the journey would cost her the little body heat she'd managed to trap beneath the covers.

She told herself no one would try to break in tonight. It was too cold. In the years she'd lived alone above the shop no one had ever tried to break in. Once a drunk fell into the front windows downstairs, but he hadn't intended to enter. This was a quiet little town most of the time where folks felt safe. Crime rarely paid a call.

But what better time than tonight, with the wind blowing and no one brave enough to investigate a scream?

At the third rattle of the door, Lacy jumped from the bed and ran for the Colt. As her hand touched the handle of the gun, a cold wind barreled through her apartment. The back door swung wide open, clamoring against the wall.

Lacy held the weapon in both hands and faced the wind. She might freeze, but she'd protect to the death what was hers.

A tall figure in a dark wool coat stood before her wearing a hat low, blocking his face from view. He filled the opening. The short cape of his coat flapped in the wind like a flag.

She raised the gun and tightened her finger around the trigger.

The stranger stomped into her kitchen as if he had a right to be there. Swearing at the storm, he raised a gloved hand to shove the door closed. The dove-colored gauntlet shone pale in the moonlight.

Leveling the gun to his chest, she stepped forward. Only the yellow braiding of his hat cords kept her from firing.

"Cavalry," she whispered remembering that only army cavalry wore yellow on their uniforms. "Infantry wear blue, artillery wear scarlet," she repeated her facts as if writing an article and not facing an intruder.

The trespasser glanced up. Icy blue eyes stared from beneath the shade of his hat.

"Walker!" She almost didn't recognize him. His chin was covered by a short, black beard, but even in the shadow of his hat, she would never forget those eyes. Cold, heartless eyes, that asked nothing and gave even less.

He jerked his hat off and tossed it on the kitchen table. "Shoot me, Lacy, if that's what you plan to do, or put that old cannon away. I'm in no mood to waste time being threatened by my own wife."

Lacy blinked as if he might disappear.

Walker unbuttoned his coat and hung it on a peg behind the door as though he knew it would be there waiting for him.

He was slightly thicker, she thought. Ten pounds, maybe twenty. His hair was longer, curling over the stiff collar of his uniform jacket. But he was no less handsome, no less frightening.

"What are you doing here?" she asked without lowering the gun.

He glanced at the Colt, then faced her directly. "Let's get something straight right now, dear wife. I have no desire to be in this town. In fact, if I had my way I'd never step foot within a hundred miles of Cedar Point." He pulled off his gloves and tossed them atop his hat. "But it seems Sheriff Riley knows someone who is acquainted with my superior officer. He sent a letter demanding I come home to protect my wife from a man she has apparently confessed to killing once."

Lacy wasn't sure if she were more upset that he came home unwillingly to protect her, or that Sheriff Riley had interfered. At this point, if she had only one bullet it would be a toss up which one to shoot. "I didn't ask him to have you come. I can take care of myself."

Walker looked at the gun. "I can see that."

She lowered the Colt. "You've no need to stay. You can return to your post, wherever that is. I'll be fine."

The deep frown didn't lift. "Would that I could," he answered as if arguing with her. "But it seems I've been given thirty days leave and was forced to take it."

"Thirty days," Lacy echoed. Thirty days with Walker would be an eternity. The few minutes she'd spent with him two years ago had taken her months to recover from. He hurt her. He humiliated her. And worst of all, he'd done exactly what she'd asked of him. He'd made her his wife in more than name.

"Don't look so terrified. I spent three days getting here and it will take me the same amount of hard riding to return, so you've only got twenty-four days of the hell of my company."

"You can't stay here!" Lacy looked around her little apartment crowded with her things. With her life.

"I can't stay anywhere else." His gaze followed hers. He didn't look any happier to be here than she was to have him. "What kind of guard would be posted outside the perimeter? Plus, if I remember this town, within hours everyone will know I've arrived and it would look strange for a husband to stay at the boarding house when his wife sleeps alone."

The little warmth in her body turned to ice. "You're not sleeping with me!"

For the first time, his frown spread into a smile. "I don't remember your being of such a mind the last time we were together. If memory serves, you were the one who insisted on sharing my quarters."

"The only time we were together," Lacy corrected.

"The only time we will ever be together. You don't want a wife, remember?"

As he watched her carefully, she added, "Maybe we are divorced. Maybe I've told everyone you died."

"You haven't," he answered too matter-of-factly to be guessing. "And stop shivering with fright. I'm not here to attack you, Lacy. I'm here to protect you."